DEREK LANDY

AMERICAN MONSTERS

HarperCollins *Children's Books*

First published in Great Britain by HarperCollins *Children's Books* in 2016
Published in this edition 2017
HarperCollins *Children's Books* is a division of HarperCollins*Publishers* Ltd,
HarperCollins Publishers
1 London Bridge Street
London SE1 9GF

The HarperCollins website address is:
www.harpercollins.co.uk

Derek Landy blogs under duress at
www.dereklandy.blogspot.com

3

ISBN 978–0–00–815711–1
Derek Landy asserts the moral right to be identified as the author of this work

Typeset in Joanna MT Std by
Palimpsest Book Production Ltd, Falkirk, Stirlingshire

Printed and bound in Great Britain by
Clays Ltd, St Ives plc

MIX
Paper from
responsible sources
FSC **FSC C007454**
www.fsc.org

FSC™ is a non-profit international organisation established to promote
the responsible management of the world's forests. Products carrying the
FSC label are independently certified to assure consumers that they come
from forests that are managed to meet the social, economic and
ecological needs of present and future generations,
and other controlled sources.

Find out more about HarperCollins and the environment at
www.harpercollins.co.uk/green

This book is dedicated to Morgan.

You've changed, man...

1

THE DEMON WAS TALL and strong, red-skinned and beautiful, and she had two black horns that curled up from her forehead. She sneered, and even her sneer was beautiful. "You really think you're getting out of this alive?"

Amber ignored the whisper, ignored her demon-self, ignored everything that wasn't real, and stepped through the darkness of the department store.

A creature stood on the glass counter ahead, trying on sunglasses and gazing at itself in the mirror on the display spinner. This was real. As bizarre as it was, this wasn't a hallucination. Amber could tell the difference now. The critter was maybe two feet tall, its body and head covered in light brown fur. It stood on spindly legs and its arms were thin. It turned this way and that, admiring itself, gurgling happily. It had a wide, wide mouth, and a small snout. When it took off the sunglasses, its eyes were big and blinking.

Amber had never seen a bogle before. Hadn't even seen a drawing of one. It was, she supposed as she got closer, kind of cute, like an adorable Disney animal. It certainly wasn't anything like she'd imagined. She'd broken into this Walmart expecting to be greeted by a horde of vicious monsters – not a solitary, cute and furry creature trying on sunglasses at night.

But, even so, she shifted. Just in case. Her body transformed, and now *she* was the red-skinned beauty; *she* had the strength, and the height, and the horns. She passed a mannequin wearing the same outfit as her – yoga pants and tank top – but while the mannequin's outfit was flashy orange on grey, Amber's was black, and she wore it better. She didn't want to spook the bogle, though, so she gave a low, soft whistle before emerging.

"Hey there," she whispered, moving even closer. "Hey, little guy."

The bogle looked at her. It cocked its head, made an inquisitive gurgling sound.

"Who's the best little bogle?" Amber continued, smiling, showing it her empty hands. "Who's the cutest little imp? Is it you? *Is it?*"

The bogle figured it might well be, because it grinned happily, its long tongue flopping out of its mouth.

Amber couldn't help but return its smile. She hoped her fangs wouldn't scare it off. "I'm looking for your master," she said quietly. "Could you take me to him? Could you do that?"

The bogle waddled to the edge of the countertop and held its arms out for a hug.

"You *are* a cutie," Amber said. "Maybe when I'm finished with your master I could take you with me. Would you like that? How does a life on the road sound to you? Sound good?"

The bogle chittered, and Amber chuckled. She doubted that Milo would approve of her keeping a pet in the back of the Charger, but he was in some other part of the store, and so his opinion was rendered invalid.

"Then it's a deal," she said. "You take me to Paul Axton and I'll adopt you."

It looked at her with its huge eyes and she almost scooped it up there and then, but something stopped her. Maybe it was how eager the bogle was for her to get closer, maybe it was that wide, wide mouth with all those teeth, or maybe it was the fact that the bigger its eyes got, the more red veins Amber could see in all that white.

Whatever the reason, she hesitated before picking it up, and the bogle didn't like that. It didn't like that one bit.

Its little hands grew little claws and it swiped at her and Amber jerked back. A trail of blood ran from the narrow cut on her cheek.

She stared at the bogle. "You little dipshit," she said.

It leaped at her, a frenzied ball of fur and teeth. Amber batted it away and stumbled as the bogle hit the ground and immediately resumed its attack. She evaded it as much as she could, throwing things in its path, jumping to avoid its swipes, but it was closing in and suddenly she had nowhere left to go. She kicked at it and missed and it leaped at her leg, tried to dig its claws into her flesh, but beneath the yoga pants her skin grew black scales, and the bogle bounced off. Right before it hit the ground, Amber managed to land a solid kick that sent it hurtling into the shadows.

She ran for the DIY section, listening for the telltale patter of tiny, evil feet. She heard a noise and turned, saw nothing but gloom and darkness. She backed up, her foot nudging something heavy. A man, lying there, and covered inexpertly in hockey jerseys. She crouched, clearing them away, revealing first the security-guard uniform and then the face. His mouth was open in a silent scream, and his eyes were missing.

Amber straightened, and a bogle landed on her shoulder – a different one, with darker fur – and she cursed and swiped it off. More of them were on the shelves above her, flinging themselves down with delighted yips of sadistic pleasure. One landed on her head, its claws getting tangled in her hair. She yanked it off, held it by its leg as it twisted and snapped, but another one came down right on her horns, impaling itself and squealing as it writhed.

Amber drop-kicked the one in her hand, tore the other one off even as she felt its blood trickle down to her scalp, and stomped on it till it shut the hell up.

She stared down at the mess she'd made, couldn't help but feel like she was beating up teddy bears.

There was a high-pitched whine and a bogle came at her with a goddamn electric saw. She jumped back, tried to kick it, but it was too fast. Her scales would *probably* protect her against the saw, but she didn't want to test that theory. She jumped on to a display table that proved as wobbly as a rickety boat, and the bogle circled her like a shark with a whirring, serrated disc for a fin. Around and around it went, cackling madly, going faster and faster, but then it must have tripped, because suddenly the disc vanished and the cackling stopped, and chunks of fur and flesh flew up and the saw cut off.

She stayed where she was, making sure it wasn't a trick, but then another bogle rammed into the table legs and Amber found herself leaping off, getting a foot on to something in the dark and springing off *that*, before crashing into the sports section. She got a foot tangled up and fell, bringing down a rack of sportswear around her.

She stayed on the ground for a moment, groaning. There was

movement around her, stifled cackling, and when she looked up she saw a bogle holding a golf club.

"Bwuuh!" it squealed, and swung the club right into her face.

Black scales formed before the impact, but it still hurt like hell, and Amber rolled sideways, grabbed a shelf and pulled herself up, turning just in time to take a baseball bat right to the jaw. She whirled, tripped over her own feet and went stumbling, overturning a display of tennis racquets.

The bogle with the baseball bat chortled, leaped off a display of catcher's mitts and scuttled away. Amber let it go, focusing instead on remaining upright.

When her vision stopped spinning, two small figures came into view, standing on the overturned display and brandishing racquets. These bogles were wearing toddler tennis clothes – the one on the left wore white shorts with its T-shirt, while the one on the right wore a white pleated skirt. They even had headbands.

The first bogle threw a ball high into the air – only it wasn't a ball: it was one of the security guard's eyes – and when the bogle swung the racquet the eye exploded on contact. The bogle howled in dismay, and now the one in the skirt threw its eyeball into the air, swung the racquet and connected beautifully. The eye hit Amber in the face with a wet smack, and she charged after them. The bogles jumped down and ran away, screaming.

She frowned when she heard a strange sort of gurgling behind her. Recognising a distorted version of the Rocky theme tune, she turned to watch a bogle wearing boxing gloves emerge from the darkness.

"You're kidding," she said.

The bogle shuffled forward, threw out a series of jabs, moving its head from side to side as it got closer.

"This is insane," Amber said loudly. "Who's dressing you? Are you dressing yourselves? How do you even know that movie?"

The little boxer-bogle paid her no heed as it closed in.

Shaking her head in frayed disbelief, Amber took a step and kicked it and watched it sail away over the racks of clothes.

Then she heard a warbling voice from the other side of the partition.

"*Plahby-pluh!*"

Amber frowned, moving forward slowly.

She peered round the side of the partition, seeing nothing but gloom and display stands. She carried on.

"*Tooty-plahb!*"

Then she saw them, maybe eight or nine, lined up in formation on the floor ahead, all of them wearing football helmets that covered most of their bodies.

"*Bloe! Blah! Blee!*"

The bogles charged forward and the quarterback stepped back and Amber just had time to catch the glint of the pistol in its hands before it opened fire. She dived out of the way even as the recoil flipped the quarterback head over heels, and then the helmets were flung off and the rest of the bogles came at her with the butcher knives they had been concealing underneath.

She cursed, rolled away from them, her scales deflecting some early slashes, but they were too fast. In an instant, they were all over her, knives stabbing downwards. She turned over and over, but they kept their balance like they were goddamn log rollers or something. Amber's clothes were being hacked to shreds, but her scales covered her, head to foot. Some of the little bastards were attempting to force the tips of their knives in between her scales to get at the skin beneath. The ones on her head were trying to stick their knives in her eyes, her ears, her mouth.

Amber thrashed, knocked a few off, struggled to sit up and then a tsunami of bogles descended on her. She managed to turn over on to her belly, tried to crawl, but they flattened her to the floor again.

Then their master walked into view.

"Aw crap," she muttered.

2

MIDDLE-AGED AND SAD-LOOKING, PAUL Axton dragged a cheap plastic chair behind him. He sat on it, and looked down at Amber.

"So you're the Shining Demon's new representative," he said. "Prettier than the last one, and that's no lie. Astaroth's demons tend to be the best looking — have you noticed that? I could have been one of you, you know. I could have asked to be a demon, to be tall, and strong, and handsome. Red, too, and horned, but you can't have everything. Of course, I didn't ask to be any of those things. I just asked for the ability to communicate with these fascinating creatures."

Amber wanted to respond, but the fascinating creatures kept trying to stick knives in her mouth.

"Naturally, I've heard about you," he continued. "You discovered your demonic heritage only a few months ago, didn't you? Which means you're sixteen years old. That's the age when all this happens. When you go through your... *changes*. But, instead of a heart-warming family moment, your parents proceeded to hunt you clear across the country. Bill and Betty Lamont. Quite a notorious couple, in certain circles.

"Interestingly, though, they are not the only parents who like to eat their young. Lions, polar bears, certain types of prairie dogs... they all indulge in infanticide when the mood takes them. Lots of others, too. And that's just the mammals. But only demons like your parents have absorbed the strength of their offspring in such a *blatant* fashion.

"How long has it been going on? A hundred years? More? You had a brother and sister, didn't you, that your parents and their friends consumed? I can barely imagine what that must have felt like. That rush of power. That taste of immortality. And then it was you on the dinner platter.

"Only you turned the tables, did you not? Now that you're Astaroth's representative, the hunters are the hunted, and the hunted is the hunter. Although, obviously, in view of your current situation, the hunter is back to being the hunted again. The circle of life is rarely kind."

Axton chuckled thinly. "Once upon a time, I was something of an anthropologist – now I am so much more. I have devoted my life to the study of creatures like these bogles – creatures too vicious to survive in today's world. Take you, for example. Those scales are wonderful. Not reliable, though, are they? I've found, in my studies, that they are tied to your unconscious instincts. Yes, you can control them to a degree, but I bet they've let you down before, haven't they? When you needed them most? Have you ever asked yourself why?"

Amber just stayed where she was. The bogles started going after her eyes again so she squeezed them shut, kept her head down. Some of them, on the lower half of her body, were still trying to stick their knives in between her scales. She struggled to control her temper.

"It's all subconscious," Axton was saying. "If you think you ought to be punished in some way for sins you have committed, or are about to commit, your scales will let a little damage in. It's really quite interesting, linked as it is to one's own self-loathing. How about you, young lady? You must have done some rather dubious things to have been made the Shining Demon's representative. How much do these sins affect you? How much do they eat away at you?"

Amber tried to block out his words, but he was right. Her scales should have protected her from Elias Mauk the day before they reached Desolation Hill, should have protected her fingers from his hammer. In the battles she'd been in since, sometimes the scales shielded her from the punch, the slash, and sometimes they didn't. They'd failed her before. If they failed her now, she'd be little more than a pincushion to these creatures.

"It's all about doubt," Axton said. He had a miserable voice. Everything about him – his voice, his slumped shoulders, his sad little belly – screamed loser. More than that, they screamed lost. Defeated. "That's the killer, isn't it?" he said. "The moment a little bit of doubt creeps in, it all starts to go wrong."

Panic flared as Amber felt the scales on her stomach start to slowly retract. She tried to command them, to regrow them, but more retracted in an instant. She pressed her belly to the floor, did her best to pretend to be calm, but more scales were disappearing. A knife scraped her red skin and drew blood.

This guy. Axton. This asshole. Talking about doubt. Talking about her scales failing her. He did this. He put these thoughts in her head and now they were there, they had taken root, and the more she tried not to think of it, the more she thought of it and the more her scales retracted.

"*Whumba de na poebee,*" Axton said, and the bogles grumbled, but paused in their stabbing.

Amber raised her head, looked up at him. "You control them."

"Me?" said Axton. "No, not at all. But I communicate, and they listen. Aren't they wondrous? Terrific mimics. Although I think they may have picked up some bad habits from watching all that TV."

"You know why I'm here," she said.

Axton nodded. "Because I made a deal with the Shining Demon, and I welched."

"He sent me to bring you back."

"And you're surprised I'm resisting?"

"Nope," she said. "Not surprised at all. Expected it, to be honest. Was surprised by the freaky little monsters you've got running around, though."

Axton smiled. "Didn't see them coming, did you?"

"I did not," Amber said, feeling the air on her skin as more scales retracted. The small of her back was now bare, and she expected to feel a knife plunge into her flesh at any moment. "You're a clever man," she said.

"I am?"

"Got me doubting myself."

He chuckled. "It's all true, though. Astaroth can't have you *too* unstoppable, you see. You demons need chinks in your armour, both figuratively and literally."

Her arms. Her arms were bare. Amber could feel the bogles' claws digging into her skin now. She could feel the cold steel of their knives pressing between her shoulder blades.

"He didn't just grant you the ability to talk to these little bastards, did he?" she asked, even though she was pretty sure she knew the answer.

Axton shrugged. "I can talk to anything and anyone."

"Including me. You're getting me to calm down. The more I calm down, the less scales I have."

"We're just having a conversation."

"While you're getting ready to kill me," said Amber.

"That's by the by, is it not? I'm not a violent man."

"How many people have you killed?"

"There are plenty more people to go around, young lady. There are only a few of these bogles. Although, admittedly, they do breed incredibly fast." Axton nodded to a bogle that sauntered towards him, holding its bloated belly. "They need very specific nesting conditions in order to lay their eggs, however. A very particular environment that provides both a viable temperature for birth and food for the offspring."

"Yeah?" said Amber. "And where's that?"

Axton blinked. "Why, on you, of course."

3

AMBER GLARED. "DON'T YOU dare."

"It's actually a very beautiful process," said Axton.

"I swear to Christ," she responded, gritting her teeth, "if it lays its eggs on me I'm gonna break every goddamn bone in your body."

Axton smiled with reassuring banality. "It's not going to hurt, if that's what you're worried about. Well, it will, but it'll be over before you know it. They are rather fast eaters."

"It's not about the pain, Paul. I just have a rule that forbids anything from ever laying its eggs on me, that's all. It's a personal thing."

"It's nature, young lady," Axton told her. "It's the circle of life."

"If it were the circle of life, it would keep happening to me. But this, this right here? This'd be the first time a little furry freak laid their eggs on my body, so it's not the circle of life, it's just gross."

"It won't take long."

Amber watched the pregnant bogle get closer. "Which part?" she asked.

"Any of it," said Axton. "They have an accelerated hatching rate."

Amber took a deep, calming breath. "Paul, you pay attention to what it is I'm saying to you."

The pregnant bogle moaned.

"Too late, I'm afraid," Axton said. "*Fahl-ahey booshop.*"

Amber felt dozens of little hands grabbing her, and before she could lash out she was flipped on to her back. The bogles swarmed over her once more, their knives tearing through the lower half of her tank top, poised to pierce her red skin as her scales continued to slowly retract.

"I wouldn't move, if I were you," said Axton. "Their eggs can be laid on a freshly killed corpse, but it's certainly not the ideal way to do it."

Some of the other bogles lay down, forming steps to allow the pregnant one to waddle up on to Amber's bare belly. The bogle poked and prodded and Amber growled, and got a couple of blades nicking her throat for her efforts.

Finally, the pregnant bogle squatted down, right over Amber's navel, and closed its eyes and started straining.

The scales on Amber's face were now fully gone, and the knives had more places to threaten. It was Axton's voice that was doing it, even more than his words. His voice was getting into her head, lulling her defences to sleep.

"Someday I want their eggs to be laid on me," Axton said. "To be a part of this, to be such an integral part... that would be the ultimate honour."

"Take my place, then," Amber said quickly. "Come on, time's a-wasting."

"I'm afraid not," said Axton. "They were going to use the body of the security guard, but now they have you. I can only hope that someday soon I prove myself worthy of being a nest."

The pregnant bogle grunted, dumping a reddish-tinged liquid on to Amber like someone had upturned a bucket. The smell hit her and Amber clamped her mouth shut and stopped breathing as she turned her head away.

Axton was weeping. "Nature's miracle," he said.

Amber looked back at the bogle as its straining got more intense. Its belly bulged, and as the egg protruded Amber tried to go to her happy place. But she didn't have a happy place. All she had was the floor of a department store at night, and the furry monster that was laying its eggs on her belly.

The first egg plopped out. It was grey and mottled, covered in a thick, mucus-like liquid. It settled on her belly.

The bogle strained again, and a second egg began to appear.

"How many?" she muttered between clenched teeth.

Axton raised an eyebrow. "Sorry? What was that?"

"How many eggs?"

"Ah," he said. "Typically six, though I have seen some bogles lay nine."

Amber lay there and tried not to breathe through her nose as more eggs plopped out, joining the sticky mess on her belly. A group of bogles stood close by, their eyes on the eggs. They all wore ties around their necks, and stood like expectant fathers. They were short, furry and they all looked the same.

The pregnant bogle was done and it collapsed, but there were others to catch it before it hit the ground. They held the bogle overhead, like it was solemnly crowd-surfing, before dumping it behind a display. Amber counted the eggs. Seven of them.

"How long?" she asked Axton.

"Mere moments," he answered, jotting something in a little

notebook. "Try not to move. They'll emerge feeling nauseous if you move too much." He checked his watch.

One of the eggs cracked, and Axton scribbled furiously.

A clawed fist punctured the shell from the inside, and the baby bogle squeezed its mucus-coated, furry head through the gap. It looked around with huge, crazy eyes, drawing a chorus of *ooooohs* from the assembled crowd. A fist burst through another egg, and another, and suddenly it was a race to see who'd be the first one out.

Amber didn't bother keeping track, but one by one the baby bogles emerged, already scratching Amber's belly with their sharp claws. When the last baby hatched, there was a cheer from the tie-wearing bogles, and Amber watched as one of them handed out cigars. Another of the little bastards had a lighter, and soon they were all puffing away like proud fathers, chattering in that nonsensical language of theirs.

Amber watched them puff those cigars, watched the cloud of smoke slowly rising...

An alarm went off and the sprinklers activated and the bogles, every one of them, looked up to see where all the water was coming from. Amber turned over, brushing the chittering babies to the floor, and scrambled up. Axton saw her coming and shrieked. He ran and she followed, knives flashing at her heels. He slipped on the wet floor and she grabbed him, swung him round, used him as a shield as the bogles closed in.

"Tell them to back off," she ordered, and gave him a violent shake. "Tell them to back off!"

"*Ah ween oh shah!*" Axton cried over the sound of the alarm. "*Ah ween oh shah, kah plemby!*"

The bogles kept coming.

"What did you tell them?" Amber snarled into his ear as she dragged him backwards.

"I did what you asked," Axton said. "They're just not obeying."

"Why the hell not?"

"I don't know," said Axton, listening to the bogles babble. "I... I don't think they like me."

"Seriously?" said Amber, spitting water.

"Also, they don't like getting wet. That's one of the rules. It puts them in a most disagreeable mood. So this..." He looked up at the sprinklers, still spraying water. "This is bad."

As one, the bogles screeched in homicidal rage, and swarmed in. Amber spun, Axton right behind her.

They ran and slipped and scrambled and fled, and the bogles screeched and snapped and swiped and pursued. The water shorted out something over in the home-entertainment aisle, throwing sparks into the air like fireworks. The bogles stopped running and stared in wonder, and Amber and Axton ran on, deep into the grocery section.

Amber threw Axton behind a freezer in the middle of an aisle and fell to her knees beside him.

She grabbed the front of his shirt and twisted. "How do we stop them?"

"We run," said Axton, still panting. "We get in a car and we drive away. They won't be able to follow. They can operate machinery, but not very well. It's their short attention spans – they're always crashing."

"We're not going to just leave them here," Amber said. "They'll kill people. They'll spread."

The water cut off, but the alarm kept wailing, and Axton blinked at her. "So?"

"So I don't want innocent people to die," she told him.

"What do you care? You're Astaroth's representative. Saving innocent people isn't exactly your job."

"Yeah, well, I'm changing the terms of my employment. How do we stop them?"

"We can't," Axton said. "There are too many."

Amber resisted the urge to throttle him. "Can we draw them all into one place? Is there something they can't resist? Catnip for bogles?"

"Not... not really."

She leaned in. "You hesitated. There is something."

"I... well, I've always worked hard to keep them away from alcohol. They have an... unhealthy reaction to it."

"Unhealthy how?"

Axton looked conflicted, and Amber punched him.

"Ow! Why did you do that?"

"Because you have a face I like to punch, and you're holding something back."

"Fine," he muttered. "I introduced five bogles to alcohol in a controlled environment in order to study the effects it might have on them. None survived."

She frowned. "Alcohol kills them?"

"No, alcohol gets them drunk. Really fast. Once they're drunk, they argue and kill each other. At first, I thought it merely heightened their violent tendencies. Then I realised it just made them bigger jerks than they already were."

"They get drunk, they annoy each other, and they fight until they're all dead," said Amber. "Okay, that's a definite weakness. So how do we get them to drink?"

"Well... that shouldn't be a problem. You just need to show them booze, and they'll do the rest."

Amber jumped to her feet, took Axton with her.

"So what's the plan?" he asked as she dragged him after her. "You're going to lead them to the drinks? Where will I wait? I can wait over there, if you want."

"You're coming with me."

"Is that strictly wise? As you have seen, I'm not very good at physical confrontation."

"Is it my fault you sold your soul in order to be a bigger nerd than you already were?"

"I – I guess not."

"Hey!" Amber shouted over the wail of the alarm. "Hey, bogles! Here we are! Come get us!"

Wet bogle heads popped up and out from around corners, and suddenly the aisles were swarming with them, their little feet splashing in water as they came.

Amber pulled Axton backwards and they ran, past the frozen meats and the chips and the sauces, and plunging down into the wine, spirits and beer section. They got to the very end before stopping and turning, just in time to see the bogles come round the corner like a wave, rolling towards them.

Then the little bastards noticed where they were, saw the bottles of booze all around them, and the wave slackened, and became smaller, and eventually stopped. The alarm cut off. A happy, gurgling cheer rose from the bogle ranks, and Amber and Axton stepped backwards, forgotten about.

It took fifteen minutes of revelry, arguments and carnage

before the last bogle slumped to the ground, impaling itself on a broken beer bottle.

"So sad," Axton said, wiping away a tear. "Such a tragic waste."

"They wanted to kill you," Amber reminded him.

"True," said Axton, "but you can hardly blame—"

Amber slugged him across the jaw and he dropped, unconscious.

"No," she said. "I guess you can't."

She returned to the sports section, found the activewear and picked out a dry pair of yoga pants and a tank top to replace her own ripped, wet clothes, then slipped her feet into a new pair of sneakers. By the time she was dressed, her scales were once again under her control. She took hold of Axton's shirt collar and dragged him towards the exit.

She was halfway there when she stopped, hauled Axton back a few steps, then let him drop. She wandered over to where Milo Sebastian was tied to a large display table.

"Hey," she said.

"Hey," said Milo. Like the rest of him, his dark hair, shot through with grey, was wet. That, combined with the stubble on his square jaw, made him look like a mature aftershave model who'd just emerged from the pool.

"Sorry about the sprinklers," Amber said.

"That was you?"

"Kinda."

"And all that singing and screeching?"

"I got them drunk," she told him. "The bogles. Got them drunk and let them kill each other. Vicious little bastards."

Milo grunted. "Yeah. Axton?"

She turned one of her fingers into a claw, and cut the ropes. "He's over there. He was studying them, can you believe it? I get the feeling he knew way too much about their mating habits. Do you know they lay eggs?"

"I do," said Milo, standing and wiping the slime off his chest. "I do know that."

"They laid eggs on you, didn't they?"

"Yeah," said Milo. "You?"

"Nope," she said. "They didn't. They tried, but I got free."

"You're lucky. It was... disgusting."

"I can only imagine," said Amber. "The clothes section is behind me. You can get yourself a dry shirt. Maybe one that isn't ripped. I'm going to deliver Axton."

Milo nodded. "Meet you back at the car," he said, and walked away.

She dragged Axton out into the parking lot, heard the sirens approaching. The Kingston Valley Fire Department was not the fastest to respond to possible emergencies, it had to be said. Amber dumped Axton behind a wall and used her claw to open a cut on her palm. Blood flowed freely and she turned on the spot, forming a circle of blood around both Axton and herself. When the circle was complete, the blood caught fire, and they weren't in California anymore.

4

THEY WERE IN A castle with high stone walls that vanished into the darkness overhead, walls that were decorated with tapestries and punctured by stained glass. A cold wind blew through the castle, and carried with it the screams and sobbing of the damned. Amber threw Axton from the circle of fire, and he woke as he landed.

It took him a moment to realise where he was, and then he spun, eyes wide.

"No," he said. "Please."

Footsteps approached, from one of the five arched doorways ahead of them. Axton tried to scramble back into the circle, but Amber stepped out, pushing him away, as Bigmouth led Fool into the chamber.

The meat beneath Bigmouth's peeled-back skin glistened like a freshly made wound, and blood still trickled from the hooks that held those layers of skin in place. His lower jaw, reattached to his skull with thread and wire, swung with every step he took. Behind him came Fool, a thing without gender dressed in a patchwork robe, blinded by the lengths of glass that still pierced its closed eyes. Its bald head was covered in ash and its mouth was smeared with lipstick. It bared its glass-shard teeth as it sniffed the air.

"Amber Lamont," it said. "And... Ooooooh. Axton, Axton, Paul Axton. I remember you, Paul Axton. You tried to cheat my Master. You tried to run."

"It was a misunderstanding," Axton said. "I swear that's all this is, a simple misunderstanding."

"Then why run?"

"I panicked. I got scared. There's really no need to—"

Amber smacked him to shut him up. "I need to see Astaroth," she said. "Just a word. That's all I want."

Fool frowned. "Pertaining to what matter?"

"Pertaining to me, Fool."

"I will tell Lord Astaroth you are here," said Fool, and tugged on Bigmouth's chain. Bigmouth scrambled ahead and Fool followed, disappearing through a wide crack in the wall. Amber didn't know the shortcuts the way Fool did – she barely knew how to take the long way round – so she shoved Axton ahead of her and started walking.

When they got to the giant doors, Fool and Bigmouth were waiting for them.

"Lord Astaroth is ready to receive you," said Fool.

The doors swung open, and Amber dragged Axton into a large hall with mirrored walls, in the centre of which were ten steps that led up to the throne of the Shining Demon. And there he sat, Astaroth, gazing down at them, orange light swirling like lava beneath his skin.

Axton dropped to his knees. "My Lord Astaroth. Forgive my stupidity."

Astaroth ignored him, looked instead to Amber. "You grow impatient, it seems."

Her eyes flickered to Fool, who kept its head down. "Not

impatient, Lord Astaroth, just... eager. You sent me to track down my parents, but every time I get close I have to go after people like this."

"And that upsets you?"

"I just... I feel like if I could focus on my parents, I'd be able to get them to you a lot quicker."

"And you want your vengeance, naturally."

She saw no point in lying. "Yes," she said.

"You are impatient," said Astaroth, "yet, to me, not even a moment has passed since your parents were born. You place far too much importance on the passage of time, as if time has any bearing on this place, or those who dwell here. Your parents will not escape me. That is all you need to know."

Amber bowed. "Yes, Lord."

"There is something else you wish to say."

She looked up. "My Lord?"

"Speak, girl."

A hesitation. "I've been carrying out my duties, my Lord, but on occasion I've had to call on the extra strength you provided in order to do so."

"You have been consuming the vials of my blood."

"Yes."

"How many?"

"Two, my Lord."

"And you want more."

"No, my Lord, actually, I... I don't. Your blood makes me stronger and it's... intoxicating, but I've been, uh, I've been seeing things. And hearing things. Hallucinations. I was—"

"You worry that you may be losing your mind," said Astaroth.

"Yes, my Lord."

Astaroth smiled. "You are my representative. As such, you must be open to different ways of thinking, to new ways of processing information. My blood is helping to expand that capacity."

"So I'm not going crazy?"

"Oh no, you most definitely are. But, as long as you stay useful to me, you will remain alive."

"But... but Lord Astaroth..."

"Begone, little creature," said the Shining Demon, turning to Axton. "I have other matters to attend to."

Amber hesitated, but left before Axton started screaming. She didn't like the screaming.

5

Amber returned to the wall behind Walmart, and the circle of fire around her died and she stayed where she was, her hands curled into fists. Bright light raked the air in rhythmic sweeps, announcing the presence of the Kingston Valley Fire Department. Right about now, perhaps, they were discovering the eyeless remains of the security guard inside, or maybe they were gazing in puzzlement at the dozens of little furry bodies lying in pools of water and whiskey.

Amber left them to it. She didn't know what happened when the civilian world encountered the horrors of the Demon Road. She didn't know who they called or what they did. She didn't care.

She hopped the wall, made for the Dodge Charger parked by the kerb. The trunk popped as she neared and she reverted. Gone was the six-foot, red-skinned goddess, and here was her shorter counterpart, the girl with her brown hair in tangles and her belly stretching her tank top. Her face lost the high cheekbones and the perfect nose and the plump lips as it settled into its normal, less beautiful shape. Months ago, this reversion would have depressed her, but these days there was someone out there, a girl with tattoo sleeves and a smile as wicked as her sense of humour, who found this version of Amber quite beautiful indeed.

The thought of Kelly made Amber smile. But then she remembered their last conversation, when Kelly had found out that Amber had agreed to become the Shining Demon's representative, and the smile faded and died.

She opened one of her bags, took out sweatpants and a T-shirt, pulled them on over her activewear. Then she rooted around for her phone, finding it right at the bottom. She'd had it for three weeks and already the screen was cracked. She stuffed it in her pocket, closed the trunk and got in the Charger.

"All done?" Milo asked as he turned the key. The Charger started with a roar.

"Of course," she said.

They headed away from the flashing lights. "He say anything of note?"

Amber shook her head. "Not really."

"Did you tell him what's bothering you?"

"He's not my therapist."

"Did you mention the hallucinations?"

"I did. He said it's to be expected."

"So it's a side effect he didn't bother to tell you about?"

"We didn't really have time to go into specifics, Milo. The blood makes me stronger, but it also does other things. He says it opens me up to a new way of processing information."

"What does that mean?"

"I don't know."

Milo didn't say anything for a bit. "The blood is dangerous. You've had, how many, two vials so far, since we left Desolation Hill? So that's two in four weeks."

"The situation called for it each time."

"I'm not disagreeing. You last drank a vial four days ago. Have you had any hallucinations since then?"

Amber looked out of the window. "No," she said.

"You haven't even been hearing things?"

"I told you, Milo, don't worry about me. We don't need to worry about the blood, all right? Astaroth said so. He said no more hallucinations. He said I'm fine. So now the only thing we have to focus on is hunting down my parents."

"And breaking your contract with Astaroth," Milo said.

She sighed. "Yes. That too. Could you stop lecturing me now? You're not my actual uncle, you know. We just say that so people won't look at us weird. I don't need a lecture, I don't need to be mollycoddled, and I certainly don't need to be reminded of how much trouble I'm in."

"Okay."

"Can we get off that topic now?"

"Sure thing."

"Thank you."

"So how is the boss?"

Amber's temper flared, but she kept it down. "Can we please not call him that?"

Milo glanced at her. "What are we supposed to call him?"

"Astaroth. The Shining Demon. A Duke of Hell. The Great Burning Asshole. I don't care, just not the boss. Why are you giving me a hard time about this? It's your fault that I'm working for him in the first place. If you hadn't got yourself caught, I'd never have had to trade my servitude for your life. I saved you, and all I get from you is grief. Jesus Christ, I do not need this."

They drove on in silence for a bit. It was nice, the silence, but then Milo had to go and ruin it.

"Ever think that maybe you shouldn't have saved me?" he asked. "Ever think that maybe I deserved to be in Hell after all the innocent people I killed?"

"No, Milo," she said, feeling stupid for losing her temper, "I didn't. You lost your way. You sold your soul to the Whispering Demon, whatever his name is—"

"Demoriel."

"Whatever. You sold your soul to him – you must have had your reasons – and he made you a demon. The people you killed when you were the Ghost of the Highway, they... they..."

"Are you going to tell me they don't count, just because I can't remember them?"

Amber sighed. "No, I'm not going to say that. Obviously, they count. Obviously what you did was... was evil. But that was twelve years ago. You've changed. And I'm sorry if you think I should have let Astaroth hand you over to Demoriel for ten thousand years of torture while Astaroth tortures me, but I don't, and, while I'm paying your salary, you will do what I—"

"You haven't paid me in over four weeks."

"Really?"

"Really. I'm not sticking around because of the money. I'm sticking around because I promised Imelda that I'd keep you safe, and because I'm not going to just abandon you when you need backup."

"Oh. Well, thank you. I'm not going to abandon you, either."

"Right."

"So it looks like we're stuck with each other."

"Yes, it does."

"So can we stop talking about this now? It's late, I'm tired, and I'm cranky, and I've still got bogle juice on my belly."

"I thought you said they didn't lay their eggs on you."

"Yeah, well," she replied. "I was just trying to make you feel special."

They drove to the very outskirts of Kingston Valley, and pulled in at the *Catching Z's* motel, an L-shaped building with a diner out front. The Charger rumbled as they passed a massive old truck cab occupying two disabled parking spots, and they parked up near the manager's office.

They each grabbed their overnight bags and headed inside, found the manager reading a battered paperback behind the counter. He had large ears. The rest of him failed to register with Amber because of the largeness of his ears. They were very large ears.

"Two rooms, please," Milo said. Amber dropped her bag at her feet and put the money on the counter.

A girl came in – pretty, blonde, around Amber's age. She stood beside them at the counter, picked up a brochure and flicked through it.

"You have room service?" she asked the manager when he came back with the keys.

"Sorry?" the manager said.

"Room service," the blonde repeated. "Do you have that here?"

"Uh no."

"So I'd have to leave my room in order to get food? I don't know, man. Seems like a lotta work. Why don't you do room service?"

"We, um, we don't have a kitchen."

"All I'd be looking for would be a sandwich or something. You can make a sandwich, can't you? You don't need a kitchen to make a sandwich." The girl sighed. "I don't know. I like the look of the place. It's nice. It's got a nice ambience. I like what it's called. Catching Z's. But the room service thing... that might be a deal-breaker." She drummed her fingers on the counter as she made up her mind. "Listen, I'll check with some of the other motels in the area, and if they don't do room service, either, I'll come back here. How about that?"

The manager nodded dumbly, and the blonde picked up her bag and walked out.

"Takes all kinds," Amber said to the manager, but barely got a grunt in return.

Milo leaned a little closer. "You realise she took your bag, right?"

Amber looked down at the space her bag had been occupying. "Ah balls."

6

AMBER HURRIED OUT OF the motel office, caught a glimpse of the blonde disappearing round the corner. There was no one else around so she shifted. She ran to the Charger, jumped and got a foot on the edge of the hood, then sprang, reaching the roof of the motel. She kept low as she jogged across the rooftop, anticipating the blonde's path. She dropped down the other side, reverted to normal, and waited a few seconds, until she heard running footsteps. Then she stepped out and the blonde shrieked and leaped backwards, lost her footing and fell.

"I think you have my bag," said Amber, looking down at her.

"Holy crap!" the blonde said, not even trying to get up. "How did you do that? You nearly gave me a heart attack! How did you do that?"

Amber picked up her bag. "This is mine."

The blonde lay back, flattening herself out on the ground. "My nerves are shot. Gimme a second."

Amber couldn't help but smile. "You okay?"

"No. I'm really not."

"Sorry for scaring you."

"You should be."

"But you did steal my bag."

"That doesn't give you the right to scare me."

"Kinda does, though."

The blonde sighed, then sat up. "You're lucky I didn't pee myself."

"I think you're the lucky one in that regard."

"These are my only pants. You'd have had to buy me a new pair."

"I don't think I would have, but okay. Do you need a hand?"

"I don't accept charity."

"I meant, do you need a hand up?"

"Oh. No, but I'll take some charity if you have any." She got up, rubbed her butt. "That hurt. You're faster than you look."

"I'd have to be."

"So what are you gonna do? Turn me in?"

Amber frowned. "Turn you into what?"

"Turn me in to the cops, dummy."

"Oh," said Amber. "No, not really."

"Right," the blonde said, and looked around. "Then do you want to buy me dinner?"

"Uh... is this how you treat everyone you steal from?"

"Just the ones who look like they might say yes." The blonde grinned. "Go on, say yes. I haven't eaten all day. Just buy me a burger. A cheeseburger. And fries with ketchup. And a Sprite. And maybe some pie for dessert. And a sandwich to go. You owe me at least that."

"I don't owe you anything."

"Shush now."

"Listen, I've had a long day, and I'm really tired."

"Are you hungry?"

"I... well, yeah, but—"

"Then it's settled," the blonde said, clapping her hands. "I won't steal your bag and, in return, you buy me food. What a wonderful bargain we've struck."

Amber said goodnight to Milo, dropped her bag in her room, and joined the blonde girl in a badly upholstered booth in the diner. They ordered, and looked at each other.

"Name's Clarissa," the blonde girl said.

"Amber."

"I like your name."

"I like yours, too."

"Thanks," Clarissa said. "It's not my real name, but I picked it because I always liked it. There was a show I used to watch on reruns, and her name was called Clarissa and she had a happy family and friends and everything, so when I left I said I know, I'm gonna be like her. She always seemed to have her life in order, in a *Clarissa Explains It All* kinda way."

"You ran away from home?"

"*Home* is a bit of a stretch. *House with abusive stepdad* is more accurate. What's your story?"

"I guess I ran away, too."

"That guy you're with," said Clarissa. "Boyfriend?"

Amber laughed. "No. Friend."

Clarissa shrugged. "That's cool. Must be nice to have someone watching your back."

"It is. How long have you been, y'know...?"

Clarissa widened her eyes, like it was a scandalous notion. "Homeless? A year. Well, just under. It's really everything you'd expect. You get to sleep under the stars, the world is your bathroom and the people are... peachy. Non-stop fun is what it is."

Amber searched for the right words. "I guess you've met all kinds on the road."

"That I have, Amber," said Clarissa.

"Same here. Some of the people I've met have been scarier than others."

Clarissa nodded. "I can relate."

"You meet some real monsters out there."

"Yep," said Clarissa. "Some complete jerks."

The drinks came, and Amber watched Clarissa pull the straw out of her glass and gulp the Sprite down. It had been so long since she'd spoken with someone who hadn't been, as Glen would have put it, *touched by darkness*, that it now seemed weird to conduct a normal conversation.

Weird but nice.

Clarissa drained her Sprite and Amber pushed hers over. "Here. I'm not thirsty."

Clarissa didn't argue, but this time she kept the straw in and sucked at a more civilised pace. "Where you from?"

"Florida," Amber said. "Orlando."

"Disney World."

"Yep."

"Always wanted to go," said Clarissa, "and my dad always said he was gonna take me. But then he got cancer, the kind they don't cure. And, when he was gone, no one wanted to take me anywhere."

"My parents are evil," said Amber.

"That must suck."

"So must losing a dad you actually love."

41

"Yeah. Anyway, toilet break."

Clarissa slid out of the booth. The moment she was gone, Amber's demon-self slid in. Amber immediately looked at her hands.

"Think you've found a new friend, do you?" her demon-self asked. "I wouldn't bother getting to know her. She's going to abandon you. Like Kelly abandoned you, and Imelda abandoned you..."

"Milo's still here," Amber muttered, not raising her eyes.

Her demon-self grinned. "Did you really buy that bullshit? He's waiting for payday. The moment he gets his money, he's gone. Just like all the rest. But then they're the lucky ones, aren't they?"

"Shut up," Amber mumbled.

"Unlike Glen," her demon-self continued. "You meet this poor Irish boy in the woods, he thinks you're going to help him, and what happens? He dies anyway, and comes back as a bloodthirsty corpse. You feel that gnawing sensation, in your belly? That's what guilt feels like. Honestly, with a friend like you, does anyone really *need* enemies?"

Amber looked up to argue, but her demon-self was already gone.

Clarissa got back just in time for the burgers, and Amber ordered more Sprites.

"Something happen?" Clarissa asked.

"Sorry?"

"It feels like something happened while I was gone. You okay?"

Amber forced all thoughts of Glen to the back of her mind, and smiled. "Nothing's wrong," she said. "Just thinking about stuff, that's all. So do you have plans?"

"For world domination?" Clarissa responded with a mouth full of cheeseburger.

Amber smiled – genuinely, this time. "Or just in general."

"Dunno." Clarissa thought as she chewed. "Wouldn't call them plans, I guess. More like hopes. Such as, I hope I don't spend the rest of my life homeless. I hope I don't die on the streets. I hope I get rich somehow. The usual hopes and dreams and idle fantasies, y'know?"

"Totally."

Clarissa's burger started to slide out of its bun. She frowned, tried to poke it back in with a French fry, then resorted to using a finger. "What about you?" she asked. "You ran away from home, you're with a friend who watches your back, you're staying in motels... You seem to be keeping it together more than most. What's your plan?"

Amber looked puzzled for a few moments before she answered. "I... guess I want my freedom back. I agreed to do a job I didn't want to do, and now I have to figure out how to trick my way out of it."

"And how do you manage that?" Clarissa asked.

"I don't have a clue. It's a whole lot of trouble."

Clarissa peered at her. "You're, what, sixteen?"

"Seventeen tomorrow, actually."

"Well, happy birthday for tomorrow, then. And you're young – you've got the rest of your life ahead of you. You'll be fine."

"And how old are you?"

"Turned seventeen three months ago," Clarissa said, grinning. "There's no hope for me."

They ate, and chatted, and Clarissa used the bathroom twice because of all the Sprite. Then Amber paid and they left the diner, emerged into the night air. They looked around, a little awkwardly, before Clarissa wiggled her eyebrows.

"Hey," she said, "thanks for the food."

Amber gave her a thumbs up, then felt stupid. "Sure," she replied.

Clarissa nodded to the Charger. "Don't suppose there'd be any room in that car for one more, would there? It gets pretty lonely out here and... Naw, forget it. The look on your face says it all."

"I'm sorry," said Amber.

"It's fine," Clarissa said, waving her hand dismissively. "It was a crappy thing to ask."

"No, it wasn't," said Amber, "and I wish I could say yes. But the last person to hitch a ride with us... it didn't end too great for him. We have a habit of getting into trouble."

"I'm used to trouble."

"Not like this you're not."

Clarissa shrugged. "Hey, forget it. Thanks for the food, and I'm sorry I tried to steal your bag." She started walking.

Amber called after her. "Where you going?"

"Moving on," Clarissa said, turning and walking backwards. "I'm that little doggy, y'know the one? Wherever I go, I make a new friend? That's me."

"Where are you sleeping tonight?"

Clarissa spread her arms wide. "The world is my bedroom."

"I thought the world was your bathroom."

"It can get messy, I'm not gonna lie."

"I'll get you a room here."

Clarissa laughed. "No, Amber, really, it's fine."

"Why not?" Amber said. "They're cheap rooms, Clarissa, and

I have the cash. What, you'll take food off me, but not a bed for the night?"

Clarissa stopped walking, but shook her head. "I have principles."

"Do your principles hate pillows?" Amber asked. "One night where you can sleep in a bed, behind a locked door? One night when you're safe? Are you really going to turn that down?"

"Safety does sound nice..."

"Come on," Amber said. "I'll even get you a room with a shower."

"A shower?" Clarissa said, skipping back to Amber. "For realsies?"

"For realsies."

"Golly!"

They stepped into the manager's office and Amber got Clarissa a room key.

"Meet you for breakfast in the morning?" Clarissa asked, swinging the keychain around her finger.

"We'll probably be gone by then," Amber said. "We tend to leave early."

"Oh," said Clarissa. "Well, okay then, so I guess this is goodbye."

"Guess it is."

They looked at each other.

"You're a really nice person, Amber."

"And you're pretty cool."

They hugged, and Clarissa went to her room and Amber strolled back to hers. But, right before she slid the key into the lock, she heard the fluttering of clothes from somewhere above.

Glen.

7

AMBER SHIFTED AND CLIMBED on to the *Catching Z's* roof. She saw him watching her, pale in the saturated night. Thin. Had he always been this thin? She couldn't be sure. The weak breeze didn't stir so much as a strand of his brown hair. His face, frozen now in his eighteenth year, was mournful.

She moved towards him and he turned.

"Stop," she commanded.

He hesitated, one foot over the edge of the building.

She bit her lip, and reverted. All horned up, she had a tendency to shoot her mouth off, but something like this required a little more empathy. "Why are you doing this?" she asked gently. "You've been following us since Cascade Falls. You followed us to Alaska and back. I've checked online. I've seen the reports in the towns we've passed through. I know you've been killing people."

Glen didn't move. Didn't turn. Didn't answer.

"Milo thinks you're following us because Varga's dead, and you don't have a — a vampire family. Is that true? Is that why?"

She moved a little closer. "Glen, you helped me in Desolation Hill. You took care of Kirsty. Thank you for that. But you can't keep doing this. You can't keep killing and you can't keep following us. You helped me, but I can't trust you. I'm sorry. I don't know what you're going to do – if you're going to help me or attack me. Maybe if you'd talk to me, you could make me understand."

Glen offered no response.

"I don't know what it's like to be where you are right now," Amber said, softening her voice. "Milo says... he says vampires don't have a soul. Glen, if he's right, I have no idea what you're going through."

A whisper passed on the breeze. She couldn't be sure where it came from.

"I want to help you," she said, "but I don't know how. I don't know if I'm able. Glen, I don't even know if this is still you. I want to believe it is, but I've got no way of telling if you're here because you feel you belong with us, or if you're just obeying some vampire instinct. Help me. Talk to me."

A moment passed, and Glen stepped off the edge and vanished.

Amber waited to see if he'd return, but after a few minutes she started to feel silly, and she went to her room and locked the door.

She showered, finally washing away the last of the bogle juice, and put on shorts and a T-shirt. She sat with her back against the headboard, iPad on her lap, and logged into the *Dark Places* forum.

TempestROCKS said...
Anyway, I gotta go to bed. Peace y'all!

Sith0Dude said...
Night, Temp!

Mad Hatter99 said...
Bye!
Ima gonna go 2.

The Dark Princess said...
Hiya

Sith0Dude said...
Don't go, Hatter, there's no one else chatting. I'll be all alone.

Mad Hatter99 said...
Princess! Welcome back! Haven't seen you in AGES!

The Dark Princess said...
Been busy! How you doing?

Sith0Dude said...
Hi, Dark Princess.

Mad Hatter99 said...
I'm good! Will I be seeing you at the con? It's only 2 weeks away!

The Dark Princess said...
Don't think so. I'd love to but might be on the other side of the country by then!
Hi, Sithy.

Mad Hatter99 said...
That SUCKS!
You spoken to BAC? I keep missing her.

The Dark Princess said...
Not surprised. Australia's a day ahead of us or something.

Sith0Dude said...
BAC is from Australia? I thought she was from Austria.

Mad Hatter99 said...
Stupid timezones.

Sith0Dude said...
I keep talking German to her. No wonder she never replies.

Mad Hatter99 said...
You know German, Sith?

Sith0Dude said...
Sort of. Not very well. My uncle works part time as a Hitler impersonator.

Mad Hatter99 said...
Is there much demand for that?

Not really. It's why he only works part time.

It's late, guys, so I'm gonna go. Just popped in to say hi! Night now!

Amber powered off the iPad and raised her eyes to the TV. The son of a New York police chief had gone missing. Reporters feared the worst.

She switched off the TV, climbed into bed, turned off the light, and let her eyes close. Her thoughts drifted in the oasis of quiet in which she now found herself. So very quiet. So very incredibly, impossibly quiet.

Amber opened her eyes and looked at the window. Headlights swooped by. She couldn't hear any engines, though. It must have been one thick window to block out that noise. Thick door, too. Hell, thick walls. In every cheap motel she'd been in, the walls were so thin the only thing keeping the ceiling from collapsing was the mould.

She turned over, closed her eyes again. Sleep caught her like a hand around the ankle, and dragged her down.

And, as she slept, she dreamed and, in her dream, Amber had a birthday party. They were in her house, back in Orlando. It was hot, and everyone was sweating.

Her parents were there, and a boy and girl around her own age that she didn't recognise.

Her demon-self was also sitting at the table, looking bored. "Why do I have to be here?" she asked. "Your dreams are as dull as you are."

Nobody paid her any attention. This was Amber's special day, and Amber was beaming.

"Happy birthday, sweetie," said Betty. She started cutting the cake. Blood spilled out but nobody cared.

"Our little girl has grown up," said Bill. "This is a big day. A momentous day. An important day. A succulent day. A mouth-watering day. A big, juicy day."

He talked on, and Amber's smile failed and she turned to her demon-self. "Who are they?" she asked, indicating the boy and girl.

Her demon-self sighed. "Don't you know anything?" she said. "It's James and Carolyn. Your brother and sister."

"Oh," said Amber.

James sat at the table with his head down. He had a collar around his neck, with a chain attached to it that Bill held like a leash. "I live in the attic," he said.

Carolyn sat with a faltering smile on her face. She was wearing a light summer dress, and white gloves. "I live in my head," she said.

"Where's Molly?" asked James.

"What did they do with Molly?" asked Carolyn.

Betty pushed a plate across to Amber, spilling blood on the tablecloth. The slice of cake had a heartbeat, and, with every beat, more blood pumped out.

"Are you ready for your present?" Betty asked. "I know you wanted a pony."

Amber frowned. "I never wanted a pony."

"So we got you a pony," said Betty.

"I don't want one."

"Bill, go fetch the pony, would you?"

Amber's father, who had shifted into his demon form without Amber noticing, let go of the chain and went into the kitchen to fetch the pony.

With their father gone, James tore off the collar and bolted for a door that hadn't been there a moment ago.

Amber got up, went to the door, glanced into the kitchen to see her father eating a dead pony. She stepped through. She wasn't in Orlando anymore. She was outside. The sun was shining and it was pleasant, and Amber wasn't sweating.

She found James sitting beneath a tree with a blonde girl wearing an old-fashioned dress. She was teaching him to read.

Amber's demon-self stood beside her. "They found each other," she said. "He escaped and hopped on a train and off he went, exploring the outside world, and they found each other. Do you think it's love? I think it's love."

A voice drifted by on the wind, someone calling for Molly.

The girl got up quickly. "I have to go," she said. "I'll meet you back here tomorrow, okay?"

"Yes, please," said James, and held out the book for her to take.

"You keep it," said the girl. "Practise."

She smiled, then she ran off, and James smiled and looked at Amber.

"Her name's Molly," he said. "She likes me and I like her."

"So I see," said Amber.

"Tomorrow someone is going to snatch her," said Amber's demon-self.

James's smile faded. "I know," he said. "A tall man in black clothes. He drives a carriage for funerals."

"A hearse?" Amber prompted.

"Yes," said James. "A hearse. I'm going to help her. She's the first person ever to be kind to me, and I like her so I'm going to help her."

Amber nodded, and it was night and they were outside a wooden building with a sign that said Stromquist's Undertakers & Coffin Makers, and the undertaker, a tall man in black clothes, was walking towards them, his face twisted in anger.

Amber woke.

She thought about the dream, but her thoughts started to rebound in this quiet room. This unnaturally quiet room.

She got up, went to the window. Tapped it. Double-paned? Triple-paned? Something more? She went to each of the walls, rapped her knuckles against them. The sound was dull. Heavy. She stood in the middle of the room. So what? It was a motel beside a diner. Of course noise pollution would be a problem. Of course they'd have had to tackle it.

She clicked on the light and sat on the end of the bed, caught her reflection in the mirror. She didn't look convinced. She looked like there was something nudging at her thoughts.

Amber went over to the mirror. It was screwed to the wall. Okay. Made sense. Some people might want to steal a mirror. It could happen. It could even be a thing. Mirror-thieves, for example – that ever-growing threat to motel owners everywhere. Screwing the mirror in place was a perfectly acceptable thing to do and she accepted this. Although, by doing so, the motel owner did make it impossible to check behind the mirror. Not that there would be anything behind it. Nothing except more wall. Not a hole, that's for sure. Definitely not a camera. Nope. This was just an ordinary mirror. Nothing two-way about it.

Amber sat back on the bed and looked at the mirror for another minute.

There was an ashtray on the nightstand, even though the motel was one big no-smoking area. It was heavy in her hand. Glass. Nice and thick. She threw it at the mirror and the mirror smashed.

"Yep," she said softly to herself.

Behind the mirror was a hole in the wall. It was covered with more glass, and Amber had a pretty strong suspicion that it was glass as thick as the window. No camera, though, and no pervert standing there. She walked over and peered through. Beyond the hole was an unlit corridor.

She straightened. So the *Catching Z's* manager liked to peep. Gross, an invasion of privacy, but okay. Probably liked to take pictures, too. Gross, gross, gross, but whatever. But there was still something more. Something extra.

Chasing a half-formed thought, she pulled back the sheets on the bed, exposing the mattress to the light. All the stains she would have expected, plus a whole bunch more. Darker too.

Dried blood. And lots of it.

8

AMBER COULDN'T SAY SHE was surprised. This was a motel on the Demon Road, after all. It was bound to have had the odd murder or two. Or three. Or whatever.

She pulled on a pair of jeans and sneakers and walked to the manager's office. He wasn't around. No one was. She went into the room at the back. A cluttered desk, an old computer, a broom closet and plenty of filing cabinets. Inside the broom closet were mops and buckets and a shelf full of bulbs and various bits and pieces one might need as the manager of a dirt-cheap motel such as this. But all of this stuff, every last thing, was on the left side of the closet. The right side was bare. Amber pressed her hand to the wooden wall and it rattled. She pushed, and the wall swung open.

She stepped through.

The corridor smelled of stale sweat and men. She passed the holes, peeking through each one she came to. She saw Milo, already asleep. He looked agitated. She knocked on the window, but he didn't wake.

She heard someone cry out, and hurried round the next corner to a window as the lights came on. It was Clarissa's room. Clarissa herself was curled up on the bed, clutching her hand.

There was a switch on the wall and Amber pressed it, and a door clicked open beside her. She pushed it wide – it was heavy – and Clarissa looked up, saw Amber come in, and jumped off the bed, wobbling slightly.

"What are you doing?" she shouted.

Amber tried to get her to calm down, but the door swung shut behind her. There was no handle. There was barely a seam.

"What's going on?" Clarissa shouted again.

Amber turned back to her. "We may be in trouble," she said.

"Where did you come from?"

"It's the manager," Amber said, "the guy from the front desk. He's got a tunnel behind the rooms. He spies on people."

"But why are you here?" Clarissa asked, panic edging her voice.

"Clarissa, listen to me. I didn't mean to scare you. I found the tunnel, I followed it, I heard you scream and I pushed the door open."

"That's the wall!"

"It's also a door. I'm on your side, okay? Why did you scream?"

Clarissa hesitated, deciding whether or not to trust Amber. Then she picked up her jeans and pulled them on. "I went to turn on the bedside lamp and it gave me a shock," she said. "Faulty wiring or something. I could have been killed. I'm definitely gonna sue. Why were you back there?"

"I went investigating," Amber said.

"Investigating the manager?"

Amber picked up the glass ashtray and hurled it at the mirror.

Clarissa jumped back, then saw the window, and the man behind it who wore a surgical mask with a snarling mouth drawn upon it. Even Amber jumped at the sight of him.

The man scuttled off, and Clarissa marched forward.

"Hey!" she shouted. "Hey, asshole! What the hell is your deal?"

"Come on," Amber said, heading for the door. "We'll catch him when he runs."

She took the chain off the door and turned the handle and the floor gave way beneath her. Clarissa grabbed her, held her, and Amber dangled for a moment before Clarissa pulled her back.

"What the hell?" yelled Amber, once she had her feet under her once again. They peered down into the hole. It was a four-foot drop on to metal spikes.

"Are you kidding me?" Clarissa whispered. "Are you kidding? What the hell kinda place is this? That could've killed you!"

"I think that was the point," Amber said.

"But why? What does he have against you? Or me? He doesn't even know us! Why would he want to kill us? Oh Jesus, we're gonna be killed. We're gonna be killed."

"Stay calm, Clarissa."

"That's not my real name."

"Yes, it is," said Amber. "*Clarissa Keeps Her Cool*, okay? All right? That's what's happening right now."

"Okay," Clarissa said. "Okay."

Amber looked around. "Move carefully," she said. "If he had a trapdoor there, he could have one anywhere."

Clarissa's eyes widened, and she jumped on to the bed. "Quick!" she cried.

Amber held up a hand to calm her. "That's okay," she said. "You stay there. I'll find a way out."

"What about your friend?" Clarissa asked. "Call him!"

"My phone's in my room," Amber said. "But don't worry – I'll get us out of this."

Stepping carefully, Amber went back to the hidden door. Now that she was this close, she could see the join.

"Can you open it?" Clarissa asked.

"Don't know yet."

"There must be some way to open it."

"Not necessarily," Amber said. She pressed her hands against the wall beside the door, fingertips probing the wallpaper. "Ah," she said.

"What?" Clarissa asked. "What is it?"

Amber jabbed at the wallpaper with rigid fingers, poking a hole through it. She tore it back, revealing a section cut out of the wall. She peered through.

"What's in there?" Clarissa asked. "What can you see?"

"Metal," Amber said. "Springs. Hinges."

"Is there a button?"

"I think so. At the very back."

Amber put her arm through. There was plenty of space to move within the wall – the entire section seemed to be pretty much hollow. She stretched her arm out straight, her shoulder jammed into the hole and her face pressed up against the wall.

"Almost got it," she said, her fingers brushing something metal. She grabbed it. It moved. "There," she said, and pulled.

There was a sound like heavy swords clashing, and pain seized hold of her arm and wouldn't let go, and Amber screamed.

Clarissa was at her side in an instant, but Amber barely recognised her, such was the agony and the panic that stabbed through her mind. Clarissa was shouting and trying to pull Amber's arm free, but whatever had her held her tight and wouldn't let go.

Clarissa ran back, out of view, and Amber's demon-self whispered in her ear.

"This is it," she said. "The day you die. Squealing like a pig, bleeding to death. Has your arm been chopped off? Feels like it has."

"Get away from me!" Amber roared, and her demon-self was gone and Clarissa was there, holding a lamp. She tore off the shade, smashed the bulb, and rammed it, again and again, into the wall next to Amber's arm. The cheap wood started to give way.

Amber stopped screaming. Her bottom lip trembled violently. She wanted to puke and pass out.

Clarissa kept ramming the lamp into the wall, widening the hole that Amber had put her arm through. Clarissa dropped the lamp.

"We're gonna pull your arm out," she said. "You hear me?"

"No," said Amber, "no, no, no..."

Clarissa reached through, took hold of something, easing the pressure off Amber's arm.

"Jesus," Clarissa said. "I think it's a bear trap."

The bear trap, or whatever it was, jarred against the opening and Amber cried out again, but Clarissa didn't stop, and together they pulled the trap from the wall. Amber sank to her knees and Clarissa laid the trap on the floor, its metal teeth holding Amber's arm tight. There was blood. A lot of it.

"You're gonna be okay," said Clarissa. "You're gonna be... Christ... you're gonna be okay."

"You're going to die like a pig," said Amber's demon-self, standing behind Clarissa. "And you're going to leak all over this fine carpet while you're at it. I hope you're happy, young lady." She laughed. "When your parents hear that this is how you died, they are going to be so unimpressed."

Amber snarled.

"Clarissa," she said. "Towels."

"What?"

"Towels. Soak them. Hot water. Go. Now."

Clarissa nodded, leaped up and ran to the bathroom, and Amber shifted.

Still snarling, she brought her knee in to brace the bottom of the bear trap, and she gripped the upper teeth with her good hand. Growling at the pain, she pulled the jaws apart, and withdrew her arm. She let the jaws snap closed again, and reverted before Clarissa came out of the bathroom.

"Oh my God!" Clarissa said. "You did it! How did you do it? Jesus!"

Amber sat back against the wall, sweating profusely and clutching her arm.

"Can you stand?" Clarissa asked. "Can you make it to the bed?"

Amber nodded, and Clarissa helped her up. They were halfway to the bed when the hidden door opened behind them, and two men came through.

The first one wore the surgical mask with the snarling mouth drawn on it. He'd cut a hole between the teeth, though, and from this his tongue darted like a pink, slippery rodent that

Amber immediately wanted to pound, whack-a-mole style. He held a chainsaw. Behind him came the *Catching Z's* manager. He was grinning.

"Let us go!" Clarissa shouted to them. "You nearly killed her! Let us go!"

The nutcase in the mask tittered, and yanked on the cord. The chainsaw's sudden roar made Clarissa scream, but instead of jumping back she ran at them, flailing.

The nutcase stumbled backwards, cursing under his mask, but the manager swung a punch that sent Clarissa tumbling over the bed. They turned their attentions to Amber, and Amber shifted.

The pain subsided and she could move her hand again. She snarled at the nutcase, watching his eyes widen over his mask. The manager looked like he might cry.

"You picked the wrong girls tonight," Amber said, and lunged.

The nutcase in the surgical mask tried to use the chainsaw to keep her away, but she punched him with her good fist, square in the chest. He flew backwards, swinging the chainsaw wide. Amber ducked. The manager wasn't so fast. The chainsaw bar hardly grazed his neck, but it was enough to cut through to the meat. Blood splattered and the chainsaw fell and sputtered out and the manager stumbled against the wall, hands at his neck, his eyes open wide in shock. His legs gave out and he slid down to the floor and died with a last spurt of blood and a gurgle.

The nutcase in the surgical mask bolted out of the door. She stopped herself from going after him, turning instead to Clarissa, who was getting to her feet. Amber reverted, gritting her teeth against the oncoming pain.

Clarissa's eyes widened when she saw the manager and all that blood. "You did that?"

"No, not me," Amber said. "The other guy, the one in the mask, he tripped, and this one kinda... fell into him. We got lucky."

"That's more than luck," said Clarissa. "That's a goddamn miracle. You okay? How's your arm?"

"It'll be fine," Amber said. "My friend, he's a medic. He can stitch me up."

"You mean you don't wanna go to the cops," Clarissa said. "Don't worry, I get it. I'm not gonna tell."

"Thank you. Seriously. Now come on. Let's get the hell out of here."

9

AMBER WENT BACK TO her room. Unsurprisingly, she didn't sleep that night.

She covered the broken mirror, shifted into demon form and took a sip, merely a taste, of Astaroth's blood. The warmth flooded her body and the pain went away, and she lay on the bed.

Her thoughts wouldn't slow down. They careened through her synapses, pinging off the walls of her brain like overexcited children. She thought about the guy in the surgical mask, thought about catching him in a bear trap just to see how long he'd last. She'd quite enjoy seeing those metal teeth spring shut on his head.

Morning came without incident, the room gradually becoming brighter. A half-hour before she was due to get up, she fell asleep, which was just typical. The alarm on her phone went off and she muted it, grumbling. She reverted and examined her arm. The wounds had reduced to the lightest of scars, and most of the pain was gone.

She dressed in jeans and a loose top. She didn't bother with the activewear today. It was too warm, and she wasn't in the mood. She stood by the door and took a selfie, then checked the room to make sure she wasn't leaving anything behind.

Reassured, she picked up her bag and walked to the diner. Milo was finishing up his breakfast at the table at the back. She joined him, and the first thing she said was, "Where the hell were you last night?"

Milo took a sip of coffee. "In my room," he said. "Sleeping. Where the hell were you?"

"You didn't notice how quiet the rooms are here? You didn't realise how everything is soundproofed?"

"I didn't notice much of anything. I was, as I said, sleeping."

"So you didn't notice the mirror that was screwed to the wall, or you didn't notice the mattress that was—"

"I'm just going to save us both some time here," Milo said. "I didn't notice anything. I got to my room and I fell on the bed and I went to sleep, pretty much immediately. So are you going to tell me what has you so angry, or are you going to let me drink my coffee?"

"I was stuck in a booby-trapped room last night." Amber pulled up her sleeve, showing him her scars. "The manager and his nutcase friend like to watch people falling into their traps, apparently."

Milo looked at her, his expression calm apart from the clenched jaw. "They did that to you?"

"Bear traps, trapdoors, lamps that give electric shocks... probably a lot more sick stuff that we never even got to experience."

"We?"

"Clarissa was there. The girl from last night."

"Did she make it?"

"She's fine. And, before you ask, she had no interest in going to the cops. They'd probably just send her home, and that's the last place she wants to be. I put her in a cab, gave her some money and a bonus as, I don't know, hazard pay for meeting me. I'll call the cops once we're on the road, tell them what's been happening here."

"Where are they now?" Milo asked, signalling the waitress for the cheque."

"The cops?"

"The manager and his nutcase friend."

"Oh. The nutcase ran off." She paused a moment. "The manager's dead."

Milo nodded. "How?"

Amber didn't like the look on his face. She didn't like the suspicion that she'd gone too far.

"It wasn't my fault," she said. "They came at me with a chainsaw. The nutcase caught the manager in the neck. I didn't have anything to do with it."

"Did you shift?"

She hesitated.

"Amber?"

She sat forward, angry but keeping her voice down. "What did you expect me to do? They had a *chainsaw*."

"They both saw you shift, and one of them got away."

"Now you're telling me I *should* have killed them?"

"No. You've got to be more careful about who sees this stuff. What about the girl?"

"She didn't see anything."

"You're sure?"

"Yes. My secret identity is secure."

The waitress came over and Milo paid, gave her a smile that sent her away happy.

"That," Milo said, once they were alone again, "was a hell of a night you had."

"Thank you," said Amber. "Yes, it was."

"We should probably get going."

She folded her arms. "I'd hate to make you rush your coffee."

"Don't worry, it's not very good."

"I was being sarcastic."

"I wasn't. It's really not very good."

They left the diner and got in the Charger. As usual, despite the heat of the day, the inside of the car was cool, and it welcomed Amber as much as Amber welcomed it. They pulled out on to the street, drove towards the highway. When they neared it, Milo glanced at her. "Which way?"

Amber closed her eyes, focused on her parents. Bill and Betty Lamont swam into her thoughts in all their glorious perfection, with their bright smiles and trim frames and casual attitude to murdering their kids. It didn't take long for the compass that had grown in Amber's gut to start tugging her in their direction. She pointed.

"East," said Milo.

She opened her eyes, sat back in her seat. "Apparently."

"No actual address?"

"That's not how it works."

He shrugged. "Just thought this time might be different."

"Why would it be?"

"I'm an optimist, Amber," he said, taking one of the on-ramps. "I think every time will be different."

They took the I-10 out of California. It was nice being able to use the highways and interstates again. They weren't the ones being chased – not this time. Amber wondered if her parents were feeling the same kind of desperation she'd felt when they'd been the ones in pursuit. She hoped they were.

It took a little under six hours to get to Phoenix. They arrived in the early afternoon and had lunch at the House of Tricks, right on the patio. Amber had the cheesecake for dessert. It was astonishing. Milo stuck a candle in it while she ate, and lit it.

"Happy birthday," he said.

"Do I get to make a wish?" she asked.

"So long as you don't expect it to come true."

She smiled, and blew the candle out. She didn't bother making a wish.

Milo had a non-alcoholic beer and they sat there for a bit, enjoying the breeze and the trees, until Amber's gut pulled them back to the car and on to the road.

While they drove, she slept, and dreamed, and in her dream she was back at Stromquist's Undertakers and Coffin Makers. She found her brother sitting with his head down. "I went to the police," he said. "I told them. I thought they could help."

Amber heard gunshots, and she ran to the corner of the building, saw a police officer in an old-fashioned uniform stumbling back, trying to reload his revolver. The tall man in the undertaker clothes stalked after him, tossing away the lifeless body of the cop's partner.

The cop managed to fire once more, straight into the undertaker's chest, before the undertaker smacked the gun out of his grip. Then the undertaker held up his hand, and his palm opened, revealing teeth, and he clamped his hand round the cop's throat, and the cop cried out, tried to pull away, but the taller man was too strong. Blood ran down the cop's neck, staining his uniform, and the undertaker stood there, eyes closed.

James walked up behind Amber. "He's a monster," he said. "Sucks the life out of people."

"A vampire," she said. "He's called a vampire."

James shrugged. "Don't know the word. If you say so. He still has Molly, somewhere in there. I've been trying to get in. Yesterday I grew claws. I might be a monster, too."

"Our parents are the monsters," Amber said. "Not us."

He shrugged again, and, while the undertaker was busy feeding on the cop, the door to the funeral home opened behind him. Amber's demon-self beckoned James through, and he ran over and slipped in.

Her demon-self walked over to Amber.

"Is this real?" Amber asked her. "It feels... real. But not."

"It's a dream," said her demon-self. "The Shining Demon's blood is letting you latch on to the memories of your dead brother from 1914. Pretty freaky, if you ask me."

"So that was him?" Amber asked. "That was really James?"

"No. It's a dream of James. God, you're stupid."

"So why am I dreaming this?"

"Because you always dream of your dead siblings before you die," said her demon-self. "Didn't you know that?"

Amber woke suddenly. She was still in the Charger. They were still travelling.

"You okay?" Milo asked, without taking his eyes off the road.

"Fine," she said, straightening up. "Just a dream."

"You were talking in your sleep."

"What'd I say?"

"Don't know. Couldn't make it out." He glanced at her. "You sure you're okay? You look like you've been crying."

She frowned, and wiped tears from her cheek.

"Huh," she said.

10

THEY DROVE FOR THREE days, closing in on her parents with every mile they covered, before something new twisted in Amber's gut.

"No," she muttered.

Milo glanced at her. "What?"

"Nothing," she said, and immediately the pain started.

She whacked her closed fist against the dash. Milo didn't say anything, but he looked displeased.

"Got another one," she said through clenched teeth. "That way."

"South."

"Yeah."

"So we're letting your folks get away again?"

"It's not my choice, Milo. Like you said, Astaroth's the boss, and when the boss tells you to do a job you do the job, or you're put through a hell of a lot of pain."

Milo nodded, and when they came to the next off-ramp they left the highway. Immediately, the pain went away.

"Who is it?" Milo asked.

She closed her eyes, pushed her irritation to one side, and focused. A face and a name swam into her thoughts.

"Your old buddy," she said. "Elias Mauk. I have to collect his offering."

Milo grunted. "This ought to be fun."

It was torture, to deviate from their mission when her parents were so close, but they got to where they were going by nightfall, and Amber fired up the iPad to find out where exactly that was. Apparently, they were just outside of Senoia, Georgia. From what she could see, their immediate surroundings consisted mostly of trees.

They got out. The air was sweet with the scent of pine. Amber shifted and the smell got even sharper.

"Now where?" Milo asked.

"Not sure," she said. "When I'm miles away, I know exactly which direction to go in, but when I'm this close it all goes kinda vague. What do you say we follow the path?"

It was little more than a trail through the trees, and Amber led the way. They heard shouts in the distance and knew they were going in the right direction.

They came to a clearing. Elias Mauk stood with his back to them. He wore a faded boiler suit and a grubby baseball cap, and he was looking up the hill at a cabin surrounded by moaning, groaning, shuffling dead people. Amber waited for Milo to get in position, and then she shifted and stepped out.

"Hello, Elias."

Mauk whirled, eyes widening. His hand went to the claw hammer in his belt, but Milo was suddenly behind him, gun pressed to his head.

Mauk froze.

"So good to see you again," Amber said, smiling brightly.

"The last time we spoke was, like, *ages* ago. Remember that? Remember when you broke all my fingers? You remember?"

Wary of the gun to his head, Mauk sneered. "Yeah," he said, in that hoarse voice of his. "I remember."

Amber took the hammer from his belt. "This is it, isn't it? This is the one you used? It definitely looks like the one you used to break my fingers, but what do I know? I'm no hammer expert. I barely know how to use one." She held it up. "This is the end you hammer with, right?"

Without waiting for an answer, she ducked down and swung the hammer into his right knee. Mauk howled, clutching his leg even as he collapsed. His cap fell off and he rolled over it.

"Yep," said Amber, "that's the end you hammer with."

"You little bitch!" Mauk yelled. "I'll beat your head in! I'll crack your skull like an egg!"

"Like this?" she asked, and tapped the hammer off his forehead, right on the band of burnt skin that ran around his skull. He rolled back, hands alternating between his head and knee, like he couldn't decide which hurt more. Eventually, he settled on his head.

"I don't like being called names, Elias. Don't do it again, you understand me?"

He glared up at her.

"You can't kill me," he said. "You tried shooting me and I got right back up again, didn't I?"

"Technically, it was Milo who shot you," Amber said.

Mauk switched his gaze to Milo. "Traitor. We used to be partners."

"I don't remember anything about that," said Milo, "but I doubt it's true. Even when I was a bad guy, you would have annoyed me."

Mauk barked a laugh. "And what are you now — a hero? That's laughable! *Laughable!*"

Amber nodded. "Laughable, he says."

"Repeated it, too," said Milo.

"So you just know he meant it."

Mauk glared at them both, but the hammer and the gun kept his retorts unspoken. He got up slowly, and they didn't move to stop him. "So that's why you're here, is it?" he asked, straightening. "You want a little revenge? What are you gonna do — you gonna break my fingers now? Maybe my toes, too?"

Amber made a face. "I do not want to see your feet, Elias. That's gross. Feet are the worst part of the human body. We're not here to get revenge on you. This isn't personal. It's business. I see you looking around as I'm talking. First of all, that's very rude. Second, are you expecting someone?"

Mauk smiled. "You could say that."

"And you think the arrival of this person will, what, save you? So obviously it's someone pretty scary, am I right?"

Mauk's smile grew wider.

Amber's matched it. "You're not waiting for the Shining Demon's representative, are you?"

Mauk's smile faltered. "How did you know?"

"Because that's why we're here. You're talking to Astaroth's new representative."

"Bullshit."

"Afraid not."

Mauk turned to Milo. "Bullshit."

When Milo didn't bother to respond, Mauk looked back at Amber. "How?"

"I proved myself," said Amber. "Now I speak with Astaroth's

voice. You get that? I'm like a red, sexy pope with horns, so you'd better not tick me off, bearing in mind that I already don't like you."

"You think I'm gonna cower?" said Mauk. "You think I'm gonna bow and scrape to you, you little tramp? You screwed up my plans and it's because of you, it is *because of you*, that I am back here in this Podunk little nowhere town!"

Amber took a step forward. "I'm sorry," she said, "did you just call me a tramp?"

Mauk faltered. "What?"

"Did you just call me a tramp?" she repeated. "After I just told you not to call me any more names, you actually stood there and called me that?"

"It's just a word—"

"No," said Amber. "It is a word targeted at women. It's meant to demean and belittle. Are you trying to belittle me, Elias?"

"I don't know what you're—"

"Because it looks like you're trying to belittle *me*, Astaroth's representative here on this mortal plane," she interrupted. "It looks like you're trying to insult me, even though to insult me is to insult the Shining Demon."

"No, it isn't," Mauk said quickly.

"Yes, it is," said Amber. "Even though his fury is my fury and his wrath is my wrath, you still insulted me."

"I'm... I'm not gonna bow or—"

"Yeah, you said that already."

"What, uh, what do you—?"

"What do I want?" she interrupted. "Is that what you were going to say? What do I want? What do you mean, what do I want? I'm Astaroth's representative. What do you think I want?"

He swallowed. "The, uh, the offering?"

"Yes, Elias. Exactly. I'm here to collect the offering."

"Well, I have it," said Mauk. "I have it ready for you."

"You think," said Amber.

Mauk looked puzzled. "What?"

"You think you have the offering," Amber said. "You think you've done enough to satisfy the Shining Demon for another year. It's my decision as to whether or not that's true."

"Oh," said Mauk.

"You'd better hope it's a good offering, Elias. I am not in a forgiving mood right now."

He nodded, and took a leather pouch from his boiler suit. Amber snatched it from his hand, opened it and peered in. She didn't wrinkle her nose in disgust, even though she wanted to. She pulled the strings, closing the pouch.

"It'll do," she said.

"What's going on up there?" Milo asked, nodding towards the cabin.

"Just, uh, just a little bit of fun I'm having," Mauk said.

Amber showed him her fangs. "What kind of fun?"

Mauk cleared his throat. "Uh, just a bunch of college kids. They think they're surrounded by zombies who want to eat their flesh. Those dead bodies up there don't want to eat anything. They're just doing what I tell 'em."

"And what's the point of this display?"

"The point? I don't know what you..." Mauk suddenly chuckled. "One of the boyfriends, he got bit, and you know what the others did? They smashed his skull in. Even his girlfriend." Mauk laughed. "Goddamn morons."

Amber watched the corpses as they pounded on the

boarded-up windows. "You're going to kill everyone in that cabin?"

"It's what I do," said Mauk. "Although this is the first time I've done it like this. I thought it'd be a nice change from bashing their brains in with a hammer, and it is, but I don't think I'll be doing it again. Takes a lot of effort to keep the dead bodies going, especially when I'm having a conversation."

"So sorry for distracting you," said Amber. "Any particular reason you're going after the people in that cabin?"

"Do I need reasons?" he asked. "Hell, no, I don't, and you can't say that I do. Astaroth made it very clear when we agreed to this deal that I can kill whoever the hell I want to. You ask him, you go ahead and ask him."

"I don't have to," said Amber. "I know the terms of your contract better than you. I'm just curious as to who would deserve this kind of death."

"Deserve's got nothing to do with it," said Mauk. "They were there. That's all the reason I need." He frowned. "What, you got a bleeding heart for these morons? How can you be Astaroth's representative if you've got a bleeding heart for the innocent?"

"Better a bleeding heart than a bleeding nose," Amber said, and banged the hammer into his face.

Mauk stumbled back, blood pumping, and she dropped the hammer and took the trail back to the Charger. Once she was there, she cleared a space in the grass around her.

"What do you reckon?" she asked Milo as he walked up.

"About what?"

"The kids in the cabin."

He frowned. "Your parents are close, and we've already spent enough time on this little detour."

"But we can't just leave, can we? Come on. Kelly was right – being Astaroth's representative is, like..."

"Morally reprehensible," said Milo.

"Jesus," she said. "You don't have to be a dick about it."

"That's what she said."

"She didn't use those exact words, though. But anyway, yeah... It is kind of, y'know, reprehensible, in a way. Even if I *was* forced into it – which I most definitely was – and even if I am searching for a way to stab him in the back and get out of it – which I most definitely am. But just because I'm working for the bad guy does not mean I can't do good things when I see the opportunity. In fact, I kinda have to, to make up for it."

Milo narrowed his eyes. "You're talking about being a hero."

"No, I'm not."

"Yes, you are," said Milo. "Doing good deeds. That's what heroes do. That's what Kelly and Ronnie and Linda and Warrick do."

"And the dog."

"We're not heroes, Amber. We don't have that luxury."

"But... but, if we don't at least try to be, then I'm going to be a villain," she said. "I don't want to be a villain, Milo."

He glared at her. "Yeah," he said. "Okay."

"Be right back," she said, drawing a talon across her palm. She let the blood drip, forming a circle around her. The circle flashed into flame and Milo was gone and the Charger was gone and she was back in the Shining Demon's castle.

"Fool?" she called. "Fool, come on, I haven't got all day."

When she got no answer, she left the chamber, picked the corridor with the windows to hurry down. She was halfway along when Bigmouth came shuffling out of the shadows.

"Where's Fool?" she asked. "Hello? Edgar? Listen, it doesn't matter. Can you take this to it?"

Bigmouth shook his head.

"Just hand it over – it'll be fine."

He scribbled on the slate around his neck, and showed her. *Can't. Not allowed.*

"Then where is Fool?" Amber said angrily. "I'm in a hurry, Edgar. Bring it here, now."

Bigmouth scribbled again.

Not Edgar. Bigmouth. I am only Bigmouth now.

She sighed. "Fine. Bigmouth. Could you get Fool, please? Could you do that?"

Bigmouth nodded, and shuffled away.

Amber looked out of the window, over the forest of twisted trees, across the river, to the palace of the Blood-dimmed King that stood high and proud in the vast city, with steeples like daggers slicing into the dark sky. A cold wind came from that palace, and it brought the screams with it. She could only imagine the suffering going on behind those walls.

Footsteps made her turn, as Bigmouth guided Fool towards her.

"Finally," she said. "Where were you? Never mind, I don't even want to know. Here, I have an offering for you."

"Not for me," said Fool. "For the Master."

"Yes, that's what I meant, for you to give to him." She held out the pouch. "This is from Elias Mauk."

Fool bared its glass-shard teeth. "Don't like Elias Mauk. He shouted at me and kicked me."

"He is a bit of a tool, all right. You'll take this to Lord Astaroth?"

"Of course," said Fool, accepting the pouch with both hands.

Amber didn't bother to thank him; she just turned and hurried back to the chamber. She stepped into the circle of fire, stomped her foot on the flames and the fire went out and the castle vanished and she was back beside the Charger.

She walked back up the trail, past the point where they'd met Mauk, and carried on. She found Milo standing at the treeline, looking at the corpses shuffling around the cabin. Even from here, she could hear the raised, panicked voices of the kids inside.

"Where's Mauk?" she asked.

"Got bored and went home," said Milo, and looked at her. "Everything go well in Hell?"

"Fine. What's the plan here? How do we stop them? Destroy the brain?"

"That won't work."

"How do you know?"

He jerked his thumb to the left, where a headless corpse was walking into a tree. "It's not the brain that Mauk controls," he said. "It's everything."

"Well, okay," Amber said, her hands growing to talons. "I guess it's lucky I'm in the mood to slice and dice."

She strode over to the nearest corpse. "Hey there," she said, and it turned, and she slashed at it until every muscle was severed, and it lay on the ground in a moaning, trembling heap.

One down.

11

THEY HEADED NORTH-WEST, PASSING through Nashville, St Louis and then on through Kansas City. With every roadside marker and town sign they left in their rear-view, they drew closer to Amber's parents. She could feel it in her gut. She could feel them, their presence, a heavy sensation that kept on building. She hoped they were running. She hoped they were hiding. She hoped they knew someone was tracking them down. She couldn't wait to see their faces when they realised it was their own daughter.

Somewhere outside of Topeka, they stopped off for food. Amber had no intention of confronting her parents on an empty stomach. As she ate, she focused her mind.

"They're a few hours away, that's all."

"And you're sure you're ready?" Milo asked.

"Of course I am. What kinda question is that?"

He shrugged. "It's just there's a difference between chasing them down and actually catching them."

"Yeah," she said. "Catching them will be a lot more satisfying."

"Okay."

Amber sighed. "You obviously don't agree."

"I neither agree nor disagree."

"Which is so helpful, by the way."

"I'm just saying, while you're chasing them, you can be all gung-ho about it, but when you catch them... it suddenly becomes real."

"I'm ready for real."

"Just checking."

"You think it'll be too much for me? I confronted them in Desolation Hill and I was good. I'm not going to choke now, right when I can end it."

"Can you, though?"

"Can I what?"

"End it?"

"Of course. You don't think I'm going to have the biggest smile on my face when I deliver them to Astaroth?"

"Maybe you will," said Milo, "but what happens after?"

She finished her lunch and pushed her plate to one side. "What happens, happens. That's what happens. You ready to go?"

"Sure."

Amber paid for lunch and they left. She spotted a convenience store across the street. "Be right back," she said. "Just getting water."

Milo gave her a half-wave and walked to the Charger as she crossed the road. As usual, he'd parked it out of sight – down a side alley this time, behind a dumpster. Always careful, that Milo.

The store's small parking lot had one car in it – a rusty death trap with an *I Brake For No One* bumper sticker on the rear window. A bell tinkled above the door when Amber entered, but the middle-aged slob in the grubby T-shirt barely looked up from behind the counter. Amber went to the back of the store, grabbed two bottles of spring water and a Coke.

The bell tinkled again and a man and woman entered, both in their forties, both in suits. The woman was small and tidy, and carried herself with the air of someone who was used to people doing what she told them. The man was tall and languid, but Amber spotted a holstered gun beneath his jacket. She stayed where she was, hidden by the shelves.

"Hello, sir," said the woman.

Amber peeked out as the slob behind the counter scratched his belly. "Don't like cops," he said.

"We're not cops," the woman replied.

"You look like cops."

"But we're not. We're Federal Agents. I'm Agent Byrd. This is my partner, Agent Sutton."

They showed him their IDs.

The slob was unimpressed. "Hate Feds more than I hate cops."

"Do you like fire fighters?" the taller one, Sutton, said. "I have a friend who's a fire fighter, maybe you'd like him."

The slob shrugged. "Got no beef with fire fighters. They fight fires."

"They do," said Sutton. "It's kinda their thing."

"But I don't like cops, and I certainly don't like Feds."

"This is fascinating," said Byrd, "but we're not actually here to talk about which branch of the Emergency or Law Enforcement Services are your least favourite. We're looking for some people."

"Don't mind ambulance drivers, neither," said the slob. "Paramedics and such. My brother was a paramedic."

"Is that so?" Byrd asked, sounding bored.

"No," said the slob. "He was a meth addict. I just tell people he was a paramedic because that's an actual job and it's a good one. Being a meth addict isn't really a job."

Sutton nodded. "More of a vocation." He showed the slob a photograph. "We're looking for two people, this girl and a man, driving a black 1970 Dodge Charger."

Amber's eyes widened.

"Yep," said the slob.

"Have you seen them?" Byrd asked.

Amber got ready to bolt for the Fire Exit door behind her.

"Nope," said the slob.

Byrd folded her arms. "Would you tell us if you had?"

"Well," said the slob, "that depends now, doesn't it?"

"It does?" Byrd said.

"On what?" Sutton asked.

"On what you can do for me," the slob answered.

The agents looked at each other, then back at the slob.

"I'm sorry," Byrd said. "What?"

"I know how these things work," the slob informed them. "I scratch your back, you scratch mine."

Amber watched Sutton frown. "But yours is probably really hairy."

"Sir," Byrd said, "that's actually not how things work. We are Federal Agents in pursuit of two suspects in a string of murders. If we ask you for information, you are obligated to tell us what you know. *That's* how things work."

The slob looked at her. "But I don't know anything."

She sighed. "Okay. Fine. Thank you."

"But if I did..."

Byrd pinched the bridge of her nose. "Yes?"

"...then we'd obviously need to come to some sort of arrangement."

Sutton leaned on the counter. "Have you or have you not seen people who may fit the description we gave you?"

The slob looked confused. "When did you give me a description?"

"Like, one minute ago."

"What did you say?"

"A man and a teenage girl, driving a black Dodge Charger."

"That's not really a description, though, is it? It's their genders, an age, and a mode of transport."

Sutton took out the photograph again and held it up. "This girl."

"What about her?"

"We're looking for her."

"Who is she?"

"It doesn't matter who she is. Have you seen her?"

"Who?"

Sutton pocketed the photo. "We could arrest you, you know."

Byrd shook her head. "Sutton, we're not going to arrest him."

"Why not? He's being a jerk."

"You can't arrest me for that," said the slob. "I know my rights."

"Do you?" Sutton said. "Do you really?"

"I know some of them," said the slob. He frowned for a moment, then brightened. "Thou shalt not steal."

"That's a commandment. That's a commandment you just said, not a right."

"I've got a right to freedom of the press."

"You're getting things mixed up now."

"I've got the right to congregate," the slob said.

"There's only one of you."

"I've got the right to freedom of assembly."

"That's the same thing," said Sutton, "and there's still only one of you. You don't know your rights at all, do you?"

"I've got the right to remain silent."

"That's only if we arrest you."

The slob didn't respond.

"Oh, for Christ's sake, are you not talking to us now? Seriously?"

The slob shrugged and kept his mouth tightly shut.

Byrd took a folded bill from her pocket, put it on the counter and pushed it over. "Sir, here's twenty dollars. Have you seen the people we're looking for?"

The slob picked up the money. "No."

"You're sure?"

"To be sure, I'd have to see a fifty."

"Come on, Sutton," Byrd said, and walked out.

Sutton followed, but turned at the door. "I hate you," he said.

"I hate all Feds," said the slob.

"I just hate you."

"I can live with that."

Sutton walked out.

Amber watched them get in their car. When they were reversing away, she approached the counter.

"Thank you," she said.

The slob looked at the counter, then frowned and looked up at her. "For what?"

"For not saying anything."

"When?"

"To the FBI."

Milo stepped into view and the slob's eyes widened. "You're the girl they're looking for!"

"You seriously didn't realise that?" Amber asked.

He lurched off his stool and stumbled to the door, but Amber blocked his way. The slob shrieked and detoured, knocking over a display of small paint cans. They got under his feet and he crashed to the floor.

Amber left the slob crying in a heap, crossed the street, headed into the alley and got in the Charger.

"Why are the FBI looking for us?" she asked.

Milo frowned. "Sorry?"

"Two FBI agents came into the store just there, looking for us. Sutton and Byrd, they said their names were. They didn't know I was there, but they had a photo of me. Why would they be after us?"

Milo thought for a moment. "Might have something to do with all the dead bodies we leave behind."

"I can't fight an FBI agent, Milo. They're the good guys."

"I'd hesitate to call any government agency the 'good guys', but I see your point."

"How did they find us? We've been in this town for, like, an hour. How have they caught up with us so fast?"

"I don't know," said Milo, "but let's do our best to leave them here, what d'you say?"

The Charger roared to life.

12

THE HEADACHE THAT HAD threatened since Pattonsburg caught up with her in Eagleville, a steady, sharp throb above her right eye that got so bad she had to turn her head so that Milo wouldn't see the discomfort on her face. She felt her hand start to tremble so she jammed it under her leg and put all her weight on it. She knew what was coming next. These were the kinds of tremors she got from drinking Astaroth's blood.

"Why haven't you told him about me?" her demon-self asked from the back seat.

Amber ignored her. Green fields whipped by.

"He knows you've been hallucinating," her demon-self continued, "so why not just tell him? Is it because you don't want him to think you're nuts? I'm afraid it's too late for that. Or wait, do you not want him to take those last four vials away from you? Is that it? Because you're still planning on drinking them, right? Even though you know they'll turn you nuttier than a fruitcake? You're still going to drink them because you want to be strong when you meet your folks again."

Amber glanced over her shoulder. Her demon-self smiled.

"Hey, I wouldn't blame you. I'd want to be as strong as

possible, too. They're sneaky, your parents. Maybe even sneakier than you."

Amber went back to ignoring her.

"That truck is moving pretty fast, isn't it?" her demon-self said.

Amber frowned, and turned again. The back seat was now empty, but an old, massive truck filled the rear window.

"Noticed him, too, huh?" Milo muttered.

"A bit close, isn't he?" she asked. "Fast, for an old wreck."

"That's a Peterbilt," said Milo. "Good trucks."

"Yeah? Do they come with brakes?"

Milo grunted. He signalled to pull off the road, but the Peterbilt didn't slow down. Then its headlights came on and filled the Charger with red.

"Ah dammit," was all Milo had time to say before the truck rammed into them.

The world jolted and Amber braced herself as Milo put his foot down, and they started to pull away.

Then the truck surged, rammed them again and the Charger swerved violently and Milo fought to keep it under control. The Peterbilt drew up alongside them. Amber risked a peek at the driver. From her angle, she didn't see much – just his glowing red eyes – before the truck veered into their lane. The Charger bounced off in a shower of sparks and screaming metal and spun into the fields and the Peterbilt kept going, blasting its horn as the car rocked to a sudden stop.

Amber took a moment to check herself and Milo did the same.

"That was one of Demoriel's demons," Amber said. "He had the same glowy red eyes as you and everything."

"Yeah," was all Milo said.

He got out and so did she. The back of the Charger was crumpled. The side was scraped and dented. A side mirror hung off. Amber tried fixing it back in place.

"Think it's a coincidence?" she asked as she did so. "Maybe he was coming this way, anyway, and saw a chance to be an asshole."

"Maybe," said Milo.

"But you don't think so?"

"I do not."

"What do you think?"

Milo scratched the stubble on his chin, his eyes on the empty stretch of road. "I think the Hound dragging me to Hell might have put me back on the Demonic radar. Astaroth might not have handed me over, but it seems pretty obvious that Demoriel knows where I am now."

"So you've got a demonic trucker after you."

"Looks like."

They got back in the Charger. It started first time, and Milo steered them to the road and they took the first turn they came to.

"How much extra trouble are we now in?" Amber asked.

"Hard to say," Milo answered. "Probably a lot. You still got a fix on your parents?"

She focused on them, and nodded. "Keep going the way we're going," she said. "We're close."

After an hour of driving, and Milo constantly checking the rear-view mirror for the truck, Amber straightened up.

"Turn here," she said.

They moved off the road, up a dirt track with trees on either side. They crested a hill and a large house came into view.

"They're in there," said Amber. "Maybe."

They kept going, approaching the house from the rear. It was more than a house, she could see that now. There were added wings and a cross on the roof.

"A church?" Milo asked.

But she recognised it. "It's a funeral home," she said. "Stromquist's Undertakers and Coffin Makers."

He frowned at her. "How do you know?"

"I... I saw it in a dream. My brother was here."

They passed a garage containing a gleaming hearse, came round the corner and parked out front. They got out. The building – wooden walls painted white – was surrounded by trees. There were no other cars that she could see.

Amber went round to the trunk, took a small box from her bag and opened it. Inside were four vials of Astaroth's blood. She slipped one into her pocket and closed the trunk.

"You okay?" Milo asked.

"I'm fine."

"You dreamed about this place?"

"Never mind that."

"Is this another one of Astaroth's side effects you didn't tell me about?"

"How was I supposed to know it meant anything? Up until this moment, I thought it was just a stupid dream. Now I don't know what to think, so can we just focus on my psycho parents, please, and leave this stuff till after?"

"Sure," Milo said, clipping his gun on to his belt.

They approached the door. It stood open. Inside, out of the sun, it was dark. Milo took his gun from its holster and flicked the safety off.

"Stay behind me," he said, and stepped through the doorway.

There was a flash and a crack and suddenly Milo was in the air and hurtling backwards. He hit the ground and rolled and Amber dodged, ducked down, eyes searching for the attacker, ready to lash out the moment they showed their face.

Milo groaned.

"You okay?" she shouted. "Milo! You okay?"

"Goddamn it," she heard him mutter.

"Who is it? Where are they?"

He turned on to his back, and groaned again. "No one's there."

"Then what happened?"

"Booby trap," he said.

"You sure?"

"Pretty sure."

Amber waited a moment, then straightened up. Keeping well away from the door, she hurried over to Milo, helped him stand.

"Jesus, that hurt," he said. "You didn't happen to dream that, did you?"

"I don't dream the future," she said. "Just the past."

"The future would be more useful." He looked around. "Where's my gun?"

"I think it fell into the house," Amber told him. "What kind of booby trap was it?"

"An old one." He limped back to where he'd been standing, examining the door frame. "See this? It's called a mur du sang. It's a demon thing."

She peered closer, seeing what looked like a line of dried blood going all the way up and around the frame. "What's it do?"

"Stops uninvited guests from getting into places they're not invited," said Milo. "It's a blood barrier. Only family can pass through."

Her eyes narrowed. "So me, then."

He nodded. "They want you alone."

"I'm tempted to give them what they want."

"Let's not — how about that?"

"Does it protect the entire building?"

"Only the entrances they've managed to coat."

"How many doors and windows into this place? If there's a lot, maybe we'll get lucky and they've already died of blood loss."

Milo nodded again. "Because we are known for how lucky we get. Could you get me my gun back, please?"

It lay within arm's reach.

Amber hesitated. "And you're sure this won't work on me?"

"Pretty sure."

"You don't sound it."

"I'm very sure."

"A second ago, you were pretty sure."

"That was a second ago. I've had time to re-evaluate and I've upgraded my certainty to *very sure*. Now will you please get me my gun back?"

Amber took a breath, then shifted into her demon form and reached in, picked up the gun without being thrown off her feet. She straightened up. "You got a lot of attitude for someone asking me for a favour." She gave it back to him and Milo holstered it. "So how do we get you in?" she asked. She spat on her finger and tried rubbing the blood off. It didn't even smudge. "You know one place I bet they haven't sealed? The fireplace."

"I'm not dropping down the chimney," said Milo.

"You could be like a scary Santa Claus with a gun."

"Not doing it."

"I should just go in myself."

"That's what they want."

"Yeah," she said, keeping her voice low, "but they don't know I'm Astaroth's representative, do they? And all I have to do is drink that vial and whatever they have planned for me will just, like, bounce off me and I'll have them. They're in there, Milo. They're literally waiting for me to grab them."

"First of all," said Milo, "your parents are never to be underestimated. Ever. They're like you that way. Second, how do we know they haven't figured out your new job title yet? They've obviously been expecting you – the mur du sang would seem to suggest that – and they might even know about your recent upgrades. They could be counting on it."

"Milo, we're wasting time talking about this, so here's the plan. I go in. If they come running out, you shoot them. Deal?"

He hesitated.

"Come on now," said Amber. "I've just thought up a plan in which you get to shoot someone. You must be at least a little happy about that."

"Okay," he said, "you go in alone. But drink that before you do."

"Naw, I think I'll wait," she responded. "I want to see their faces when I drink it."

"Amber..."

"What, now you're trying to make me drink it? I'll be fine, okay? Trust me." She took out her phone and turned with her back to the door.

"What are you doing?" Milo asked.

"Selfie," she said, taking the picture.

He stared at her, and she gave him a smile, put the phone away, and stepped in.

The funeral home was cold, and old, and very formal. Wood panelling and polished floorboards. Framed paintings on the walls. Antique furniture. Tasteful carpet.

Her dead brother stepped out of the doorway ahead. "This is where they killed me," he said.

Amber's heart hammered so hard in her chest it was like it wanted to break free. She blinked and he was gone, and she carried on walking.

Her parents were nearby, but when she was this close to them it became impossible to tell which direction she should take. She thought about calling for them, then decided against it. They could be right around the corner. Her fingers became claws and she took the next right.

The tall man from her dream stood before her. For a moment, she was going to just walk on by, but she looked into his eyes and stopped. He wasn't a hallucination. His black suit was a different, more modern style and he was older then he'd appeared in the dream. His face had settled into a permanent sneer and his grey hair was now white.

It was unsettling, talking to someone she'd first seen in a dream, but she could handle it. When she was horned up, she could handle anything. "You're hiding my parents," she said.

"I am hiding nobody," he responded. His voice was deep. Hollow.

"I know they're here."

"They are," he said, "but I am not hiding them. I have simply given refuge to some old friends."

"You don't really want to count my folks as your friends," said Amber. "People who do that usually end up dead."

The sneer twisted a little. "Death holds no mystery for the likes of me, young Amber."

She faced him with her hands on her hips. In any other circumstance, he'd be one hell of a creepy bastard. "They told you about me, then."

"They told me you are the Shining Demon's lapdog."

Amber shrugged. "They figured it out, did they? And I wanted to surprise them with the news. So are you Stromquist? I feel like I know you, and yet we've only just met. Stromquist the bloodsucker, am I right? You wanna step outside with me, Stromquist? It's a lovely sunny day. Let's work on your tan."

Stromquist grimaced slightly. "They said you've developed a smart mouth recently. They said before your skin turned red, you were quieter. Less confident. I think I would have liked you better back then."

"Blame the teenage hormones," Amber said. "So are you done distracting me? Because you can talk all you want and delay me all you like, and they can put up their murder songs—"

"*Murs du sang.*"

"—whatever, they can put up their *murs du sang* to isolate me from Milo, but it won't do them one teeny-tiny bit of good."

"Ah," he said.

"What? Ah what?"

The thinnest of smiles on Stromquist's lips. "You think the *mur du sang* was to isolate *you* from *him.*"

Amber looked at Stromquist, tried to spot the bluff in his eyes. "Balls," she said.

His chuckle was not a pleasant one, and it followed her as

she spun and sprinted back the way she'd come. She burst out into the open air. Her father was on his knees in all his red-skinned glory, and standing behind him was Milo, gun pressed to Bill Lamont's head.

Behind Milo was Betty, holding a gun of her own to Milo's back.

13

"HI, HONEY," SAID BILL.

Amber flipped him off, and Bill laughed, showing his fangs.

"I'm going to forgive that," he said. "Just this once, I'm going to forgive such a blatant show of disrespect. I understand that everyone is very tense right now. Betty, how are you feeling at this moment?"

"Like I want to kill someone," Betty said.

"And Mr Sebastian?" said Bill. "How are you feeling?"

Milo ignored him and looked at Amber. "I shoot him, she shoots me. You can get her then."

"Let's not be hasty," said Bill. "This is a perfect time to chat, wouldn't you say, Amber? To catch up? A lot has changed since the last time we spoke. You've gone from running from the Hounds of Hell to being one. Even better, you're Astaroth's representative. Yes, yes, we know about your new role, we found out, and I don't mind admitting it... it makes me proud. Betty?"

"Our little angel," said Betty, "going from a part-time job in the Firebird Diner to the vengeful right hand of a Duke of Hell. If the others were still alive, I would probably be boasting about this."

"Bet you never thought you'd be one of those parents," Bill said, still smiling.

"Never in a million years."

"What," said Amber, "the hell are you talking about? Seriously? These are your last few moments of life and you're wasting them talking about nothing?"

"You wouldn't kill us," said Betty, acting wounded. "We're your parents."

"I would," Amber said, "and I will. The Shining Demon wants me to drag your souls back to Hell and that's what I intend to do."

"We understand that," said Bill, "but we have a counterproposal for you."

Amber moved forward. "Talk all you want, Bill. It's not going to change anything."

"Then it won't hurt to listen, will it?" Betty asked. "It won't hurt to consider another idea."

"I have no intention of listening to anything you have to say," Amber told her.

"That's because you don't know what we're going to say yet." Amber stopped moving and waited.

"We've been running for weeks," Bill said. "I'm not going to lie to you, sweetheart – things got rough. We were running out of places to hide, running out of things to try. If you had been anyone else, yes, this would be the end for us."

"But he made you his representative," said Betty. "I don't know why but I can guess. He probably thinks it's fitting. It probably appeals to his warped sense of humour, if Astaroth can be said to have a sense of humour. But why he did it doesn't matter. What matters is he did, and it's the first mistake he's made in a very long time. Centuries."

"I found you, didn't I?" Amber said. "He couldn't have been too far off the mark."

"Oh no, we're not questioning your ability," Bill said. "You've surprised us again and again until, to be honest, we've come to expect miracles from you. But he picked the wrong person to be his representative because now – now – we have someone on the inside."

Amber frowned. "I'm... sorry, what are you saying? You're saying you're happy it's me because...?"

"We're family," said Betty. "We stick together."

Amber couldn't help it. She burst out laughing.

"Are you insane?" she managed eventually. "Are you seriously suggesting that we're on the same side now?"

"Why not?" said Bill. "This is a golden opportunity, sweetheart. It's beyond perfect. Astaroth believes that the animosity you've built up towards us, for whatever reason, will prevent you from even considering working with us."

"'For whatever reason'?" Amber echoed. "You've been trying to kill me."

"And now you're here trying to kill us," he responded, "so I'd say we're even, yes?"

"You tried to kill me first."

"Well... I hate to say it, Amber, but you're sounding awfully immature right now."

"You are," Betty agreed.

"This is an insane conversation," said Amber. "You two are nuts."

"Have you thought about this?" Betty asked. "Have you thought about what comes next, after we're dead? What, you think you'll be happy, scurrying from one madman's offering to the next? You think your destiny is to be a lackey of the Shining Demon?"

Amber gave the most indifferent of shrugs. "Haven't really thought about it," she lied.

"Of course you haven't," Betty said. "You're young, you're impulsive, you live in the moment... and that's wonderful. It is. But we're thinking of your future, of all our futures."

"And you have to admit," Bill said, "when we work together, we work well. The three of us took down a Hound of Hell without any weapons. That's teamwork, Amber. That's family. That's what we're going to need if you're going to sneak us into Astaroth's castle undetected."

Amber sighed. "That's what I'm going to do, huh?"

"We can take him down," said Bill. "We catch him unawares, when he's vulnerable, and, if we work together, he'll never see it coming."

"So we kill the Shining Demon," Amber said. "The three of us. And then what?"

"Then we're all free," said Betty. "We no longer have to run. You no longer have to work for him. We can live our lives."

"As one big, happy family?"

Betty smiled sadly. "If you like. We know it's going to take you some time to forgive us for what we did, but we're willing to wait. These last few months have been a revelation, sweetie. We're seeing you in a whole new light."

"We're proud of you," said Bill.

"You've grown so much," Betty said, nodding. "You've become this astonishing young woman. I think, honestly, you needed this to happen."

Amber looked at her. "I needed you to try to eat me? Really?"

"In order for you to evolve. Yes."

"Wow," said Amber. "Just... wow."

"The old group is gone," said Bill. "Imelda and Alastair and Grant and Kirsty... we started this with them. We were solid. Unstoppable. Or so we thought. We lost sight of who we were – all of us, except for Imelda. She remembered what it was like to be a good person. A decent person. Her actions, the things she did, reminded us of who we used to be."

"We can be those people again," said Betty. "They were our family – now *you* are our family. The three of us against the world."

Amber laughed. "I can't actually wrap my head around what you're saying. Milo, what about you?"

"I think if I shoot him," he said, "and she shoots me, you can get her then."

"Valuable input," said Amber. "I like it."

"Please believe us," said Betty.

"Oh, I do," Amber said. "I believe that you are one hundred per cent genuine. I believe you are arrogant and nuts enough to think that I would ever, *ever*, want to be on your side after everything you've put me through."

"We are, admittedly, imperfect people."

"You murdered my brother and sister, Mom. You ate Imelda *alive*. My entire life is a lie, it's a joke, and my death would have been the punch-line if you'd had your way. So no, we're not going to be working together. Instead, I'm bringing you to Astaroth and he's going to flay your soul until it's as thin as your conscience, which is pretty goddamn thin."

"We just want you to think about this," said Bill.

"I've thought about it," Amber said. "And my answer is: bite me."

Milo moved suddenly, shifting as he spun, his skin turning the deepest, most impossible black, the kind of black that drank in the light around it. He struck Betty's arm an instant before she fired, and the bullet hit the ground, but as he spun Bill spun, and powered into him. Milo got a shot off as they stumbled, and Betty cried out, clutching her leg. Something hit Amber's shoulder as she went to help. It was an arrow.

Somebody had shot her with an arrow.

She looked up and saw a man standing in the trees, a bow in his outstretched hand, and a second arrow came arcing through the air towards her. It thudded through the half-formed scales on her chest and she grunted, stepped back and wobbled. She fell to her knees.

Milo, red light spilling from his eyes and mouth, dropped his gun. When Bill reached for it, Milo kneed him in the face and grabbed it again. Betty fired and Milo jerked, and she fired again and that one twisted him, tripped him, made him fall. She missed with the third shot and stumbled on her injured leg.

"Leave it!" Bill said, scooping her up. "The hillbillies will keep them busy!"

Bill took off running, his wife in his arms.

Milo raised his gun to fire, but an arrow found his thigh.

More people now, emerging from the trees. Amber watched them come. They held bows and arrows and hatchets and machetes. Four men, one woman, all dressed in faded rags. All misshapen. She knew at once who they were. Kelly had mentioned a run-in with an inbred hillbilly family who lived in the Sacramento Mountains – a run-in she'd barely survived. The Gundersons. Apparently, they ate people.

"More goddamn cannibals," Amber muttered, getting to her feet.

An arrow whizzed by her neck, snagging her hair on its way. Milo fired at them as they came running. He was still on his back, though, and now reloading. Amber walked stiffly over, unable to take her eyes off the arrows in her chest and shoulder for more than a few seconds at a time, and grabbed the collar of Milo's shirt.

She dragged him backwards across the ground as he resumed firing, sending the Gundersons scrambling for cover. They got behind the corner of the funeral home, and, with Amber's help, Milo stood. He growled, and reverted, sagging back against the wall. Blood soaked through his shirt.

"It bad?" she asked.

"Probably pass out soon," he said. "You've got arrows in you."

"Mm-hmm."

"This is going to hurt." He reached out and she braced herself. He took hold of the arrow in her chest with both hands, snapping the shaft. He did the same with the other one. "We're going to need a knife to get the arrowheads out," he said. "If we live that long. I saw five people in rags." He snapped off the arrow in his own leg.

"The Gundersons," Amber said, waiting for the pain to pass. "They eat people."

"More goddamn cannibals," he muttered. "We get to the Charger, we get out of here."

The pain wasn't passing, so she tried to ignore it and peered round the corner. "They're at the Charger."

"Then we kill them," Milo said. "What do you know about them? They living or dead?"

"Living, I think."

He slid a fresh magazine into his gun. "I got nine bullets left. Almost two each."

"Providing you don't miss. Crap, they're coming."

"This might be a good time to drink that vial."

She nodded, dug her hand in her pocket. "Oh."

He looked at her. "No."

She peered around. "I dropped it when the arrow hit. It's right there. On the ground. I can get to it, though. If I run, I can... okay, I can't get to it. We have to move."

She got Milo to his feet, then helped him hobble into the trees.

"All right," he said. "I'll meet you back at the car."

"What? We're not splitting up — are you crazy?"

"It's the only move that makes sense," he said. "They'll catch us if we're together. You go it alone, you have a chance to stay ahead of them. I go it alone, I have a chance that they'll go after you."

"Oh, that's great, that is. Thanks."

"We've got to be practical," Milo said. "Splitting up gives us the most options to get out of this alive."

"But—"

"No arguments. No time. Go!"

He shoved her and took off the other way, and she heard the Gundersons shouting to each other, and she cursed, and ran.

14

The woodland was quiet.

Amber came to a halt, panting only slightly despite the speed she'd been moving at and the distance she'd covered. She'd easily outrun the Gundersons, but now her thoughts were on Milo. No gunshots yet, so they hadn't caught up with him. Hell, maybe he'd evaded them completely. If she was lucky, the Gundersons who were coming for her would just get themselves lost, and she could sneak round them and get back to the car before they realised what was going on. They were inbred hillbilly hicks, for Christ's sake. How much of a threat could they be?

An arrow thudded into the tree next to her face.

"Shiiiiit," she breathed as she pushed herself off. She ran low, zigzagging through the brush, scales rising on her skin. Another arrow hit those scales and ricocheted off. She couldn't even tell where the bowman was. It was like the goddamn trees were shooting at her.

Another arrow whistled by her ear and she tripped on a thick root sticking out of the dirt, but turned her sprawl into a roll and scrambled up, scampering on all fours, lunging through a wild, thorny bush. On the other side she ran down the slope, each step becoming a leap, each leap taking her farther than the one before. She hit a branch and spun and fell and flew, rocks and dirt blurring beneath her, branches whipping as she sailed through the air like she was never going to come down.

But she did come down, hard, all the wind knocked out of her, and now she was rolling uncontrollably, uncontrollably rolling, down and down and over and under and the ground and the sky and the ground and the sky. She crunched into a tree and came to a stop, laden down with pain and fractured ribs, despite the scales that had formed, and she lay there, gasping, trying not to moan too loudly. Now that she was out of immediate danger, her scales retracted.

An arrow found her forearm and she found the breath to scream.

Amber saw the bowman coming down the slope after her as she somersaulted backwards. She threw herself behind a tree and started crawling through the bushes. Once she was behind cover, she looked at her left arm. The tip of the arrow had gone straight through.

Gritting her teeth, she snapped the arrowhead off, took hold of the other end and pulled it out. She couldn't help it. She screamed.

She heard the bowman laugh.

Moving again. Keeping low. She didn't hear him behind her but she knew he was there. He was quiet. Silent even. Not like Amber. She was like a goddamn elephant, the noise she was making. He was having no trouble tracking her, and sooner or later she was going to stumble into his sights and get an arrow between the shoulder blades – unless she stopped running and started fighting back.

She kicked off her sneakers and jumped, her hands and feet becoming claws that dug into the tree. She climbed quickly, despite her injuries, disappearing into the branches. She stayed there, listening for the footsteps. When they came, she held her breath. The bowman came into view, another arrow nocked and ready to let loose. He stepped over her sneakers, looked around.

Amber let go and dropped, but she banged into a branch on the way down and this gave the bowman enough time to jump out of the way. She landed as he drew back the string and she froze. The bowman grinned. At this range, even with her scales up, an arrow would smash through her heart like it was nothing more than a balloon.

"Up," he said.

Amber stood slowly.

"Walk," he said.

As they made their way along the trails set into the woodland, she tried looking for a way out. The bowman was close enough so that she couldn't run, but far enough so that she couldn't reach him without getting an arrow for her trouble. So she walked.

They headed back towards the funeral home, then took a detour that led them to a clearing with an old shed surrounded by rusted farm machinery. There was a truck here, too. It was rusted beyond measure, but held together with rope and chains and metal patchwork. Somehow she just knew that this truck belonged to the Gundersons, that this was how they had come down from the mountains.

The bowman made her kneel and put her hands behind her back. He tied her wrists with rope. She didn't mind that. It wouldn't take much to get free, not with claws like hers. Then he put a sack over her head. She didn't like that.

But she stayed where she was. The inside of the sack smelled bad, like rotting vegetables. Around her were sounds of movement, of footsteps. Voices too.

Someone pulled her to her feet and turned her so that her back was against the truck. The sack was pulled from her head. She blinked.

The bowman was gone. In his place was the woman with the hatchet and a bald man.

"So you're Amber," the woman said. Her eyes were too far apart and she had whiskers on her chin and a bald spot. Apart from that she fine-looking. "I am pleased to make your acquaintance, Amber. My name is Aphrodite. You've met some of my family. The boy with the bow, that was Ares. The dumb one here is Apollo. Say hello, Apollo."

Apollo, the one with the large, bald head and the bulging eyes, was too busy inspecting whatever he'd gathered in his hands to look up.

Aphrodite Gunderson sighed. "No discipline, that boy. Lack of a strong male role model in his life, that's what I put it down to. Ares, he went after your friend and he took the youngest with him. Between you and me, Hermes was born weak. In the head, you know? Maybe Ares will see him straight, but I doubt it. I can see a drowning in that boy's future." She said it sadly, but not *too* sadly. Another Gunderson wandered into view, carrying a pitchfork. He disappeared into the trees.

"That my eldest, Poseidon," said Aphrodite. "Wields that pitchfork like a trident, yes he does."

"I don't want to hurt you," Amber said.

Aphrodite laughed. "*You* hurt *us*? You got so many arrows in you, you look like a damn porcupine!" This seemed to be the funniest thing in the world to Aphrodite, and she practically doubled up with laughter.

Amber waited till she'd finished. "You attacked me," she said. "You attacked my friend. You're helping my parents. You're a long way from home and you've already used up your three chances. Walk away now, while you still can."

Aphrodite peered at her. "You wouldn't be... *threatening* me now, would you, Amber?"

"Look at me, Aphrodite. I'm a demon, just like my parents. Except I'm stronger. I am the Shining Demon's representative. You don't want to piss me off."

Aphrodite smiled. Her teeth were yellow, and had gaps. "Demons don't scare me," she said. "Some old great-great-grandpappy of mine, he made himself a deal with the Devil. Don't know which one, don't care. Then he got himself a woman, and he liked being a demon so much that he wanted to pass it on to his kids. It was at this point we figure he got it into his head to keep the bloodline pure, if you know what I mean."

"So you're as inbred as you look," said Amber.

Aphrodite's smile became a grin. "Very likely. We got generation upon generation up in them hills – weird to look at, sure, but strong, healthy. We got demon blood in our veins. But, even we got to admit, the gene pool is running pretty shallow lately. So we been shifting our focus. We met your folks back in the 1970s, and we been friendly with them ever since. Know why?"

"Because you're all psychopaths?"

Aphrodite chuckled. "I can see why you'd think that, but no. Reason we been friendly is because of the kids – like you. Your folks've used us in the past – we've lost some beloved members of our family to their whims. Take today, as a for instance. They called us here – a long way from home, like you said – and they told us to wait, on the understanding that if and when things went sour, we'd step in while they ran. They don't care if we die. Fact is, I believe they reckoned you'd have us killed long before we got the chance to kill you. May even be counting on it. But you know why we still do it? You know why we still come? It ain't cos we're stupid. It's the opposite. For years, we been trying to snatch one of you away, right from under your parents' perfect noses, and take you back with us. And now look. It's finally happened."

Amber frowned. "What?"

"You got some good hips on you," said Aphrodite. "Child-bearing hips is what they are. You are what we call *breeding stock*, young lady. So you're coming back with us to replenish the gene pool."

"You can't be serious."

"You don't have much of a say in things, just to warn you in advance," Aphrodite said. "And that fella with you, we'll take him, too. I got a loada womenfolk back home."

Amber nodded. "I see," she said.

"Do you?" said Aphrodite. "What is it you see? Can you tell me that?"

"I just mean – that's it, then. That's the end of the conversation right there."

Aphrodite hooted. "Is it? Is it really?"

"Yep," said Amber, her claws slicing through the rope.

15

APHRODITE YANKED THE HATCHET from her belt a lot faster than Amber was expecting. She ducked the first swipe, the scales on her arm deflected the second, and then she shoved Aphrodite away. She dived to the ground, scrambling beneath the truck as Aphrodite came after her with the hatchet. She crawled all the way under, got up on the other side, saw Poseidon and his pitchfork too late. Her scales rose, but the prongs sliced right between them, into her injured left shoulder and out the other side, pinning her to the wooden panelling on the truck. Amber howled in pain. Poseidon didn't let go. He grinned at her screams.

Aphrodite came running, fury contorting her face. More scales rose on Amber's upper body and arm as she fended off the hatchet. Aphrodite dropped back, breathing heavily.

Apollo wandered up, holding Amber's vial of blood. He popped the stopper out, sniffed it, stuck his extraordinarily long tongue in to taste, then whipped his head back. A grin spread.

"What's that?" Aphrodite asked. "What's that you got there? Give it to me, boy!"

Apollo shook his head, guarding the vial jealously.

"Apollo!" said Poseidon. "You share that out now! You share it!"

Apollo shoved the vial into his mouth and bit down. Astaroth's blood spilled down his chin and Apollo's eyes widened as he chewed the glass.

"You goddamn degenerate," said Poseidon.

Apollo's bones cracked and his veins stood out under his skin. Blood vessels burst and his bulging eyes bulged wider. He fell to his knees, his body distorting, a strangled cry escaping his lips.

"What was in that?" Aphrodite demanded. "What was in that bottle, you little witch? What did you do to him?"

Apollo's left eye burst, spraying his cheek with viscous fluid, but he barely seemed to notice. Aphrodite screamed in anguish and renewed her attack on Amber.

"I'll kill you!" she hollered. "I'll hack you into bits!"

In her anger, Aphrodite came too close and Amber managed to rip the hatchet from her grip. Amber kicked her away and threw the hatchet at Poseidon. It didn't embed into his skull or anything, but it knocked him off balance and he stumbled.

Amber took hold of the pitchfork, gritted her teeth and pulled it out. She almost fell to her knees, but Poseidon was lunging at her and she flipped the pitchfork, driving it into his belly as he came. He gasped, but his momentum took him forward and Amber jabbed the end of the handle into the ground. He was taken off his feet like a graceless pole-vaulter, before toppling sideways into a pained, mewling mess.

Aphrodite grabbed Amber's horns from behind, dragged her back with surprising strength, screaming obscenities the whole time. Amber tore free and spun, stumbled, got a knee in the face for her efforts. She fell and Aphrodite got on top, straddling her, bloodying her knuckles on Amber's scales. She grabbed a rock, crunched it down on to Amber's forehead, tried to do it again, but Amber caught the rock in her hand. She slashed through Aphrodite's leg with her other hand, then pulled the rock away and struck Aphrodite across the temple.

Aphrodite sagged and Amber pushed her off, tried to stand, but Aphrodite wasn't done yet. She wrestled her as Amber struggled to straighten up, pulling her hair and trying to get her back down to the ground. Aphrodite went for her face, but her dirty fingernails slid off the scales that had already formed, and Amber got enough space between them to hit her. Aphrodite pinwheeled back, nudging against Apollo, focusing her rage on Amber —

— and then Apollo stood and batted his mother away with a single swipe that crushed her against the truck.

Apollo fixed his remaining eye on Amber, and charged. They went down in the twigs and the dirt. Amber turned over, slashing at Apollo as he crawled on top of her. She shunted herself back, kicked him in the face, did it again, and when she drew back her knee to do it a third time he moved forward, his face pressing against the sole of her foot, his full weight on her leg. His hands gripped her. He bore down.

Her foot became a claw, each toe a multi-knuckled talon tipped with a three-inch nail. She flexed and clenched, and those nails pierced Apollo's cheeks and skull, slicing into his brain.

Apollo went rigid, and then he breathed out, and his remaining eye closed. Amber put her other foot on his chest and pushed him off her and stood. She wiped her foot on his shirt, doing her best to get his blood off. She didn't look at his face. She didn't want to see what she'd done.

She followed the trail as far as a small bridge, then saw a building through the trees. The funeral home. Wary of stumbling across Ares and his arrows, she stayed low as she crept towards it. At the treeline, she scanned her surroundings. No sign of Ares or his brother, or Amber's parents, or even Milo. She could see the Charger from where she was, though.

Taking a deep breath, she broke from cover, and ran hunched over until she could use the funeral home itself as a shield.

She approached the Charger carefully. On the far side the smallest of the Gundersons, Hermes, lay with his throat ripped out.

Out of the corner of her eye she saw movement, an arrow, but Milo crashed into her from behind and the arrow skimmed her cheek. They hit the ground and rolled behind the car. Red light spilled from Milo's narrowed eyes.

"They're dead, Ares," Amber called. "Your mother. Apollo. Hermes. Poseidon is bleeding out as we speak. You want to die here, too?"

"I'll kill you!" Ares shouted. "I'll kill you and scalp you and wear your ears around my neck!"

Amber took a peek. She couldn't see him. "Who's going to take their bodies back to the hills, Ares? If you die here, who'll take them home? Who'll bury them?"

"We don't bury our dead!" Ares screeched. "We eat them!"

Amber shrugged, more to herself than anything. "Makes sense," she muttered.

She jumped at the first gunshot. Three more followed, and Ares broke from cover, fumbling with his bow. He turned to loose an arrow back into the trees, but more gunfire dropped him. He started crawling across the trail, reaching for his fallen bow.

The FBI agents, Sutton and Byrd, stepped from the treeline, guns trained on him.

"Don't do it," Byrd called.

Ares had his bow in his hand now, and he had an arrow nocked and he tried getting up on one knee and they fired until he was dead.

Then they turned their attention to the Charger and stalked towards it, guns at the ready.

"Drop your weapons!" Sutton shouted. "Raise your hands and step out where we can see you!"

Amber glanced at Milo. He was getting himself ready for round two. She heard Byrd cry out and looked back, saw Poseidon lunging at them with his pitchfork. Blood drenched his shirt and every step was a stagger, but he was a dangerous opponent and the agents knew it. Sutton fired twice into his chest and Poseidon swung the pitchfork across his face. Sutton spun, yelling in pain, as Byrd emptied her gun into Poseidon's back.

Amber and Milo jumped into the Charger. The engine roared and Milo slammed his foot down and they got out of there in a cloud of swirling dust.

16

AMBER WAS BACK IN the funeral home, but it was 1914 and the corridors were maze-like in complexity. She was trapped, with no way out, with no idea which way she'd come. She heard people shouting, and then James and the blonde girl, the one named Molly, sprinted by.

"Run, Amber!" James yelled. "Run!"

She looked back. Her parents walked after them, smiling.

Amber tried to shift, to protect her brother, but it didn't work, and now her demon-self was beside her.

"I'm not going to help you," her demon-self said.

Amber started running, terror filling her throat. Her parents were still only walking, but they were gaining.

She turned a corner, saw James helping Molly out through a window. He closed it behind her, ignoring her calls for him to follow, and he started running again.

"Come on!" he shouted. "This way!"

But he ran straight into the arms of Alastair, and as much as he kicked and struggled there was no getting free now. Amber's parents closed in, and so did Kirsty and Grant and Imelda, and they ignored Amber and grabbed James and pulled him apart.

They sank their teeth into his flesh, even Imelda, and Amber shut her eyes as her brother screamed, and when she woke up she was in a nice hotel and there was blood on the sheets and someone knocking on the door.

Grumbling, she got up and caught her reflection as she pulled on a complimentary robe. Red, and horned. She reverted, checked her wounds. Mostly healed. She was a little stiff and a little sore, but, apart from that, fully functioning, and she invited the room-service people in. They laid out her breakfast and she even gave them a tip before they left.

While she ate, she searched the TV channels for a mid-morning rerun of In the Dark Places, or maybe even When Strikes the Shroud, but settled for the news. They were still talking about the police chief's son in New York. Amber switched over to Adventure Time reruns.

She took a shower. A long, hot one. Her body ached. Removing the arrowheads had not been a pleasant experience. She'd chosen this hotel last night because she could not face a stay in another dingy motel, not when she had so many injuries to recover from. It was an expensive room, but worth it. Milo had spent the night in the Charger. He did all his best healing there.

Amber dried off and examined herself. Not bad. Another few hours and there wouldn't even be scars left.

There was another knock on her door – this time it was the laundry-service people, returning a pile of her freshly pressed clothes. She dressed in jeans and a Spider-Man top and packed the rest into her bag. She laced up her spare pair of sneakers and left the hotel. Milo was waiting for her outside, standing by the gleaming Charger. As usual, not a scratch on either of them.

She nodded to him. "Morning."

"Have you thought about what they said?" he asked.

Her head dipped. "Can we just say good morning to each other? Can that be how we start our day?"

"Sure," Milo said. "Good morning. How did you sleep?"

"Very well, actually. How about you?"

"Like a log. Did you have breakfast?"

"I did. It was lovely."

"That's good. That's nice. Have you thought about what they said?"

"What who said?"

"Your parents."

"They said a lot."

"And have you thought about it?"

"What part? Their proposal? Don't tell me you think I should work with them."

"No," Milo said. "But you're looking for a way to double-cross Astaroth. It's worth thinking about."

"No, it isn't. They want me to walk them into his castle so they can kill him? They can't kill him. He's a Duke of Hell – they're not gonna be able to just stroll up and stab him in the back."

"Their plan isn't a good one, I agree, and I don't think you should even consider working with them. But there must be something here you can use against both Astaroth *and* your parents."

"Do you have any idea what that might be?"

"Not... yet."

"Then will you let me know when you do? Because I will be all ears, believe me."

"I just want you to consider your options."

She looked at him over the car roof. "What options? Seriously, what are they? Where are they? I can't run. He knows where I am at all times. If he ever wants to find me, he just thinks about me and *boom*. How do you hide from someone like that?"

"I don't have the answers, Amber. I'm just asking the questions."

"I don't have the answers, either, Milo." She went round to the trunk, which opened for her, and dumped her bag inside. "But I do know that teaming up with my parents for whatever reason would only lead to their crushing, inevitable betrayal. Those two only care about each other."

"I'm not arguing with you there."

She closed the trunk. "But, like I said, if you can think of a genius plan that will get me out of this deal with no strings attached and no one wanting to kill me over it, please do not hesitate to share this miraculous insight with me." She got in the car and buckled up.

Milo joined her a moment later, and they pulled out on to the road and drove.

"Wow," he said.

Amber nodded. "Yeah."

"That was a whole dose of attitude right there."

"It was."

"I'm a bit taken aback."

"So you should be. And what about you? What are you going to do?"

"About which part?"

"Once we catch my parents," she said. "What are you going to do next?"

"I'm going to help you get free of Astaroth."

"And then what?"

Milo took his time replying. "When this is all over? When your parents are gone and you're no longer Astaroth's representative? Then that would lead to a conversation."

"About... us?" she asked.

"I guess."

"Would you..." Amber sniffed, and shrugged. "Would you want to stay together, maybe? As a team?"

"Maybe."

"Cool."

"Depends what we do. There's no point in being a team if we don't actually do anything. Normal people with normal lives, they're not generally part of teams."

"So then what would we be if we had normal lives?"

"I don't know," he said. "Friends, I guess."

The smile burst from somewhere deep inside, and arrived so suddenly Amber had to turn her head to look out of the window. "Cool," she said.

They came to a junction. "Which way?" he asked.

She pointed.

By nightfall of the following evening, they'd made it past Minot, North Dakota. Amber told Milo to pull over near a farm. She shifted and they waited there until a man and woman walked up to them. Dressed plainly, with deep lines etched into their hard faces, they each held a black jar. Amber knew instantly what was inside the jars, and she knew instantly what they'd done to collect their offerings.

She did her best not to throw up as they came close.

Without a word, the man put his jar on the ground first, as carefully as a doting father would lay a sleeping newborn into its crib. Then the woman placed her jar beside it. A tear rolled down her cheek.

They walked back to the farm, holding hands, and then they were gone.

"Do I want to know what's in there?" Milo asked.

"No," Amber whispered.

He nodded. "Thought not."

Amber stood over the jars, made a circle of her blood that caught fire, and delivered the offerings to Fool. She didn't bother talking to him. She didn't even glance at Bigmouth.

She stepped back into the circle and the flames went out and she was by Milo's side once again. She reverted, went to the bushes and threw up.

"I need a new job," she said weakly.

17

"THAT'S AN AWFUL LOT of corn," Amber said.

Milo nodded. They'd been driving for the last five minutes through endless acres of eight-foot-high corn stalks, rising up on either side of the road.

"It's like the Red Sea," she said.

Milo glanced at her. "What?"

"The corn," she said. "We're like Moses driving through the Red Sea."

"I don't think Moses drove."

"You know what I mean. It's impressive, is what I'm saying. As far as corn goes."

"Right."

Silence began to settle.

"So," she said.

Milo kept his eyes on the road. "Yes?"

"So I've looked at the map. I've looked at where we're heading and, uh, and it would appear that we'll be passing through Montana."

"If we keep going in this direction, sure."

"Well, y'know, my parents, they're still, they're still ahead of us. Montana might even be their destination."

"Maybe," said Milo.

"I was thinking, though..."

He looked at her. "You want to go to the *Dark Places* convention, don't you?"

"Yes," she said immediately. "Well, I mean, maybe. Since we'd be in the city, anyway, I figured we could spare a few hours..."

"If your folks are in Montana, and you spend a few hours at the convention, how will you feel if we miss our chance to grab them?"

"Pretty lousy," she mumbled.

"Would it be worth it?"

"Probably not."

"So...?"

"So we'd probably be better off going after them first," she said, "and maybe catching the second day of the convention."

"We might have to miss the convention entirely."

She groaned.

"Amber..."

"Shut up," she said. "I know you're right. Shut up."

She looked out of the window again. A minute passed.

"Do you know any interesting facts about corn?" she asked.

"You're obviously very bored."

She turned to him. "But do you? We learned about corn in school. Did you know that archaeologists were able to pop corn kernels that were over a thousand years old?"

"How did they taste?"

Amber frowned. "I don't know."

"Is that the only thing you learned about corn?"

"It's the only thing I remember."

"Do you miss it?"

"Corn?"

"School," said Milo.

"Oh. No, I don't. And I can guarantee you that there isn't one person in that place who misses me, either. They probably think I've been expelled, actually, after that fight with Saffron."

"Why did you get into a fight with her?"

Amber shrugged. "Does it even matter anymore?"

"I guess not," said Milo. "Did you win?"

Amber grinned, and he laughed.

The road curved ahead and then straightened again, and a covered bridge swept into view. Painted a robust, healthy red, it stood strong and long, straddling a river that divided the forests of corn from the flat lands beyond.

"Pull over, would you?" she asked.

Milo tensed. "Your parents?"

"My bladder."

"Ah," he said, and pulled over.

Amber crossed the road, walked a few steps into the corn and squatted down to pee. Milo turned off the engine and for a moment the sound of swaying corn was the only thing she could hear. She stood, buttoned her jeans and buckled her belt, listening to another engine getting closer. She had visions of a farmer on his tractor, incensed at the idea that an out-of-towner would dare use his field as a toilet.

She left the corn, heading back to the Charger with her eye on the covered bridge. The tractor — it must have been a tractor because of the deep, heavy rumble it was making on those wooden boards — kept coming through the dark. And then a pair of headlights opened up like red, staring eyes.

The Peterbilt lunged from the covered bridge and Amber shifted and ran back into the corn, her arms up in front of her face. She didn't have to look behind to know that the truck had left the road and was coming after her. Its roars filled the world, the rumble of its tyres both heavy and dangerously fast.

Amber tripped, almost fell, had to hike up her jeans as she ran. The trucker was playing with her. He was letting her get far enough away so that when he hit her she'd go splat against the grille of his battered, rusted truck.

She stopped running and turned, crouching, getting her breath back and tracking the sound of the engine through the forest of corn. She cinched her belt tighter as she moved sideways, doing her best not to disturb the corn around her. She became aware of another engine, the Charger, somewhere to her right.

Amber stopped, and stayed very still. It became impossible to tell where the truck was, exactly. Moving somewhere to her left, she reckoned, but then the breeze wafted through the corn and suddenly it could have been right in front of her.

Then the world roared and she straightened, spun, the noise coming from all around her, and she chose a direction at random and jumped, right before the Peterbilt charged through the space where she'd just been standing. It clipped her leg on the way past, spinning her in mid-air. She hit the ground and the truck was gone, leaving a flattened trail in its wake.

Cursing with the pain, Amber got up, started hobbling, and there was another roar beside her and she flinched, almost fell, but the corn stalks swayed and parted as the Charger slid to a stop.

She threw herself in, yanked the door closed, and Milo gunned the engine and they surged forward. He wrenched the wheel to the right and she glimpsed the Peterbilt pass within an arm's length of the trunk.

Milo took them on a wide loop through the corn. They found a scarecrow but no truck.

Milo turned off the engine for a moment, and they listened to the Peterbilt driving away from them. The Charger crept out of the corn.

"Is he gone?" Amber asked, still rubbing her leg.

"I think so."

"Which way?"

Milo nodded to the covered bridge.

"Aw crap," she said. "We've got to follow him?"

"At least for the next ten miles or so. Then we have our pick of roads."

"So he's got ten miles to hide in and wait for us to drive by."

Milo didn't answer, he just pulled out on to the road. They passed through the covered bridge and carried on.

As they drove, Amber took it upon herself to scan their surroundings, 360 degrees. Behind every dilapidated shack they passed, she expected to see the Peterbilt lurking. Every clump of trees became a hiding spot. Every bend in the road an ambush point. And every few seconds she'd check the road behind.

"Amber," Milo said softly.

She looked straight ahead. A car was parked at the side of the road. They slowed, taking in the damage done to the car's exterior. The driver was slumped in his seat.

"Should we stop?" Amber asked. Her voice was so quiet. "I

don't know if we should stop. That's probably what he wants us to do."

"Yeah," said Milo, and kept going.

Amber called for an ambulance and hung up when she was asked her name.

A few minutes later, they passed a family station wagon, its back end crumpled up like an accordion. Its doors were open. No sign of the occupants.

Two miles farther on, they rolled by a pickup truck on its side. The driver had managed to get out and he'd tried to run. He hadn't got very far. They passed his body in the middle of the road.

The Charger drove on.

Past a motorcyclist who'd never stood a chance, a farmer whose truck had come apart upon impact, and a girl with a novelty licence plate on her twisted, wrecked, brand-new Mini.

And then, on the long road straight ahead of them, the Peterbilt. It wasn't speeding, it wasn't swerving, it was just trundling on like it hadn't just left a trail of destruction and death in its wake.

"He wants us to catch up with him," said Amber.

Milo chambered the first round into his gun, flicked the safety on and handed it to Amber. "Hold that," he said.

They started to speed up.

When the Peterbilt was close enough for Amber to just about make out the mud-splattered licence plate, the trucker indicated he was about to pull over. Milo eased his foot off the gas as the Peterbilt kicked up clouds of dust, rolling to a stop in the emergency lane.

"Now what's he doing?" Amber muttered.

Milo took his gun back, flicked the safety off.

"Wait," said Amber, peering through the swirling dust. "There's someone there, on the road."

"Jesus Christ," Milo said. "He's picking up a hitchhiker."

His foot hit the gas. They shot forward, speeding to the truck, and they got close enough for Amber to see the face of the smiling girl climbing into the cab.

Clarissa.

Milo pounded the horn, but the door was already closing, and the Peterbilt took off in reverse. Milo cursed and wrenched the wheel, but the back of the truck slammed into them and the Charger left the ground and the world flipped around it.

Amber barely glimpsed the Peterbilt driving on.

18

THAT NIGHT THEY MADE it to Roundup, Montana. The Charger was injured, wheezing and clunking, but it got as far as the parking lot of the motel and gratefully sank into a deep, dark sleep. Amber went to her room and showered. Her demon-self was waiting for her when she got out.

"Clarissa's dead by now," her demon-self said.

Amber ignored her.

"How's that feel, to have her blood on your hands?"

Amber shook her head. "It's not my fault."

"Of course it is," her demon-self said, laughing. "She was doing fine. Sure, she was homeless. Sure, a life like that has its risks. But it was your friendship that steered her on to the Demon Road."

"You're wrong."

"You're lying to yourself."

"We'll find her," Amber said. "We'll find her and that truck and we'll—"

"When?" her demon-self asked. "Before or after you've found your folks? Before or after you've cheated the Shining Demon? Face it, Amber, Clarissa is last on your list of priorities, so just forget about her. Put her out of your mind. She's already dead. She was dead the moment you met her."

Amber turned, ready to shout, but her demon-self had vanished.

She heard her laugh, somewhere in the distance.

She slept without dreaming.

She woke, and dressed. She wasn't in the mood to eat so she skipped breakfast, went straight out to find Milo already sitting in the shining, immaculate Charger.

"She feeling better?" Amber asked as she got in.

"Much," said Milo. "How are you?"

"That trucker guy taking Clarissa... that's my fault."

"How do you figure?"

"I involved her in this crazy life, and from now on craziness will seek her out. That's how the Dark Highway works, right?"

He looked at her, and shrugged. "Maybe."

"So it's on me. Something else to hate myself for. That's fine. I can handle it. Clarissa is now on my list of things to sort out. I'll get to her. But we are here, in Montana, to scratch my parents' names off of that list. That's how we're gonna start."

Milo nodded. "Okay. How far away are they?"

"Hard to tell, but I'd say about an hour. They're not moving. Maybe they don't know we're this close, or maybe it's a trap. Either way, that's where we're going."

"Yes, ma'am," Milo said, and started the engine. The Charger roared its health, like a great beast waking from slumber, and they left the parking lot and joined the light Sunday morning traffic.

By 10am, Amber's internal compass had brought them straight to the *Dark Places* convention.

"Shit," she said.

Milo stopped the Charger. They watched a long line of weirdly-dressed people pass through the doors.

"They're somewhere in there," she said.

Milo exhaled. "Then it's a trap."

"Obviously."

"We've already walked into one of their traps," Milo said. "It'd be unbecoming to walk into another quite so soon."

"We don't really have a choice," said Amber.

A convention volunteer walked by, waving fliers. Amber rolled down her window and took one, and the volunteer wandered off. Amber rolled her window back up.

She showed Milo the flier. "Look, the con's divided into two halls. You take the south hall, I'll take north."

"Why?"

"Why what?"

He took the flier from her, glanced at it, and handed it back. "The north hall is where all the celebrities are," he said.

"Fine," said Amber. "I want to see some. Maybe. In passing."

"We're looking for your parents."

"I'm well aware of that. But, if I happen to catch a glimpse of some of the stars of my favourite TV show, I'm gonna glimpse them. What's wrong with that?"

"You're sure you won't be distracted?"

"Positive."

"They're planning something, Amber. To come here, to wait for you... they're planning something big. We'll be split up, so you'll have to be extra careful."

"So will you," she said, "or need I remind you just which one of us they held at gunpoint last time?"

"I'm going to be on my guard," he said. "Call me if you see them."

"Likewise," she said, and headed for the north hall. As she stood in line, waiting to pay to get in, she saw Milo at the entrance to the south hall. He wasn't paying, he was just talking to the steward. They laughed, and the steward let Milo in, free of charge.

Amber scowled, and moved forward a single step.

A few hundred single-steps later, she joined thousands of people in the north hall. The aisles between the stalls heaved with people. Some wore costumes from the show. Some wore costumes from other shows. People were taking selfies everywhere.

Amber recognised every single actor giving out autographs. The popular ones had lines that stretched back until they were absorbed into the crowds. The other actors, the less popular ones, sat at the table, chatting with friends, tapping on phones or staring into space, alone in their misery. Amber tried not to make eye contact with those ones.

"Amber?" came a voice from behind her.

She whirled, teeth bared, ready to shift, and a man with a soul patch jumped back, startled.

Amber's eyes widened. "Warrick."

"*Heyyyy,*" Warrick said, his smile returning to him. "Hey there, Amber. What's happening?"

"Warrick, Jesus... You scared me."

"Likewise, Amber. What are you doing here?"

"I'm looking for my parents."

Warrick looked surprised. "Your parents are at the convention?"

"Well, yeah," she said.

He frowned. "Are they fans? Kind of a weird thing to do, what with them being on the run and everything."

"They're not fans," she said. "I don't know why they're here, but it's probably got something to do with drawing me into a trap of some sort. Why are *you* here?"

Warrick leaned closer. "We're on a case. There have been some spooky goings on and innocent lives are in danger." He paused. "Also Kelly wanted to come."

A spark flared in Amber's chest. "She's here, then?"

"The whole gang's here," said Warrick. "Ronnie and Linda should be back at any moment. Two's still out in the van – they've got a crazy No Dogs Allowed rule, but I'm gonna sneak him in the moment the coast is clear. And I mean, yeah, Kelly is here, too. She's the one you actually... She's the important one, let's say, from your point of view."

Amber tried to look indifferent. "That's ancient history."

"Really? It was only a few weeks ago."

"A lot has happened since then."

"Right," he said, nodding. "So are you still Astaroth's henchman?"

"I prefer henchperson."

"Are you still his henchperson, then?"

"I'm joking. I don't like anything with *hench* in it."

"But are you?"

Amber sighed. "I guess."

"How's that going?"

"It's a little sickening."

"Hard to sleep at night?"

"Sometimes."

"I'd say so."

"What's the case?" she asked.

"Okay," said Warrick, "so six *Dark Places* fans from around the world have all died in mysterious circumstances in the past month. They don't know each other, have never met, they're from different backgrounds and cultures, they're different ages... but they have one thing in common."

"*Dark Places*," she said.

"Two things in common, then. *Dark Places* and *Dark Places* fan fiction."

"Oh. I wrote fan fiction."

He shrugged. "There is some good stuff out there."

"Not mine. Mine was terrible."

"Theirs was pretty good," said Warrick. "Well, some of it was. But their stories had one common theme, and that was pairing off the characters of Gideon and Uriah."

"I hate Uriah."

"I don't know him myself. Kelly's the fan."

"So six *Dark Places* viewers who shipped Gideon and Uriah in their fan fiction are dead," said Amber. "What is it, the work of a prudish, serial-killer uberfan?"

"Oh, Aaliyah Brewer is much, much more than that," Warrick replied. "She's a *dead*, prudish, serial-killer uberfan."

"Like, back-from-the-dead dead or...?"

"Nope," said Warrick, "we're talking a real-live *g-g-g-g-ghost*. Well, a real dead one. Actually, no, a dead person would be a live ghost, right? So, yeah, a real-live ghost. We think she travels through the internet."

"Jesus."

"Scary, isn't it?"

"I'll say."

"Think of everything she's seen. The GIFs. The cat pictures. The porn."

"Wow."

"Yeah," said Warrick.

"But, if she travels through the internet, why are you *here*?"

"Because," Warrick said, handing Amber a convention flier, "the notoriously reclusive author of the *Dark Places* books is going to be doing an online Q&A from here later today. This'll be the first time she's been near a Wi-Fi signal in three years."

"Annalith Symmes is *here*? In the building?"

Warrick rolled his eyes. "Focus, Amber. Ghost killer, remember?"

Amber nodded and looked at the author's photograph. "You think Brewer will go after Symmes? Why?"

"Kelly says there's a line in the books about Uriah and Gideon locking eyes, and that's really been the cause of all this."

"It was a hot moment," Amber said.

"So, yeah, we think Brewer will go after her."

"Amber!" said a voice in the crowd, and a moment later Linda emerged, and gave Amber a hug.

"Hey," said Amber in response. She smiled at Ronnie as he joined them. "Hi."

"Yeah," Ronnie said.

"Come on, man," said Warrick, "you can try to be a little friendly."

"Hmm? Oh yeah, sorry," Ronnie said, and gave Amber an uncertain smile. "How've you been?"

"I've been good," said Amber. "You okay? I understand that the chances of this are actually pretty high, but you look like you've seen a ghost."

"Uh, he just got some news, actually," said Linda, and she turned to Warrick. "I'm leaving."

Amber winced to herself, and stepped out of the conversation.

"Where are you going?" Warrick asked.

"No," said Linda, "I'm not leaving the building, I'm leaving, you know... the gang."

Warrick frowned. "Our gang? This gang?"

"Yes."

"When?"

"As soon as we finish up here," Linda said. "This'll be my last case."

Warrick stared at her. "Why?"

"I just need to do something different with my life."

"Is it me?" Warrick asked. "Is it something I said?"

"No," Linda said quickly. "God, no, of course not. I've just come to the end of my time here."

"But... I don't understand. Was it Desolation Hill? Was it the haunted cabin in the woods?"

"It was neither of them," she said. "Well, neither and both and, and everything. I've been thinking about this for a while."

"This is the first I've heard of it."

"Because you're not me, Warrick."

"But we share things," he said. "Stories, secrets, toothbrushes..."

"You've been using my toothbrush?"

He ignored the question. "Why are you leaving? We make such a good team."

"I've tried that," Ronnie said dismally. "You're not going to change her mind."

"I'm sorry, Warrick," said Linda.

Warrick shook his head defiantly. "Have you told Kelly? Kelly will talk you out of it."

"Kelly knows."

He went back to looking incredibly sad. "She does?"

"She's the first one I told."

"Well, what are we doing that you don't agree with? We'll stop doing it, we will. Is it Two? Are you sick of him humping your head while you sleep?"

Linda frowned. "I didn't know he did that."

"He doesn't," Warrick said immediately.

"Well, it isn't Two," she said. "I've never loved any animal as much as I love that dumb dog. And it isn't anything you've done, either. I just need to stop this. I need to have a normal life now."

"But normal's so boring."

"I'm in the mood for boring."

"But that's like being in the mood for vegetarian quiche. I mean, what's the point?"

"It's just something I feel I have to do, Warrick. It's been on my mind for a while now and I think it's best to quit while I'm ahead, before the... oh, please don't cry."

Warrick turned away. Linda wrapped her arm round his shoulders.

"I'll keep in touch," she said softly. "I'm not going to vanish from your life forever..."

Amber looked at Ronnie. "So... serial-killer ghost, huh?"

"Yeah," Ronnie said. "That's why you're here?"

She shook her head. "Parents."

"If I see them, you're the first one I call."

She smiled and nodded, and Linda was still comforting Warrick so she said, "Need any help with the ghost?"

"Naw, we can handle it," said Ronnie. "Is Milo with you?"

"Searching the crowds."

"Cool. Kelly's somewhere around here."

"So Warrick was saying."

"She's probably at one of the panels."

"Wouldn't be surprised."

A few awkward moments passed. "If you wanted to say hi, I'm sure she'd be pleased to see you."

"Yeah," Amber said, offering a fake smile, "maybe. Heard anything from Austin?"

Ronnie brightened at the prospect of something else to talk about. "Just talking to him yesterday, actually. His parents are acting happy families, his teachers give him great grades for barely trying, and the entire population of Desolation Hill is doing its best to carry on with life as normal, while at the same time coping with the implications of no more Hell Nights. Remember the Party-Monster and Dave?"

"I remember being told about them."

"Dave got bitten by a rabid squirrel and didn't tell anyone. They found him in bed a few days later, curled up like a pretzel."

"Jesus."

"The Party-Monster got himself trapped in a coffin as part of a prank that nobody else knew about. That was on a Thursday. They found him the following Tuesday. He did not survive the ordeal."

"They both managed to get themselves killed in such a short space of time?"

"I know what you're thinking. Foul play, right? Nope. Lucy Thornton looked into it, and came up with the cause of death as being sheer stupidity in both cases."

"Wow."

"Looks like she's gonna be elected Chief of Police, by the way."

"That's good."

"Yes, it is."

They nodded, looked around at all the *Dark Places* fans passing.

"Lot of odd-looking people here," Ronnie said.

Amber chuckled. "Yeah."

They kept looking at passers-by, long after it started getting weird.

"Well," she said, "I've gotta go find my parents. If I don't see Kelly, um, tell her I said hi, okay?"

"I will," said Ronnie. "Oh, and Amber? I know she seems hard as nails, and she is, but she's been through a pretty rough few years and..."

"Yes?"

"Please don't break her heart."

Amber blinked, and nodded, and walked away.

19

SHE SEARCHED.

Her parents would stand out in a place like this. Tall and gorgeous, well-dressed and seemingly respectable, the lowly masses would give them a wide berth even in this jam-packed hall.

Amber wiped the perspiration from her forehead. It was sweltering in here, and frustrating for someone of her height. All she saw were torsos and the backs of heads. She tried to slip out of the surging current, but it snagged her back in and took her with it to the next corner. She edged to her right and stepped into the flow moving in the opposite direction, was greeted by a dozen muttered curses and then a slender, tattooed arm reached out, took her hand, and pulled her into an empty stand.

Kelly frowned at her. "What are you doing here?"

That was it. No greeting, no smile...

"Parents," said Amber, wiping her forehead again.

"Your parents are here?" Kelly asked. "Why?"

"I don't know yet," Amber said. "I couldn't even begin to imagine what goes on in their heads."

Kelly, her face a little flushed, her red hair a little mussed, was wearing an old *Dark Places* T-shirt with spots of fresh blood quickly drying.

"Uh, you okay?" said Amber. "Is that your blood?"

"No," said Kelly, "not mine."

Amber nodded. "I was talking to the others. They told me about Brewer. You really think she lives in the internet?"

"That's how she travels. It's not how she kills."

"Oh?"

"Three people just attacked me in the bathroom," Kelly said, "one after the other. They were all her."

Amber frowned. "I'm not sure I understand... Are you talking about cosplayers?"

"She infects people, Amber," Kelly said. "That's the only explanation. Her consciousness leaps from a wireless device into a living host. She possesses them, and she can hop from one to the other. Through touch, I think. Basically, it means that anyone here could be Brewer. Including you."

Amber raised her eyebrows. "Me? Wow. Well, I guess that's true, if she can possess people. It's not, though. I mean, I'm not. Her."

"Though that is *exactly* what she'd say," said Kelly.

"Crap, yeah," Amber responded. "Or she could be you. I mean, let's not forget that."

Kelly shook her head. "She wouldn't be me."

"You don't know that."

"Yes, I do."

Amber narrowed her eyes. "But isn't that just what she'd say?"

"I'm not her, Amber, because, if I were, I wouldn't have told you about her being able to possess people, now would I?"

"Oh," Amber said. "I guess not."

"So Brewer isn't me, but she could be you."

"I don't think she'd be as confused as me, though."

"You might just be pretending to be confused."

"Why?"

"To... what? To try to fool me."

"Oh," said Amber. "Yeah. Sorry, I forgot what we were talking about for a moment. So *you're* not her, and I know that *I'm* not her, so at least *we're* okay."

"No, Amber, see, I *don't know* that you're not her."

"But I do."

"And that doesn't make any difference to me."

Amber thought about it. "Okay, how about this. Come over here."

She led Kelly out of the stand, away from the main throng of people, and through a set of fire doors into the empty corridor beyond. Amber turned Kelly to face the wall, and stepped up close, shifting as she did so. She tapped Kelly's shoulder with her talons, and then reverted.

"What's this supposed to prove?" Kelly asked.

"If I were Brewer," said Amber, "and you're the only one who knows I can swap bodies, I'd take the opportunity to kill you right here, wouldn't I?"

"I guess so," said Kelly, and turned.

Amber smiled. "So we both know the other is who they say they are. That's good news. Although... I mean, Jesus, Kelly, if I *had* been Brewer, I could have killed you right there. It was pretty silly of you to let me take you to a secluded corner like this."

"Yeah, well," Kelly said with an irritable shrug, "I guess I still like you, then."

"You do?"

"Even though nothing's gonna happen while you're the Devil's lapdog. So are you?"

"Am I what?"

"The Devil's lapdog."

Amber made a face. "I'm still Astaroth's representative, if that's what you—"

"It is."

"Oh. Then, yeah, still the Devil's lapdog."

"Thought so," Kelly said, walking back to the hall.

Amber caught up with her as she went through the fire doors. "But I'm still me, Kelly. I haven't changed."

"Yet," Kelly said. "But it's only a matter of time."

"You said that, next time we met, we might be enemies," Amber said. "Do you think we're enemies now?"

Kelly hesitated. "No."

"Then I can help you."

"You've got your own stuff going on."

"My parents want me to walk into a trap. Helping you will delay that. It might even mean I don't walk into it at all. They couldn't have planned for me meeting you here. I can help you, Kelly, if you'll let me."

Kelly grunted. "Yeah, whatever."

Despite the churning in her gut, demanding that she pursue her parents, Amber brightened. "I can help?"

"Sure," said Kelly. "We're looking for a needle, and the haystack is every single person in this convention centre apart from you and me."

Amber observed the crowd. "How did you find her last time?"

"She chews her top lip," said Kelly. "Practically every picture on Brewer's Facebook page has her chewing her top lip. She does it when she's nervous, excited, angry... pretty much all the time, according to her Instagram, too. I went to the VIP section, saw a dude hanging around, chewing his lip the same way, went up and asked him some questions and he bolted."

"Good detective work."

"Yeah, well, that's what you have to look out for."

"So we're looking for a lip-chewer? In a crowd of thousands?"

"We're not going to be examining every single person, Amber. We're going to go back to the VIP area and stand guard."

Amber nodded. "That'd make sense. Okay then, let's go."

She went to move off, but Kelly put a hand on her arm. "We're going to have to be careful. She possesses people through touch."

"So we can't let anyone touch us?" Amber asked, frowning. "This place is packed."

"Hence the careful part."

"You better call the others and warn them."

"No calls," Kelly said sharply. "We won't know if it'll be a friend who answers the phone, or Brewer."

"Balls."

"Yeah."

Amber took another look at the crowd. "Okay, this is getting creepier."

"Stay close to me."

Doing their very best to avoid contact with the crowd, Amber and Kelly kept to the wall, stepping over the outstretched legs of cosplayers and the backpacks of fans.

"You still you?" Kelly asked.

"Yep," said Amber. "You?"

"Still me."

They came to a cordoned-off section of the hall within which were the partitioned walls that made up the VIP area. Staff members in convention T-shirts with lanyards around their necks stood ready to intercept any naïve fan who thought they could sneak into the temporary den of the stars.

"We could probably sneak in," said Amber.

"We're not going to do that."

"But Aaliyah might already be inside. She could be possessing one of the actors. We should sneak in and make sure they're okay."

"We don't have passes, Amber."

"So? We're not like these other fans, are we? We're resourceful. You're a ninja. I'm a demon."

"I'm not a ninja."

"But you can beat people up."

"I'm not going to beat up convention staff."

"I'm not saying beat them up, I'm just saying... We have skills. Surely we can use them to get by a few clueless volunteers?"

"Okay," said Kelly. "How?"

Amber looked around. There was one entrance to the VIP enclosure. It was guarded by two staff members.

"I don't know," she confessed.

Kelly sighed. "Come on," she said, taking Amber's hand. They left the hall, headed down a corridor towards the restrooms, then took the fire escape outside. The cooler air dried the perspiration on Amber's forehead as they walked round the side of the building.

"So how have you been?" Amber asked.

Kelly let go of her hand. "Fine."

Amber wished she hadn't said anything now. She liked it when Kelly held her hand.

"There," Kelly said. Ahead of them was an open door, guarded by a single staff member. "That's the back way into the VIP section. You distract the guard and I'll sneak in."

"How do I distract him?" Amber asked. "You want me to wave? Juggle something?"

"What are you talking about?"

"How do I distract him?"

Kelly stared at her. "You can engage him in a ridiculous conversation, Amber. Like the one we're having now. You're really good at that."

"I don't know," Amber said. "I don't think I'll be very good at it."

"Jesus, Amber, you just have to make him look the other way for ten seconds while I sneak in behind him. You can do that. Anyone could do that. A child could do that."

"Well, of course a child could do it," Amber said. "Children are cute and adorable. If they fall over, you run to help them up. When I fall over, he'll just frown at me."

"Why... dear God, Amber, why would you fall over?"

"To... to distract him. No?"

"All you have to do is ask him if he's got the time. Falling over is not required."

"Oh," said Amber. "Oh yeah. That's a good idea. But then, wait, how do I get in?"

"You don't," said Kelly. "One of us inside is all that's needed."

"Then why can't you distract him and I sneak in?"

"Because it's my plan."

"Still, though..."

"Amber, you said you wanted to help. Is that true? Do you really want to?"

"Yes. Of course."

"Then distract the guard."

Amber sagged, and nodded. She walked over. The guy was looking at his phone. He didn't even raise his eyes when she passed. She stopped and turned. He still didn't look up.

"Uh," she said.

His gaze didn't move from his phone. "Can't let you in."

"Oh," said Amber.

"VIP section," he said.

"I don't want to go in," Amber told him. "I'm just... Uh, do you have the time?"

"Seven minutes past three."

"Ah."

She looked over at Kelly, who was glaring at her.

Amber tried again. "Could I ask a question?"

"I'm not gonna let you in," said the guy.

"I'm not asking to be let in," she said. "I just want to ask a question. I was wondering about Montana. It's my first time here and I was wondering what it's like."

"You're in it," he said. "You can see what it's like. It's fine."

"Okay," she said. "That's good to know. Thanks for answering. Guess I'll be going now. Oh, now that I have you here, do you know the way to the restroom?"

"Back the way you came."

"That one smells bad. What about another one?"

"Continue the way you're going, all the way around, take three rights and you're there."

Amber frowned. "Wouldn't that take me back to the same restroom?"

"I don't know," said the guy. "I'm not a restroom expert. Please move along now."

Amber hesitated, then started walking away. She glanced back, and her legs gave out from under her and she fell. The guy still didn't look up, so she got back to her feet and made a helpless gesture to Kelly.

Furious, Kelly strode over. "Hey," she called out. The guy at the door looked up immediately. "What the hell do you think you're doing? You think this is acceptable behaviour? Where the hell is your supervisor?"

"I can't allow you—" he started to say.

"You can't allow me?" Kelly raged. "You can't *allow me*, you say? You listen to me, you little pipsqueak. I want to talk to your boss, do you hear me? To your boss!"

The guy held up his hands in a placatory gesture, turning his back to Amber as he did so. The open door beckoned her in.

"Miss, if you could tell me what this is about—"

"If I could tell you?" Kelly screeched. "If I have to tell you, then you've failed at your job! You want me to do it for you, is that what you want? You want me to do your job for you?"

Amber hurried inside.

20

SHE GOT TO THE end of the corridor and pushed open the next set of doors. She passed a table with a box of lanyards, snagged one for herself and put it over her head. Around the next corner was an open area full of tables and chairs. There was a sign on the wall: NO PHOTOGRAPHS.

Lots of people milling around, chatting. With her heart lurching and her eyes wide, she recognised most of them. Seth Dimitri chatting with Emmy-Lou Walters. At another table, Dominic Grey and Colin Phelps peering over Jessica Vaughan's shoulder, laughing at whatever she was showing them on her phone. Marc Winter sitting by himself. It took every ounce of willpower Amber had not to just rush over and scream for selfies. She had to remind herself that she wasn't here for that. She was here to protect the writer.

And there she was, Annalith Symmes, sitting alone in the corner, away from the flesh-and-blood versions of the characters she'd created. Compared to their beauty, their studied cool, she was nothing. She was wallpaper. Occasionally, her eyes would flicker to them, as if hoping for an invite to join their effortless, carefree bantering. She received no such invitation. Amber wondered if they even knew who she was.

A convention official stopped by Symmes's table, spoke briefly to her and tapped his clipboard. She nodded, he gave her a smile and departed. Amber watched Symmes take a deep breath, then get up and follow the signs for the restroom. Amber went after her, moving away from the celebrities and the volunteers who were trying to act normal around them. Symmes disappeared into the ladies' room and Amber hung about outside, making sure nobody went in after her. She tried to ignore the sound of puking.

When Symmes emerged, she was pale and sweating slightly.

"Hello," Amber said brightly.

Symmes gave her a panicked look. "I have to go onstage now? But... but the man said I had ten minutes. He said ten minutes and then—"

"You're still on in ten," Amber assured her. "I'm not here about that. I just thought I would take this opportunity to say, to tell you, and I know that you probably hear this all the time, and I swear I'm not a weirdo, but I am a huge, huge fan of yours."

"Oh," said Symmes, blinking quickly. "Thank you."

"And I was a fan long before the TV show," Amber said quickly. "A family friend, practically my auntie, bought me the first three books and I just, I devoured them. I did. All because of Imelda. Then the show happened and everything exploded and I love the show, I do, but the books... the books are really, really good."

Symmes nodded awkwardly, made to walk past and Amber jumped in front of her.

"Can I just say," Amber said, "that the female characters in your books are just the best examples of, like... they're the best representations of women that I've ever read, probably. You see all these polls and people saying that Little Women has the best characters, or Pride and Prejudice or whatever, but I think, in the modern world, In the Dark Places says more to people my age than any of the classics." She even did the air-quotes thing, and she hated the air-quotes thing.

"The classics still have a lot to say," Symmes responded. Her voice was quiet.

"Absolutely," said Amber, "but I think you're way up there with Jane Austen and her sister."

"I... I didn't know her sister was a writer."

"Wasn't she?"

"You may be thinking of the Brontës."

"Maybe I am. Who wrote Little Women?"

"Louisa May Alcott."

"I think I'm thinking of someone else."

"I think you are, yes. It was very nice to meet you."

Symmes went to move by her again, and once more Amber stepped into her path. "Before you go, actually, I was wondering if you had seen anyone, uh, suspicious, hanging around?"

"I'm sorry?"

"Suspicious," Amber repeated. "Someone maybe... lurking? Have you seen anyone lurking?"

Symmes took a step backwards. "Just you."

"Ha, yes," said Amber, "but I promise you, I'm not the one who means you harm."

Incredibly, Symmes went even paler. "There's someone who means me harm?"

"No!" Amber said. "No, God, no! No... Well, yes. I have reason to believe your life is in danger. But don't worry – I'm here to protect you."

"You?" said Symmes. "How old are you?"

Amber tried to look taller. "Seventeen. I know I may not seem like it, but I really am your best chance of getting out of this alive."

"I... I think I'll need to speak with your supervisor."

"Oh, I don't have one," said Amber. "I'm not even a real volunteer."

Symmes nodded. "Please," she said, "please don't kill me."

Amber tried to use laughter to make Symmes feel better, but it wasn't working. She stopped laughing and said, very calmly, "I promise I'm not going to kill you." That made Symmes even worse.

Then Kelly came round the corner. "There you are," she said.

Amber held her hands up. "I didn't do anything, I swear."

Kelly barely glanced at her. "Miss Symmes, I need a word, if you wouldn't mind. I have reason to believe your life may be in danger."

Symmes was almost in tears. "That's just what this girl was saying."

"Well, she was right," said Kelly, and lunged at Symmes with a huge pair of scissors.

21

Symmes shrieked and fell back, arms over her head, but, before Kelly could complete the stab, Amber wrapped her arms around her from behind and twisted, throwing her against the wall.

"Go," Amber said, picking Symmes up off the floor. "Run!"

Symmes ran, and Amber held her hands out as Kelly turned to her.

"Kelly, this isn't you."

"Damn right it isn't her," said Aaliyah Brewer from behind Kelly's snarling mouth. They circled each other. "I'm a real woman, something this stick insect would know nothing about."

"Well, okay," said Amber, keeping an eye on the gleaming scissors, "at the risk of allowing this conversation to derail, she's slim, sure, but I wouldn't exactly call her a stick insect."

"Look at her," Brewer said, lifting her top. "When was the last time she had a burger, huh? When was the last time she defiled her body temple with a slice of pizza? This, all this? This is all for them."

Amber took her eyes away from Kelly's abs long enough to frown. "For who?"

"Men," said Brewer. "She's starved herself to conform to the male perception of what makes a woman beautiful. I didn't need to do that. I was comfortable in myself and that's what made me beautiful. I didn't need male approval."

"Uh, neither does Kelly. She's a lesbian."

Brewer kept on glaring, but didn't respond.

"Anyway," said Amber, "now that we're talking, I wonder if I could persuade you to leave Kelly's body and stop killing people. Could I do that?"

"It doesn't matter," said Brewer.

"What doesn't?"

"Her sexual orientation. It has nothing to do with anything. She's still a woman in a man's world, because, in this culture of ours, it's the stick insects who get the magazine covers. That's all we see, 24/7. Image after image after unrealistic image."

"Okay, I really have to stop you there and ask what this has to do with anything," said Amber.

Brewer shrugged. "It's just something that bugs me."

"I think it might be because you live on the internet and you've probably seen some pretty unhealthy things."

Brewer shook her head. "This has been bugging me long before that. Why are you taking her side? You're like me. You should be proud of your body."

"I'm taking her side because she's not trying to murder anyone."

"You're ashamed," said Brewer.

"You realise we're having two completely different conversations here, right?"

"Admit it," Brewer said. "You hate how you look."

"If I admit it, will you leave her body?"

"Gladly."

Amber took a moment. "Then yeah, I do. I don't like being fat."

"Fat according to who?"

"I think it's *whom*. And I don't know. Other people, I guess."

"They called me fat, too," said Brewer. "Fat and ugly. The boys in my school. And the girls hardly rushed to my defence. They were too busy looking pretty and trying to fit in. Well, I didn't care about fitting in."

"I did," said Amber. "Care, I mean. I did my best to be like everyone else, but it was never going to happen. There was a girl I grew up with, she was way bigger than me. Then, after one summer, she came back to school and she'd lost all this weight. It took a few months to lose her old nicknames as well, but she did, and I watched it all and I knew that even if I did everything that she'd done, it wouldn't make one bit of difference. I still wouldn't fit in. Some of us are just different, Aaliyah."

Brewer shook her head. "If I looked like them, they'd have loved me. If I'd been a stick insect like this one, I'd have been the most popular girl in school."

Amber took a small step forward. "What about you? All I've heard from you is a rant about how much thin people suck. But what if they don't? What if they're just like you?"

"The difference," said Brewer, "is that I'd never bully anyone because of how they looked."

"Then how about you stop calling people stick insects, and leave her body like you promised?"

"I'll leave when I'm ready to leave," said Brewer.

Amber didn't know where the hell Symmes had run off to, but wherever it was it looked like there weren't any security guards there. This was up to Amber.

"Why are you doing this, Aaliyah?" she asked. "Is it really because of the fan fiction?"

"Gideon and Uriah are polar opposites."

"Aaliyah, come on... You're killing people because you object to the pairing. You've got to be able to hear how nuts that sounds."

"These characters are my friends!" Brewer yelled. "I grew up with them! I know them better than I know my own family!"

"They're not real."

"To me, they are! To me, they are *everything*. We own them. The fans, the true fans, we own those characters, and Symmes thinks she can come in and ruin all that? She thinks she can plant those seeds and — and — and absolve herself of all responsibility?"

"It's fan fiction, Aaliyah. What does it matter?"

"Fan fiction, the *good* fan fiction, is as relevant as the books. Maybe even more so, because the writers aren't motivated by greed or publishing contracts. We are pure."

"Just not the writers you disagree with."

"Gideon and Uriah don't belong together," Brewer said defiantly. "Gideon and *Balthazar* belong together."

"How did you die, Aaliyah? Aaliyah? How did you die?"

"An accident," said Brewer. She chewed her top lip.

"What happened?"

"It was an accident. They said, they said afterwards that I did it myself, that it was suicide, but it wasn't. It was an accident."

"I believe you."

"I didn't kill myself. They said I was confused and angry and..."

"It's okay," said Amber. "I believe you."

Brewer nodded.

"Aaliyah, I don't want to fight you. I've been fighting way too many people lately and I really don't want to fight you. Can we not fight? Can we not do that?"

"If you stand in my way, I'll kill you."

"Stand in your way of what? Killing Annalith Symmes? What do you think that will achieve? The TV show will go on, you know it will. It'll probably get a huge ratings boost."

"The show isn't why I'm doing this."

"Then have you thought about what happens with the books?"

"Yes. They stop, before they get a chance to slide into mediocrity."

"But if you kill her then we'll get tens of thousands of new readers, each one of them claiming to have been fans from the very start. Forums will be swamped by noobs. *In the Dark Places* will become even more mainstream than it already is."

Brewer glowered. "I hate noobs."

"I do, too. We all do."

"But she has to die."

"No, she doesn't," said Amber. "Neither did those people you killed."

"You don't understand," Brewer said, tears springing to her eyes. "They were changing my friends. They were making them do things they would never do. They were butchering them."

"They're allowed to do that. We're talking about stories here, Aaliyah. And the characters, they've already been changed. Balthazar in the TV show is not the Balthazar in the books – he's wittier."

"His eyes are the wrong colour, too."

"Well, yeah, I mean..."

"And he should be taller."

"I guess you're right," Amber said. "But he's even different from how he was in the early books, isn't he? Remember how he used to say that he'd never been in love, and then in *Tempest's Anguish* he talked all about the women he's loved over the centuries? Some people call that inconsistent, but I call it—"

"Evolution," said Brewer. "He's evolved. They all have."

"And fan fiction is just another stage of that," said Amber. "Maybe not an official stage, maybe not a canon stage, but it's still a stage of the characters' development. You've just got to... you've got to accept this, Aaliyah. And stop killing people over it. Aaliyah? You okay?"

Brewer frowned. "There's a voice in my head. A girl."

"Kelly."

"Kelly, yeah. She says... she says hi."

"Tell her hi back."

"She can hear you," Brewer said absently.

"I don't want to fight you," Amber said, her voice gentle. "I don't want to hurt you. I don't want to hurt her. Don't make me. Please."

"She's talking to me," said Brewer. "It's hard to... it's hard to focus."

"Listen to her."

Brewer shook her head. "You're trying to get me to stop. I don't want to stop. I don't want to..."

"Do you like hurting people?" Amber asked.

"No!" Brewer said, so vehemently that Amber thought she'd blown it. But then Brewer calmed. "No. I don't. But they're... they're hurting my friends."

"Balthazar and Gideon are my friends, too," Amber said.

"They're Kelly's friends. Everyone in those halls? Their friends, too. We share them. We love them."

Brewer screwed her eyes shut and wobbled a little. She dropped the scissors. "I'm all alone," she said.

"I know what that's like," Amber said, stepping forward slowly.

"I'm scared."

"I know you are. But you can't stay in Kelly's body. I'm sorry."

Brewer looked at her, tears rolling down her cheeks. "What will happen to me?"

"I don't know, Aaliyah."

"Do you think I'll be lonely, where I'm going?"

Amber hesitated. "I think you're going to a place where you'll be surrounded by friends and loved ones. They're waiting for you. All you have to do is go to them."

Brewer smiled through her tears. "Thank you," she said, but Amber didn't know if it was she Brewer was thanking, or Kelly.

Brewer's eyes rolled back in her head and Amber caught her before she fell. Moving awkwardly, she lowered Kelly to a seated position.

Someone came round the corner. Emmy-Lou Walters. Tempest herself. She saw Amber and Kelly and she frowned.

"The heat," Amber explained. "Too much for some people."

Emmy-Lou gave her a flash of that TV-star smile. "I guess it is," she said, before walking into the ladies' room.

"Was that Tempest?" Kelly asked in a quiet voice.

Amber hunkered down by her. "You okay? Kelly? Is it Kelly or is it Aaliyah?"

"It's me," said Kelly, reaching out so that Amber could pull her up. "Aaliyah has left the building."

Amber grunted as she helped Kelly to her feet.

"That was Emmy-Lou Walters, wasn't it?" Kelly asked.

"Yes."

"And she saw me all passed out and stuff?"

"That's right."

"Aw man. Did I have my mouth open?"

"You did. You looked gormless."

"Ah Jesus."

"She's really nice, though," Amber said. "We chatted a little. You okay to walk?"

"I'm fine," said Kelly. "Maybe you could introduce us when she comes back?"

"Actually, I think that'd be kinda creepy, don't you? Hanging around the bathroom, I mean? I think it's best if we just head back to the hall."

"I guess you're right," Kelly grumbled.

22

Amber and Kelly took one last look at all the celebrities, and then left the enclosure and fought their way through the crowds.

"We make a good team," Amber shouted to her over the noise.

Kelly looked back, and nodded. "Pity you're still the Devil's lapdog," she called.

Amber bounced off a huge guy dressed as an angel, found herself pressed up against Kelly from behind. "Could there be anything else that you might call me?" she asked. "I don't really like the whole *lapdog* thing."

Kelly turned to her, smiling. "You want something cooler?"

"I really do."

Kelly's smile dropped. "Devil's lapdogs don't get cooler, Amber. They get called names until they change their ways."

They broke through the crowd into the eating area.

"But I'm still a good person," Amber said.

Kelly shook her head. "You can't be a good person while doing an evil job. It's not possible."

"I'm doing my best to get out of it," said Amber. "You think I like this? I hate it. I hated having to agree to it in the first place."

"But you still agreed to it," Kelly said, and went to turn away.

Amber took hold of Kelly's shoulders, kept her in place and looked her dead in the eye. "Okay, Kelly, I like you, I like you so much and I am thrilled beyond words that you like me, too, but for the last time – I had no frikkin' choice. Astaroth was going to give Milo to Demoriel, and Demoriel would have killed him. Then Astaroth would have killed me. And our deaths would not have been painless, and they would not have been quick, and what happened to us afterwards would have gone on for the rest of eternity. I agreed to be Astaroth's representative to save my friend, to save myself and to finally stop my parents. So tell me, *tell me*, what is so wrong with that?"

Kelly looked at her, said nothing.

"You think I'm working for the enemy," Amber continued. "You think I'm working with the monsters we fight. Well, you'd have a point, if I were going to do that for the rest of my life. But I'm going to cheat the Shining Demon the first chance I get. I'm going to stab him in the back at the earliest goddamn opportunity. And you think I'm working with the killers? You think I'm working with people like Elias Mauk? I'm biding my time, Kelly. This was the only option open to me and I took it, and I'd do it again, and, if you can't understand that from way up there on your high horse, then there's obviously nothing I can say to change your mind."

Amber stopped talking. That had been a lot of words, and, now that she'd stopped, she was no longer sure any of them had made sense.

But now, judging by the look on Kelly's face, she suspected

that some of what she'd said might have actually had an effect. She just couldn't tell if it was a good or a bad one.

"I'm sorry," said Kelly.

Amber frowned. "What?"

"I'd started to think that maybe, once everything in Desolation Hill was cleared up, maybe you'd tag along with us in the van," Kelly said. "But then your parents got away and I realised you were going to be sticking with Milo and I didn't know if I'd ever see you again, and then with what Astaroth made you agree to... I got scared, Amber. I'm sorry."

"You are?"

"I wanted to call you. After I'd calmed down, I wanted to call. I should have."

"Why didn't you?"

"I should have. I was mad. I was stupid."

"Well... I mean, it wasn't entirely your fault. Technically, I *am* the Devil's lapdog."

"I'm sorry I called you that."

"You slapped me, too."

"I'm sorry I slapped you."

"I've had worse."

"Well, yeah, but it was still a rotten thing to do. I kinda panicked."

"You're forgiven. Obviously."

"You need any help?" Kelly asked. "Getting your parents? Cheating the Shining Demon?"

Amber smiled. "Sure. If you're offering."

"I am. If it's okay with you, I'll get the others and we can sit down and come up with a plan."

"Plans are cool," said Amber. Kelly smiled, hesitated, then turned and vanished into the crowd.

Amber took a seat at an empty table, sighing now that the weight was taken off her feet, and watched the people go by. She wondered suddenly if she should hide her face. If Annalith Symmes had given a detailed description to the security guards, Amber might be in for some trouble. She lowered her head, taking the iPad out of her bag for something to read.

She logged on to the forums.

The Dark Princess said...
Hey to all at the con, anyone around to meet up really quickly?? Looks like I'll be leaving soon!

Sith0Dude said...
Wish I was there.

The Dark Princess said...
Maybe next time!

Sith0Dude said...
My parents would never allow me.
How'd you get to go? Thought you weren't gonna make it.

The Dark Princess said...
Last-minute change of plans. But now I'm about to leave and I haven't met anyone off the boards!

Sith0Dude said...
Least you were allowed to go.

Amber tapped her fingers for a few minutes, and nothing new was posted. She was about to log off when BAC logged in.

The Dark Princess said...
Hiya, BAC!

Balthazar's-Arm-Candy said...
Hey, guys! Surprise! I'm in Montana!

The Dark Princess said...
Seriously??

Sith0Dude said...
Ur at the convention??

Balthazar's-Arm-Candy said...
Family vay-cay to America! Woop! Where are all my lovely peeps at?

Balthazar's-Arm-Candy said...
Princess! U here too? THIS ROCKS! Where are u? I'm lost! This place is way too big!

Sith0Dude said...
I wasn't allowed to go.

The Dark Princess said...
I'm in the north hall. Where r u?

Balthazar's-Arm-Candy said...
North hall also! But somewhere backstage!

The Dark Princess said...
U got lost backstage??

Balthazar's-Arm-Candy said...
I'm Australian! We do things backwards here! Can u come get me??

Sith0Dude said...
No one cares that I'm not there.

The Dark Princess said...
LOL sure. But I'm about to leave, so it'll only be a quick hug! Any clues to where u might be?

Balthazar's-Arm-Candy said...
Just passed a sign for Corridor 14B. That any help?

The Dark Princess said...
I can see a sign for Corridor 12A. Stay where u are and I'll find u!

Balthazar's-Arm-Candy said...
Yay! Can't wait! I'm wearing a black top!

The Dark Princess said...
C u soon!

Amber put the iPad away, checked that Kelly and the others weren't anywhere close, then followed the signs. She squeezed through the crowd and almost got stuck, before popping free like a champagne cork. She found the sign for 14B, got to a door and passed through into the empty corridor beyond. She walked quickly for the door ahead, pushing and finding it blocked. She pushed harder, putting her shoulder to it, and felt it give. She slipped through. It shut quickly, weighed down by the pile of bodies on the other side.

For a moment, all Amber saw was the blood and the unnatural angles in which the bodies, three of them, were bent. Then the clothes registered with her, and her legs gave out and she collapsed, sliding down the wall, mouth open and eyes wide and staring at the bodies of Warrick and Linda and Ronnie, dumped on top of each other like discarded rag dolls.

The door at the far end opened and Betty came through, holding Two in her arms with one red hand clamped over his muzzle. She was wearing a black top, just like Balthazar's-Arm-Candy had said she would, and she smiled, broke the dog's neck and tossed his body away.

"Hello, my little Dark Princess," she said.

23

AMBER'S VOICE WAS HUSHED. "What have you done?"

"You seem surprised," said Betty, looking beautiful with her red skin and horns. "I'll take that as a compliment. Do you know how hard I had to work at being Balthazar's-Arm-Candy? I had to watch every episode of that damn show just so I could befriend you in the forums. It was exhausting, Amber. The show isn't even that good. There, I've said it. Bombshell."

"You didn't have to... you didn't have to kill them..."

"Of course we did," her mother said. "Now you know the stakes. Now you know that we are quite serious, and that we will kill whoever we need to kill."

Amber stood, and shifted. "I'm going to tear you apart."

Betty smiled. "That's the spirit. But I wouldn't, if I were you."

Amber fought the urge to leap at her and rip her face off. "Where's Kelly?"

"You mean your little girlfriend?"

Bill stepped out behind Betty, in full demon form. Kelly lay limp in his arms.

Amber surged forward, screaming. "No!"

But her mother held up a hand. "She's alive," she said. "For now."

Amber froze, her body trembling.

"I have had conflicting feelings about being a father," said Bill. "On the one hand, no boy was good enough for my daughter. On the other hand, I was planning to kill you and eat you so, really, what did it matter? But, when we realised you liked girls, I could suddenly breathe again."

Betty laughed. "Are you shocked that we knew?"

"I'm shocked that you noticed," Amber said.

"Oh, we noticed, all right, and long before we were called in to that meeting with... what was your principal's name? Crabbe?"

"Cobb," said Bill.

"Cobb, that's it," Betty said. "Called in because you got into a fight with a friend you'd had a crush on since you were twelve years old. What happened? Did you tell her you loved her? Did she threaten to out you?"

"I was never in," said Amber. "Other gay kids are mostly worried about what their parents will think. But I grew up knowing you wouldn't give a damn. Let Kelly go."

"Obviously, we're not going to do that."

"What do you want?" Amber asked. "You want me to sneak you into Astaroth's castle? Fine. Okay, I'll do it. Let Kelly go and I'll take you right now."

"Oh no, no," said Betty. "It's not quite so simple anymore. We've been thinking. We don't want you to bring us to him. We want you to bring him to us."

"What? I can't do that."

"Of course you can," said Bill. "You're his representative."

"Astaroth doesn't leave his castle," Amber said. "He did it in your day, yes, but not anymore."

Bill nodded. "We know. We don't have all the information, obviously, but we suspect it's something to do with the mayor in Desolation Hill. He summoned and trapped Naberius, after all. Astaroth isn't going to risk that happening to him, so he's making everyone else do the travelling."

"Smart," said Betty.

"It's what I'd do," said Bill.

"So you understand," Amber said. "I can't get him to leave."

"You can't trick him into leaving," Betty corrected. "But you can still force him to."

Amber frowned. "I can't force him to do anything."

"The mayor, whatever his name was, found a way to trap a Demon, didn't he? That's where you start. Find out how he did it, and find out how they kept Astaroth's brother in that cell for a hundred years, and use this knowledge to bring Astaroth to us."

A wave of anger and desperation hit Amber and flooded her mind, but she struggled through it. To lose her temper now would be disastrous. "Jesus... why? I can sneak you into his castle easily. If you want to kill him, that's the best way to go about it."

"But we don't want to just kill him," Bill told her. "For what we want to do, we need to be able to take our time. We can't take our time on enemy ground. The Blood-dimmed King has eyes everywhere, we've heard."

"What are you talking about?" Amber asked. "If you're not going to just kill him, then what are you going to do?"

"We're going to eat him," said Betty, flashing a razor-sharp smile. "We're going to eat him and absorb his power. Doesn't that sound delicious? And it truly is the best possible resolution to all our current problems. With Astaroth gone, you'll be released from your obligations as a representative and you can spend the rest of your life here on Earth with your tattooed girlfriend."

"I... I don't know if I can do what you're asking."

"Of course you can," said Betty. "You've proven yourself to be quite resourceful when you need to be. We expect nothing less from you now."

"You have one week," Bill said.

Amber gaped. "I'll need longer."

"Then you have six days."

"What?"

"Every objection is a day less. Do you have any more objections?"

Amber kept her mouth shut.

"Good," said Bill. "If you do not deliver Astaroth to us by midnight on Saturday, we'll kill the redhead."

"Where?" Amber asked. "Where will you be?"

"Where else would we be?" Betty asked. "We'll be waiting for you in Orlando, sweetheart. We'll be waiting for you at home."

24

AMBER SAT IN THE Charger with her head down, trying not to shake, trying not to puke. Trying not to cry. Police cars and ambulances screamed past. The convention centre was six miles behind them. She wondered if the paramedics had started loading the bodies on to the stretchers yet, or if the cops were insisting that everything remain untouched, like they did on TV.

She wondered what effect this would have on *In the Dark Places*. Would its ratings suffer? Would it be cancelled? And what about Annalith Symmes herself – would she keep writing? Would she ever leave her house again?

Amber wondered about all of these things because that stopped her from wondering about Kelly.

"They'll hurt her," she mumbled.

Milo waited until all the cop cars had gone by, and then he pulled out on to the road again.

"When Kelly wakes, she'll try to escape," Amber said. "And they'll hurt her."

"Maybe," said Milo.

"I know they will."

"Maybe."

Amber wiped her eyes. "This is my fault. If she'd never met me, she'd be fine right now, and the others... They'd still be alive."

"Not your fault," said Milo. "Your parents' fault. Don't make the mistake of forgetting that."

"We have six days to do something I don't even know if it's possible to do, Milo. When I don't bring them Astaroth, they're gonna kill Kelly in front of me and that will be my fault."

"So we'll bring them Astaroth."

"It's that easy, is it?"

"No," said Milo, "but it's that simple. And let's face it, we were planning to move against Astaroth eventually, right? Our timetable has just been moved up a little, that's all. Whatever happens, I'm with you."

"You sure that's a good idea?"

He glanced at her. "What d'you mean?"

"Glen was with me all the way, and now look at him. Look at Imelda. Look at Ronnie, and Linda, and Warrick... even the damn dog. I knew Clarissa for a few hours and now a lunatic trucker has her. The only person, apart from you, that I have even remotely in my corner is Kelly, and her life depends on whether I can jump through enough hoops. If I were you, I'd dump me by the side of this road and drive away as fast as you can."

"That would appear to be the smart move," Milo said.

"They're going to kill you, Milo. Sooner or later, someone is going to kill you because you're with me."

He grunted. "I've got Demoriel after me. My life doesn't get any safer if I suddenly start to go it alone." He took out his phone, handed it to her. "Give Buxton a call."

"You think he'd be able to help?"

"I don't know, but he's the resident expert on this crap, so we may as well try."

She found Gregory Buxton's number, and pressed dial. Her first attempt rang out. So did her second. On her third, the call was answered, and Buxton's deep voice came on over the speaker. "You said you wouldn't call."

"I know what we said," Milo responded, "but things have changed."

"That right?" said Buxton. "Is Amber with you? I'm going to take it that she is. So, Amber, have you changed, or are you still Astaroth's representative?"

She hesitated.

"Yeah," Buxton continued, "that's what I thought. Listen, I was fine about helping you out when we all had the same problem, that problem being the Shining Demon, but you're taking your orders from him now. You are a danger to me. You're a threat."

"I won't go after you," Amber said. "I promise."

"It may get to the point where you no longer have the choice," Buxton replied. "I like you, Amber, I do, but there's no way in hell that I'm helping you help Astaroth."

"Well, that's the thing," Milo interjected. "This isn't about helping Astaroth. In fact, it's about hurting him. Possibly destroying him."

There was silence from the other end.

"We want to trap him," said Amber. "Trap him, wrap him in chains, and drag him out of his castle. Bring him back here, where he'll be killed."

Buxton grunted. "You're going to do all that, are you?"

"We need your help," said Milo, "but yes."

"What you're proposing is suicide. It'll never work."

They stopped at traffic lights. "But there's a precedent," said Milo. "The mayor of Desolation Hill trapped Astaroth's brother in a cell. He's bound by chains that sap his power."

"Well, there you go," Buxton said. "You don't even need my help. Just go back to Desolation Hill and take a peek at those chains."

"We wouldn't know what to do with that information," Milo responded. "Those chains are custom-made. We can't make more."

"You think I can?"

"You studied this stuff."

"I am a layman, you understand that? Not an expert. I wouldn't know where to begin."

"You know more than us," said Milo.

"Wouldn't be hard," said Buxton, "but that's not enough. I can't help, I'm afraid."

The lights turned green, and Milo accelerated. "What about the people who helped you? The people you went to for advice? Could we talk to them?"

Amber could practically feel Buxton shaking his head. "If they knew I'd passed their names around, they'd be sending people out to kill me. It's not going to happen. Although..."

Amber straightened. "Yes?"

"You already know someone who could probably help," Buxton said. "Course, she might need something in return."

"Abigail," said Milo.

"That's the one," said Buxton. "I mean, as creepy little girls go, she's one of the creepiest, but she knows her stuff. If anyone can help you get your hands on more of those magic chains, it's her. But do me a favour – do not tell her it was my suggestion."

"We won't," said Amber, slouching back in her seat.

"I gotta go," Buxton said. "Don't contact me again until Amber quits her damn job. Even then, think twice about it."

He hung up.

"Do we have Abigail's number?" Amber asked.

Milo shook his head. "The Dark Stair is a bar without a phone. We'll have to ask her in person."

"How far?"

"We'll make it there tonight."

"Then okay, let's go."

He nodded. "You got it."

She didn't want to sleep, didn't want to dream, but exhaustion pulled her down with every mile, tugged her into the car seat, and she plunged, stepping through the front door of her home in Orlando.

Music played. That song, 'Turn! Turn! Turn!' by... someone. Herman's Hermits? No, the Byrds. She was pretty sure it was the Byrds. Imelda had used to listen to sixties music all the time.

Amber walked in. The table in the living room was covered in blood that seeped from the birthday cake at its centre. Only one person sat at the table. Her sister, Carolyn. She was singing along, softly, to the record.

"Hi," said Amber. She realised she was crying. "You're my sister. Hi. I'm Amber."

Carolyn looked up and smiled. "Pleased to meet you. They're going to kill me."

"I'll help you," said Amber. "Come with me. I'll help you, I promise."

"Thank you," said Carolyn. "That's awfully nice of you, but I couldn't impose. Just let them kill me. It's quite all right."

Amber took her hand, pulled her to her feet. "We can run. The both of us."

Carolyn smiled and shook her head. "They'll be back soon. You're better off letting them kill me. Just like you let them kill Kelly."

Amber let go of her hand. "Kelly's not dead."

"She will be soon, though, won't she? I mean, one way or the other she'll abandon you. She'll either walk away of her own free will or she'll be carried away, a lifeless husk. Isn't that right?"

"I won't... I won't let that happen."

"Do you have much of a choice?"

The door was flung open, and a woman strode in, slight of frame, with grey hair. Maybe sixty-five or seventy years old, but moving like someone fifteen years younger.

"Molly," said Carolyn, turning to her with a smile, "I was telling Amber here that there's really no point in me running. My parents are going to kill me just like they're going to kill Kelly."

"Kelly's not dead yet," said Molly, the same Molly James had helped all those years before, "and neither are you. Come on now." She took Carolyn's hand.

"But I don't wish to be a burden," said Carolyn.

"You stop that talk right this minute!" Molly said. "They've taught you to be like this! They've taught you not to make a fuss! Well, you know what, young lady? Now is the time to *rebel*."

"Oh, I couldn't."

"Oh, you damn well will," said Molly, and dragged Carolyn to the door. "And you!" she said, pointing with her free hand at Amber. "You do not stop fighting, you hear me?"

Then they were gone, and the door slammed shut behind them and Amber woke to fir trees and white-capped mountains and the rumble of the Charger.

"You okay?" Milo asked.

"Fine," she responded, straightening up. She wasn't about to stop fighting. Not yet. She had Kelly to rescue, and her parents to deliver, and Astaroth to cheat.

She had a long way to go before she could stop fighting.

25

They got to Salt Lake City at a little past eleven, only to find that The Dark Stair bar closed early on a Sunday night.

"Early?" Amber raged, kicking the locked door. "Early? It's a bar on the Demon Road, for Christ's sake! The only people that drink in it are monsters and killers and frikkin' weirdos! Why the hell does it close early on Sundays?"

Milo scratched the stubble on his chin. "Beats me."

"We drove all day for this! We're in a goddamn hurry! Now what do we do?"

"We find somewhere to sleep," Milo said, walking back to the Charger.

"Sleep?" said Amber. "We can't sleep! We have six days to get Astaroth!"

"I need to rest, Amber," said Milo. "So do you."

"We don't have time!"

"We don't have a choice," Milo said. "We have to wait for the bar to open. We may as well wait in a motel and catch some shut-eye while we can. Listen to me – you're angry, you're upset, I get that. But depriving yourself of sleep will lead to sloppiness, and we can't afford to make any mistakes from this moment on, can we?"

Amber clutched her hair in big, angry bunches. "No," she said through gritted teeth. "No, we can't."

She got in to the Charger, grabbed for the seat belt, but it snagged. "Oh, for Christ's sake," she snapped, tugging harder.

"Be nice to her," said Milo, slipping into the driver's seat.

"It's a car!" she roared, slamming her fist on to the dash. "It's a stupid goddamn car! It doesn't have any goddamn feelings!"

Milo looked at her, waited for her to calm down, and Amber threw herself heavily back into the seat. "Whatever," she mumbled. She went for the seat belt again, and this time it flowed smoothly into the buckle. She felt a ridiculous urge to apologise to the Charger, but ignored it as the engine came to life and they pulled away from the kerb.

They found the nearest motel. It was small and crummy, and only had one room available. It was a twin room, at least, so Amber grabbed the key and stormed off while Milo paid. She dumped her bag by the bed nearest the window, sat down and flicked on the TV just for something to do.

She shifted and lay down. She was calmer like this. Her insides didn't tie themselves into as many knots when she was horned up. She was still in a bad mood, though. Her heart was still beating fast. She changed the channel, caught the end of a news report on the police chief's missing kid. They reckoned a serial killer had snatched him away, the same serial killer the police chief had been investigating. Bad crap happening in New York. Bad crap happening everywhere.

Another press of the button and another channel. A rerun of

When Strikes the Shroud. Amber watched a young Virgil Abernathy kick evil's ass and grinned.

Milo came in.

"Hey," she said.

He looked at her for a moment before saying, "Hi."

She changed the channel. Commercials. "Something wrong?" she asked.

"Not a thing," Milo said, draping his jacket over the chair. "There a reason you're wearing your red skin?"

She raised an eyebrow. "What, I'm not allowed to horn up in the privacy of my own motel room?"

"Just wondering why, that's all."

She kept her eyes on the TV. "I like being like this."

"So it's a comfort thing?"

"Yep." She glanced at him. "Though you look like you don't believe me."

"And you talk like you want an argument."

Amber shrugged. "You're the one acting strange, not me."

He sat on his bed. "How are you feeling?"

"Peachy."

"And how were you feeling before you shifted?"

"What's that got to do with anything?"

"Were you thinking about Kelly? Were you worried about her? Or Clarissa? Were you thinking of Linda and Ronnie and Warrick?"

"You sure know how to kill a good mood."

"Well, that's just it, Amber. You shouldn't be in a good mood. Your friends have been murdered. That's a lot for anyone to handle. That's too much, even. Some people might turn to the bottle after something like that. Some people might turn to drugs."

"Dear God," she said, sitting up, "what is your point?"

"When you shift, you care a little less, don't you?"

She glared at him. "You think you're so smart."

"I'm not blaming you."

"You're not? Oh, that's nice." She swung her legs off the bed and perched there, on the edge.

"But you're going to have to deal with what you're feeling sooner or later," Milo said.

She laughed. "Seriously? You are lecturing me about feelings? You?"

"It does strike me as ironic."

"How about hypocritical?"

Milo shrugged. "I'm just pointing it out."

"I appreciate you sharing these thoughts with me," she said, "I really do, but maybe next time you could keep them to yourself, seeing as how you don't know what the hell you're talking about?"

"Sure thing."

She got up. "You know what? I'm gonna go for a walk."

"You're going out like that?"

"That's a very dad thing to say, Milo. May I remind you that A, you are not my dad, and B, you wouldn't want to be."

"I just meant the horns, Amber."

"I know what you meant," she said, and walked out.

A voice in the back of her mind yelled at her, demanded that she revert, that she only go out in public as plain old Amber Lamont with all of her many flaws and shortcomings there for all to see. But she ignored the voice, drowning it out with the thrill that came from walking down a sidewalk in full demonic form. Cars passed. Some of them honked their horns.

She waved.

It was bullshit what Milo had said. Pure bullshit. She wasn't running from anything. She was ready to take on the world and its cousin. It was everyone else that was running from her. She grinned at the revelation.

Because they *should* run, and that's what Milo was refusing to understand. They should all run from her.

They certainly wouldn't run from the other Amber, the old Amber, the plain old dumb Amber whose clothes she was still wearing. Why would they? There was nothing fierce there. There was nothing formidable. There was only a pathetic need to both fit in to her surroundings and fade into the background.

She stopped outside a weird gothic boutique, eyes drawn to the mannequin in the window. Everything she'd heard about Salt Lake City being a conservative town, and here she was looking at tiny skirts and plastic horns.

Scales formed over her fist and she smashed the glass. No alarm sounded. She pulled the tartan skirt and *Little Devil* T-shirt off the mannequin, and changed clothes in the shadow of a squat building. She left her jeans and *Dark Places* hoody there, along with her sneakers and socks. They didn't go with her new look.

She went walking. Barefoot. It was nice, being out in the open like this with her horns on. Liberating. She didn't mind the slight nip in the air on her bare arms and legs. She didn't mind the cold at all.

She heard laughter and was drawn towards it. A few guys and a girl, all in their early twenties, chatting outside a cafe. The girl was cute. She had a pixie cut.

"Hey there," Amber said, walking up to her.

Pixie-cut laughed. "Wow. Nice costume!"

Amber grinned. "Thanks. There's a costume party somewhere around here, but I went for a walk and got lost." She shrugged. "What you gonna do?"

"I know what you could do," said one of the guys, trying to wrap an arm round her waist.

Amber pushed his hand away, focused on Pixie-cut. "You from here? This is my first time in..." She laughed. "Okay, I don't even know where I am!"

Pixie-cut giggled. "How drunk are you?"

"Like, very," said Amber, and joined in her giggles. "Am I in Salt Lake City? I think I'm in Salt Lake City."

"You are," Pixie-cut reassured her. "But don't worry, I'm not from here, either."

Amber laughed. "I heard this was a boring-ass town. Please tell me there are places to dance."

"Oh, there are," another one of the guys said. "Listen, I don't know about your costume party, but we're headed to a club, and we can get both of you lovely ladies in. Spencer's friendly with one of the bouncers."

"I don't know," said Pixie-cut, "I'm already pretty wasted."

"I'll take care of you," Amber said.

Pixie-cut laughed again. Such a pretty laugh. "Sure," she said. "I'm in."

The guys led them down the street and round the corner. The next block over there was a line of people outside a club.

One of the guys fell into step beside Amber. "That is some amazing make-up, by the way. Could I try the horns?"

"The horns stay on," Amber said.

"No problem," the guy said. "I'm Leon, by the way."

"Leon, you sure you can get us in? I don't have any ID."

"I don't have any ID, either," said Pixie-cut.

"Relax," Leon said. "Spencer, you can get them in, right?"

"Without a doubt," said the tall guy with the crappy goatee. "Of course, they're gonna owe me for all the effort I'll have to go to. Calling in favours is not something I do lightly."

"Understood," said Leon. "I'm sure the girls would be willing to pay you back somehow, if only there was a way..."

Amber turned. "I'm going to stop you right there, before your imaginations get you into trouble," she said. "We're not going to be paying you back. In any way. Seriously, you can wipe the grins off your faces."

"We weren't being totally serious about that," Leon said, still smiling.

"I must have missed the joke," Amber replied. "Thanks for showing us where the club is. We'll get in by ourselves."

Spencer looked distraught. "But... but I know the bouncer."

"Be sure to say hi to him from the back of the line," Amber said. "We're cutting straight to the front."

She took Pixie-cut's hand and carried on to the nightclub, leaving Leon and his friends behind.

"We don't have IDs," Pixie-cut reminded her.

"We don't need them," said Amber. "Have you *seen* me?"

26

AMBER GAVE THE BOUNCERS a smile and they parted for her, and she led Pixie-cut straight through to the hot, heaving crowds and the music that reverberated up through the floor. An idiot reached for her horns, tried to yank them from her head. She caught his wrist and squeezed, then shoved him away and left him there, shrieking.

She lost Pixie-cut in all the confusion, but found the dance floor, and she danced.

She'd never danced before, not really. She'd been to a few school dances, had moved awkwardly to music while trying to look indifferent, but the only time she'd let herself go like this was in front of the mirror in her bedroom. Back then, she fought to ignore how she looked. Now she didn't have to.

Amber watched herself in the mirrors that lined the far side of the dance floor. There were boys around her, men, each of them trying to be the one she locked eyes with. She ignored them. The girls on the floor separated into two groups – those who glared at her, and those who tried to outdo her. She ignored them all, all but the blonde.

The blonde strutted through the other dancers, straight to

her, put her arms on Amber's shoulders and now they were dancing together, moving to the beat, their rhythms interlocking. The blonde turned, pressed into Amber and Amber grabbed her hips. A few guys started laughing. A few started cheering.

Amber spun the blonde, grabbed her and kissed her, and the blonde kissed her back. There were a lot more cheers now. Amber ignored them all. Then a hand slid up the back of her skirt.

She broke off the kiss and turned and hit the guy so hard that his nose practically exploded on impact. There was a lot of shouting, a lot of pushing, and then someone came at her, a bouncer, and he grabbed her arm, but she lifted him off his feet. She laughed at the expression on his face, then threw him into the crowd that was forming around her. Another bouncer lunged into her path and she knocked him sideways. He went stumbling.

Then the music shut off and people were attacking her. Some of them were bouncers, but not all. They drove her back through sheer force of numbers. Once she'd regained her footing, she started smacking her way through them, breaking bones when she needed to. Someone threw a beer bottle. It missed, but Amber zeroed in on the guy and stormed into the crowd as he fled. She caught him, fingers curling over the back of his terrible shirt, and she hauled him off his feet before slamming him to the ground. She kicked him three times. The second kick spun him into unconsciousness. The third kick spun him across the floor.

A huge guy came at her, part of the door staff, at least a foot taller than Amber and a solid wall of muscle. She went to push him away, but he moved sideways, was suddenly behind her with an arm wrapping around her throat. He locked up the choke and leaned back, took her on to her toes. She tried to pull his arms away, but he was strong. Maybe even strong enough to do damage.

Scales formed around her throat and she could breathe again, but he kicked at the back of her leg and now she was sitting on the floor, the choke still on. The people watching were thinking it was over. They saw the big, strong bouncer who knew how to restrain a disorderly customer and they figured yep, that's it, it's done. The hot girl dressed as a devil and high on drugs was now out of commission. A lot of them were recording the altercation.

Amber grinned.

She flailed weakly, her hands tapping uselessly off his arms. She could hear laughter. She kept flailing, weaker and weaker, eyes fluttering closed, until she was tapping his fingers. Then she opened her eyes again, took hold of two of those fingers and pulled them back. She heard the snap of bones and the cries of the bouncer and she wrenched his arm to one side as she twirled, got to her knees. The bouncer punched her with his free hand. The scales didn't even bother to form. The blow was negligible.

She let him go and allowed him to fall back. She stood and fixed the remaining two bouncers with a look. They held up their hands, palms out. A calming gesture. But Amber didn't need to be calmed. Amber was in complete control.

She walked over to the crowd. They tried to shrink back. She snatched a phone from the hand of a guy who was filming, and hurled it across the dance floor. It hit one of the mirrors. The mirror smashed and the phone exploded.

She turned back and the crowd parted. She saw Pixie-cut, reached out to her, but the girl shrank back. Whatever. Amber left her there and exited the club as a patrol car pulled up and two cops jumped out.

"That's her!" shouted someone behind her. Amber ignored him.

Two cops, both male. One tall and skinny, the other shorter and fatter, like those black-and-white movie stars Bill used to watch. Laurel and Hardy. The thought made Amber laugh as they approached.

"Hold on there, miss," said Laurel, the tall one, extending his arm with his fingers splayed. She walked on.

Hardy, the fat one, moved in front of her. "Stop right there," he commanded. Funny little fat man, commanding her to do *anything*.

She shoved him, laughed as he fell. Laurel started shouting all kinds of things behind her, but she didn't bother turning. Then something sharp pinched between her shoulder blades and electricity shrieked through her and her legs stiffened and every muscle locked up, corded beneath her skin.

Then the electricity was gone and she stumbled against the hood of the patrol car. She turned, saw Laurel's finger tighten on the stun gun, and this time the electricity whipped her sideways. She fell, straight as a board, hit the ground with her chin and lay there, her whole body in spasm.

It cut off again and she gasped. She tried to push herself up. Pain flashed and kept coming. She tried reaching behind her, tried yanking the darts from her back. She could hear it now, the sound the weapon made. It rattled. When the rattling stopped, she gasped again and sank to the sidewalk.

"Get the cuffs on," she heard Laurel say.

27

THERE WAS A GROUP of cops waiting at the precinct, and the moment the patrol car pulled up they were dragging her out. They didn't even allow her feet to touch the ground – they held her between them, horizontally, as they marched through the doors. They didn't take her to be processed, didn't take her fingerprints or anything like that. Didn't even take the cuffs off. They wanted to get her behind bars as quickly as possible.

She let them. She didn't struggle. She didn't squirm or curse or spit or bite. She just smiled.

They must have cleared out one of the cells before they shoved her in because the others, four in all, were now over-packed with hooting, hollering drunks. Amber didn't mind. She tuned out their comments and turned to watch the officers slam the barred door closed. They were saying things, the cops, that she didn't bother listening to. Let the cops talk. Let the drunks holler. It was all noise to her.

The cops went away and Amber walked over to the bench, passing her hands down the backs of her legs as she sat. She scooted the handcuff chain under her bare feet and out in front.

Most of the cops left, leaving only Hardy and another guy. They saw what she was doing and came forward.

"On your feet," Hardy said.

She stayed sitting, stayed leaning forward, arms hanging down. She tried pulling her hands apart.

"I don't care what you're on," Hardy said, "you're not breaking out of handcuffs, all right? Get up."

Amber smiled again. "Make me."

He took something from his belt – a can of pepper spray. "Know what this is? You know what it'd do to you if I sprayed it into your face for even one second? It'd do more than ruin your Halloween make-up, that's for damn sure. Get on your feet."

Some of the drunks came to her defence, telling him to leave her alone, and Amber just increased the pressure on the handcuffs.

Hardy stepped forward, can raised and finger hovering over the button.

"You really think that's going to hurt me?" Amber asked. "How many shots of your stun guns did you need to take me down?"

"Whatever drugs you're on can make you resistant to pain," said Hardy, "but this is more than pain. This is total incapacitation."

"I'm telling you," said Amber, "I'll barely feel it. Where's Stan?"

Hardy frowned. "Who?"

"Your skinny friend. I've named him Stan. I've made up a whole life story for him. He's single, he has a pet tortoise and he does yoga. Stan, that is, not the tortoise. I miss Stan. I felt he understood me. I don't think that you get me at all, Ollie."

"Get up," said Hardy, "or I'll drag you up by those horns."

"Leave her be!" said one of the drunks. "She brightens up the place!"

Amber lowered her hands to the floor, and put her bare foot between them, resting on the chain. She raised her eyes to Hardy and the other cop, gave them a smile, and pulled her hands back towards her as she straightened her leg.

The handcuff chain snapped.

Hardy wasted no time. The pepper spray hit her right in the face even as she was standing. She closed her own hand over his, kept his finger pressing down, and redirected the spray into her open mouth. Then she tore it from his grip and grinned.

"Minty," she said, and breathed out.

The fumes hit Hardy and he coughed, eyes squeezing shut. He tried to turn away and she gave him a little shove as the second cop came at her with a baton. Scales formed on her arm as she fended off the strike, and she slammed the bottom of her fist into his forehead. The cop wobbled. She took his baton and gave him a tap to put him to sleep, and did the same to Hardy.

The drunks cheered. Most of them. The others backed away from the bars warily.

"Get the keys!" one of the enthusiastic drunks cried. "Let us out!"

Amber dropped the baton, walked out of the cell.

"Let us out!"

"Hey!"

"Just give us the keys!"

And then, just as was about to leave the cellblock, one of the drunks called out, "You bitch!"

Amber turned, walked back, right up to the cell with the loudest, drunkest idiots. Her eyes rested on a middle-aged businessman in a suit. "You," she said.

"Give us the keys."

"What's your name?"

"What's it matter?"

"It matters because you called me a bitch."

He grinned. "So what?"

"So I don't like that word."

"Then how about you not be one, and let us out."

She observed him, and shrugged. She went back to Hardy, took the key from his belt, and returned to the cell door.

"Good girl," said the businessman.

"What's your name?" Amber asked.

"Reggie," said the businessman.

"And are you going to apologise, Reggie?"

"Open the door and I'll do whatever you want," Reggie said, to the delight of his buddies.

"Apologise first," said Amber.

Reggie rolled his eyes. "Fine, whatever. I'm sorry for calling you a bitch."

She unlocked the cell and swung the door open.

"Thank you," he said, and his smile widened. "I like your horns. Something to hold on to when you're—"

Amber had known he was going to say something like that. It didn't matter that her hand closed around his throat before he could finish the sentence. It didn't matter that she applied so much pressure that he dropped to his knees, his face turning purple. It didn't matter that the other drunks jumped back, gave her space, showed no intention of rushing forward to help their buddy.

"What gives you the right?" she asked. "When you say things like that. What gives you the right?"

She released him and he fell back on his ass, sucking in air. "It was just a joke," he gasped.

"Oh," said Amber. "So it's a little harmless fun, then, is it? Especially after a few drinks? Hell, it might even be a compliment, if only I'd take it the right way."

Someone helped Reggie stand. "I don't want any trouble," he said.

Amber laughed. "Way too late for that, Reggie! Way, way too late! I'm going to ask you again, and if you don't answer I'm going to break your arms. What gives you the right to say things like that to me?"

"I swear, it was just a joke."

"If it was funny, say it again."

Reggie swallowed. "I'm... I'm sorry."

"But are you, Reggie? Are you really?"

"I swear."

She winced. "I don't believe you, Reggie. I'm sorry, I don't. I think you'd say anything to get out of what's coming."

Amazingly, he went even paler. "What's coming?"

She showed him her teeth. "Retribution."

The cells were deathly quiet now as she took a step forward. "If it really is fun, Reggie, if it really is nothing to worry about... then compliment me. Make those jokes again. No? Any of you?" She spread her arms wide. "Come on, boys, where are those wolf whistles? Here I am, in all my glory. You don't think I look good? Come on. Let's hear you whistle, wolves."

No one whistled. No one spoke.

Amber laughed. "I'm not crazy. I don't think one demonstration of awesome physical power is enough to change any of you. What good has violence ever done?" She stood there with her hands on her hips, smiling around at them. "But I'm probably going to kill some of you tonight."

There were some shouts of protest, some wails, and quite a few curse words thrown about.

"We can take her," someone said.

"We'll all rush her," someone else chimed in.

"She can't take on all of us."

Amber let her hands grow to claws.

"What the hell is she?"

"Jesus Christ."

"Help! Help us!"

There was a scuffle, and Reggie was thrown forward. Someone stuck their foot out and he tripped, went sprawling.

Silence once again.

"What do you think about that, Reggie?" she asked, looking down at him. "You've been sacrificed, my friend. The wolf, thrown to the bigger wolf. They're hoping I'll kill you and spare them. What do you make of that kind of disloyalty?"

Reggie raised himself to his knees. "Please don't hurt me."

"Too late for begging."

"Please."

"See the horns, Reggie? They mean something. They mean I'm the Devil's lapdog. A nasty piece of work. Killing you would be as easy to me as breathing."

"I'm sorry I called you names."

"We've moved beyond that, Reggie. We're into brand-new territory now. You've never been here before."

"I can give you money," said Reggie, and Amber hissed.

"Let's not cheapen the moment," she said. "Let's all embrace what is actually happening here. Let's all understand what this means. Do you understand, Reggie? Do you truly understand?"

Tears streamed down his face. "I have no idea what's going on."

"I'll explain it," Amber said, hunkering down and taking his face in her claws. "I'm going to kill you," she whispered. "And then I'm going to kill everyone else here. And then I'm going to kill every man out there who doesn't know how to be a decent human being."

Reggie whimpered.

"And it's all because of you," she said into his ear. "I want you to know that. It's all because of you."

"Please don't kill me," he whispered back. "I have a wife."

"She'll be better off without you."

"I have daughters."

"Playing the parent card with me is not your best option."

"I don't want them to grow up without a dad," he said. "Jesus, please, miss, please don't do that to them."

"That is all on you, Reggie."

She raised her eyes to the crowd, making sure they were all behaving, and she caught sight of her own face.

The Amber she once was, standing there, watching her. A little short, a little overweight. Not beautiful but not ugly, either. Another hallucination.

Amber snarled at it. "Shut up," she said. "You want this. You want me to do this."

"I don't," said Reggie.

"Not you," she snapped.

The hallucination didn't move or speak. It just stood there.

"Stop!" said someone behind her. The hallucination vanished and Amber turned, saw Laurel running up with his stun gun, but black scales were already forming beneath her T-shirt as he fired and the darts bounced off.

She jumped at him, knocking the stun gun from his hands

and forcing him out of the cell, and she followed him, snarling. Stumbling back, he drew his gun, the kind that fired bullets.

"Do not move!" he yelled.

She showed him her fangs. Showed him her claws. She took a step and he fired four times.

Amber hissed, squeezing her eyes shut, only opening them again once she realised he'd missed. From that distance.

He stared at her, the gun trembling in his hands. It still had more bullets, of course, but he seemed to have forgotten that.

She tore the gun away from him, closed her fingers around his throat and pulled him into her.

"I could kill you," she told him, anger biting at her words. "I could tear your throat out. No one could stop me. You tried to kill me, you little shit. You tried to shoot me. I should rip your head off."

Laurel was crying. He was crying at the sight of her fangs, at the sudden awareness that she wasn't wearing a costume, that those horns were real.

He was crying because she was a goddamn demon and now his whole life was turning upside down, the way Amber's life had done when she'd seen her parents kill those two cops in their living room in Florida.

She remembered the way her mom had punched through that poor cop's chest.

Amber let go of Laurel, and he sank to the ground, and she ran.

28

THEY WERE AFTER HER.

The night was alive with their sirens. Flashing lights stabbed the darkness behind her as she ran. Streets were blocked so she hurdled walls and kept running.

She sprinted by a squat building, recognised it, and veered off. The cops pulled up, tyres screeching and sirens blaring. She ran the length of the building, turned the corner and plunged into utter darkness. She found her old clothes, yanked off her skirt and T-shirt and pulled on her jeans and sneakers, grabbed her top and ran on.

There were flashing lights ahead of her now. She put on her *Dark Places* hoody and slowed down, took a breath and reverted. Ignoring the instant shame over her actions, Amber shoved her hands into her pockets and started walking with her head down.

"Stop!" a voice commanded, and flashlights blinded her and she stumbled back, a look of astonishment and fear on her face as the cops closed in.

"Not her," she heard one of them say, even as another grabbed her, stuck his flashlight right into her face.

"Have you seen anyone?" he demanded. His hand was rough. "A girl, red make-up all over?"

Amber blinked stupidly. "Make-up?"

"In a short skirt, wearing horns," the cop said impatiently.

"I haven't seen anyone," said Amber.

Running footsteps behind her.

"We've found her skirt! She has to be around here!"

The cop dragged Amber to the patrol car. "You're sure you haven't seen anyone?"

"A naked red girl?" Amber asked. "I haven't, I swear."

"Goddammit!" the cop said, releasing her. "Get outta here. Go on, move it!"

Amber nodded, hurried past them, and left them in her wake.

She got back to the motel and let herself into the room. It was dark. She went to the bathroom, got changed into a loose T-shirt and shorts. Careful not to bump into anything, she navigated her way back to her bed and climbed in. She lay there, her eyes growing accustomed to the gloom even as the tears started to roll.

"You awake?" she whispered.

A moment of quiet in the dark, when she could have been all alone in here.

Then, "Yep."

"I'm sorry," she said. "I was a dick. I didn't mean to be. I didn't want to be."

"You're under a lot of pressure."

"Doesn't make it any better," she said. They were both talking softly, like there was a third person in the room they were trying not to disturb. "And you were right. I didn't want to deal with all those horrible feelings and so I shifted. When I'm her, it's easier."

"I know."

Amber turned her head to him, but all she saw was a dark shape on the dark bed. "I don't know what to do, Milo."

"You're doing fine."

"I'm not, though. I'm really not. I'm doing terribly. My friends are dead. Kelly might be dead by now, for all we know. Clarissa too."

"I don't know about Clarissa," said Milo, "but your parents won't kill Kelly. Not yet. This is too important for that."

"I'm screwing this whole thing up," Amber said. "I'm hurting people. I hurt a lot of people tonight."

"Did they have it coming?"

"Only some of them," she said. "And even then... even then, I don't know."

"Regret is a tool, Amber. It's there to help you. It sticks in your head and you can't get rid of it. You can forget about it for a while, fool yourself into thinking you're over it, but it'll come back with a single thought, a single memory, and it'll be sharper than ever. You've got to learn to use it. It's a tool and it's there for a purpose."

"To make sure you never do it again?"

"To make you a better person," he said. "You're going to keep making mistakes. You might even keep hurting people. And every regret becomes another sharp spike, digging into your brain, reordering you, changing the way you do things. Don't be afraid of it, Amber. It's there to help."

"I... I don't want to shift again. Not for a while."

"Okay."

"I mean, I'll do it if I have to, but... but I'd really rather not."

"Then I'll do my best to make sure you're not put in that position," said Milo. "Go to sleep now. We have to deal with Abigail tomorrow. You're going to need your wits about you."

She turned over, pulled the covers up.

"Goodnight," Amber said softly.

Milo muttered something, and that was it.

29

Amber didn't dream that night.

She woke the next morning and showered while Milo went to get them some coffee and bagels. She looked at herself in the mirror. When she was like this, her legs weren't long and her muscles weren't toned and her face wasn't beautiful... but it'd do. It'd all do. It wasn't really that bad, she supposed. If Kelly liked it, that was good enough for Amber.

Rescue Kelly. Deliver parents. Cheat Astaroth.

She dried off and got dressed and waited for Milo. She sat very still, apart from her leg. That bounced. Milo came back, but by then she'd lost her appetite. They put their bags in the trunk and got in the Charger, drove the few minutes to The Dark Stair.

"How are you feeling?" he asked.

Amber thought for a moment. "Down," she said.

He nodded, and said nothing more about it.

They got out of the car, walked in off the street and took the stairs down. The darkness drank them in and still they went down, until finally the gloom lifted and they passed through, into the light. At midday, the bar was quiet, but, just like in the boring Westerns that Milo watched, it went even quieter with their arrival. Everyone turned and stared as Amber descended the last few steps, Milo behind her. She got to the bottom and looked around, and then Milo moved, quickly and without fuss, intercepting a lunge from one of the bar's patrons. Amber saw the flash of a knife and then the patron's face hit the wall and Milo was standing over him, calmly appraising the rest of The Dark Stair's clientele.

"We're looking for Abigail," Amber said, hoping her voice wouldn't crack.

"Here I am," said the little blonde girl in the pretty dress, waving to them from a table at the back. They walked over. No one else lunged out at Amber.

"Please excuse the stares," Abigail said when they sat down. "It's not often we get a Demon's representative gracing our establishment. Usually, when that happens, people start dying."

"I'm not here to hurt anyone," said Amber. "I need your help."

"Well, of course you do," Abigail said with a small giggle. "Everyone does, sooner or later."

"We want to trap a Demon," said Milo. "Chain him up for transport. Can you help us?"

Abigail didn't answer right away. "Are you sure that's what you want to do? You don't want to find someone or locate some—"

"We want chains that will hold Astaroth," Amber said. "Just like the chains that hold Naberius."

"I see."

"Can you help us?"

Abigail smiled prettily. "It's not really a question of can I, my dear. It's a question of will I, and for what price?"

"Will you?"

"I don't think so. I'll have to think about it some more, but... No, I just thought about it some more and it's still looking unlikely."

Amber leaned forward. "What would I need to do to get you to help me?"

Abigail sat back. Considered her. "There may be something."

"Tell me."

"A problem I've been having," Abigail said. "I've already sent someone to take care of it and they have failed, quite spectacularly. I'd say a Demon's representative, however, would be more than enough to get the job done."

"I'll do it."

Abigail smiled. "That's it? A promise to do whatever task I set for you? That's risky, is it not? What if I needed you to deliver to me the livers of ten newborn babies?"

Amber frowned. "Do you?"

"What would I want their livers for? No, I actually need you to do something you might well agree with, morally speaking. I need you to stop a bad man from doing a bad thing to some good people."

"Who?" Milo asked.

"Simon Cranston," said Abigail. "Or the ghost of him, anyway. Terrible man. A serial killer, killed upon arrest but risen again. You know, the usual."

"Who's he going after?"

"A small community on the outskirts of the city," Abigail said. "Maple Lake. Nice people, good people. Innocent people. He's killing them. Well, he's killing the kids. Teenagers. Why do so many people go after teenagers when they return from the dead? Why can't they take up a new hobby, like gardening?"

"Tell us about him," said Milo.

Abigail laughed. "You mean, his motivation? Oh, I don't know about things like that. He's crazy and he likes to kill. He does it at night. He's slow-moving – one of those lurchers, you know? But he's persistent, and very hard to put down. You'll have your hands full with him, I dare say."

"Why do you want him stopped, Abigail?"

Abigail blinked her big blue eyes. "Because he's a bad man, Milo."

"And what does that have to do with you?"

Abigail sighed. "It's a job I need doing. I thought you two might be perfect for it, since you get to save some lives along the way. Obviously, if you don't want to do it, I'm sure I could find you something suitably unsavoury..."

"We'll stop him," said Amber. "And, in return, you'll get us those chains?"

"I'll have them in two days' time," Abigail said. "But I will need Cranston taken care of at once. Do we have a deal?"

"We have a deal," said Amber.

She found Maple Lake on the map, and they drove there in under an hour. It was a pleasant little community, more affluent than Amber was expecting, and every direction she looked was laden down with the kind of mountainous beauty found mostly in coffee-table photography books and dime-store postcards. They were delayed slightly on their way to the main street by a procession of cars heading to a funeral.

The mood of the town was sombre, which Amber appreciated.

The smile the server gave them while they ordered their food was a restrained kind of smile, the sort used to mask pain. Amber gave him one in return.

Amber had the falafel salad while Milo had the Gorgonzola and steak quesadilla. She managed a few mouthfuls before her stomach started to churn.

"Kelly will be okay," Milo said.

Amber didn't answer.

She used the restaurant's Wi-Fi to look up Cranston, and grunted while she read.

"What?" Milo asked.

"Says here Simon Cranston used to perform at children's parties in his spare time," she said. "He used to dress up as a clown called Buddy. He gets extra creepy points for that."

Milo chewed his food. "I don't think I like clowns," he said.

She shrugged. "I don't mind them. I always liked Ronald McDonald, but that might just have been because of the cheeseburgers." She read on. "He was killed in 1979. Cranston, not Ronald. Shot twice in the chest."

"And since then he's been killing his way across America," said Milo.

Amber tapped the iPad, ran a new search. She read a bit before speaking. "The funeral we passed," she said, "was for Hailey Rylance. Cause of death not found."

"It wasn't murder?"

"Well," said Amber, "that's the thing. This article is all about the weird deaths lately. All teenagers the same age, all found dead. No injuries, no trauma... No cause of death. People are thinking it's poison, or a gas leak somewhere. Lotta people moving out of town, actually."

"How did Cranston kill?"

She flicked back. "He didn't have a signature move or anything. Gunshot. Two stabbings. Strangulation. Some bludgeoning." She looked up. "All things that leave definite marks. You think Abigail got it wrong?"

Milo swallowed the last bite of his meal, then sat back. "I don't think Abigail gets things wrong," he said. "If these are the work of Cranston, he may have just altered his MO. Pretty unheard of when you're dealing with back-from-the-dead psychos, but I guess it's possible. But something else is going on here. Abigail doesn't give one single crap about the people in this town."

"So why did she send us?"

Milo shook his head.

It got dark slowly, like the day was reluctant to give way. Maybe it knew something Amber didn't. Maybe it knew what was to come. But when it was finally beaten back, and night established its dominance, Amber and Milo began to trawl the streets, looking for a killer.

"Why don't you like clowns?" she asked as they left the main thoroughfare and headed into the outskirts of town.

"Don't know," said Milo.

"Maybe you were attacked by one as a kid."

"Maybe."

"You must have seen one, though," Amber said. "I know you can't remember anything about your life up until twelve years ago, but surely you've encountered a clown or two since then."

He glanced at her. "You're talking like encountering clowns is a regular occurrence for most people."

"I wouldn't say regular, but... I mean, you've seen them on TV and stuff, right?"

"Yes," said Milo, "on all those clown shows they have."

"So you're saying you've managed to avoid all clowns, even pictures of clowns, for twelve years?"

"I don't know what to tell you, Amber. It's a gift."

"And what if Cranston is dressed as a clown?"

"Why would he be?"

"Because it's creepy as hell," she said, "and it's just the kind of thing someone like him would do."

"Well," said Milo, "let's hope he isn't."

"Let's hope," Amber echoed, then lurched back in her seat as the Charger's headlights lit up the seven-foot clown walking across the road.

30

"HOLY SHIT!" SHE CRIED, and Milo slammed his foot on the brake.

"What? What's wrong?"

"The frikkin' clown!"

"Ah no," said Milo. "Where is he?"

"*Where is he?*" she screeched. "He's right there!"

The clown reached the other side of the road and disappeared into the bushes.

"Where?" said Milo, looking around.

She grabbed his arm. "You seriously didn't see him? He was right in front of us! He crossed the road right in front of us!"

Milo's eyes narrowed. "Have you taken any more of Astaroth's blood?"

She stared. "I am not hallucinating."

"I was looking right in front of us, Amber. I didn't see a thing. What'd he look like?"

"Huge. Seven feet tall."

"Seven feet?"

"At least."

"What was he wearing?"

"A clown costume, Milo! He was wearing a clown costume! That's how I knew he was a clown! It's Buddy! It's the clown Cranston dressed up as!"

"And how do you explain you seeing something that I don't?"

"It... I didn't hallucinate. That's not what..." Amber frowned. "Jesus." Then she shook her head. "No. I can always tell when I'm hallucinating. There's a difference."

"It's been happening a lot?"

"Never mind that," she snapped, and jumped out of the car, ran across to the bushes and plunged in. Beyond the initial mass of sharp twigs and leaves there was a trail. Amber hurried along. It took her behind a row of houses. She watched the hulking mass of the clown as he ambled towards a park area.

Milo caught up with her, his gun in his hand. "Okay, if he isn't a hallucination, then where did he go?"

She pointed. "He's right there."

"Where? At the trees?"

"No. Jesus, Milo, he's at the fence post."

Milo frowned. "That fence post?"

"You don't see him?"

"I don't."

It wasn't a hallucination. It *wasn't*.

They started running, covering the distance quickly. Amber steered Milo wide, and stopped ahead of Buddy the clown. The clown kept coming, his dull eyes not even focusing on them. Milo stepped into his path.

"Be careful," she said. "He's right there."

Milo raised the gun – and Buddy the clown just walked straight through him.

210

"Oh," said Amber.

"What?" Milo asked.

"He passed through you. You didn't feel anything?"

"Not a thing."

Amber stopped retreating. "Maybe... Jesus. Maybe I am hallucinating."

"How much has it been happening?"

"A few times. But usually it's my brother, or... or me... Never a frikkin' clown," she said, and Buddy hit her so hard he sent her rolling in the grass.

Milo ran over as Amber groaned, and Buddy walked on by.

"You okay?" Milo asked, helping her sit up. "What happened?"

"He hit me," Amber said, the wind knocked out of her. "Told you it... wasn't a frikkin'... hallucination."

"I just saw you fly backwards like you were on strings," said Milo. "You sure you're okay? Maybe you should shift."

"Not yet," she said. "Only when I need to."

"Amber—"

"Only when I need to," she said, and got up, ignoring the pain. She watched Buddy walk on. "So only I can see him," she said, "and only I can touch him. That's hardly fair."

She followed him, and Milo followed her, and they strode through the park.

"Ever heard about anything like this before?" Amber asked.

Milo shook his head. He took a silencer from his jacket and screwed it on to his gun. "I might not be able to touch him, but maybe my bullets can. Where is he?"

Amber took his arm and they jogged up behind the clown. "Right in front of you."

Milo held his gun out.

"Little higher," said Amber. He raised it until it was pointing right at the back of Buddy's head. "There. Shoot."

The silenced pistol barked and nothing happened.

"Did he fall down?" Milo asked.

"Still walking."

"You try it," he said, passing her the gun.

She frowned, feeling the weight of the weapon, then raised it and fired. The bullet tore through Buddy's skull, but instead of a jet of blood there was a small plume of dust, and Buddy didn't even break his stride.

"The bullet hit him that time," she said, "it just didn't bother him all that much. What do we do? How do we stop him?"

"You don't," said a boy, emerging from behind a tree. "I do."

He was sixteen or thereabouts, a good-looking guy in a checked shirt and ripped jeans, and he held an old-fashioned revolver in his hands.

"That won't do any good!" Amber shouted. "Guns don't work!"

"This one will," the boy said, and fired.

Buddy jerked back.

The boy fired again, emptying the gun and driving Buddy back. When the last bullet hit, he toppled over and lay still.

"What's happening?" Milo asked. "Where is he?"

"On the ground," said Amber. She looked at the boy. "How did you do that?"

"This is the gun that killed him," the boy said.

"How did you get it?" Milo asked.

"I stole it," said the boy. "The officer died a few years ago, but his wife kept all his things. I found her. Took the gun. I...

I can't believe it worked." He laughed and cried at the same time. "I can't believe it worked."

"I'm Milo, this is Amber. What's your name?"

"Jason Osmont," said the boy. "Thank you so much for your help."

"I don't think we managed to be of any help whatsoever," said Amber. "This was all you."

"Not just me," said Jason. "There have been a lot of us. I'm just the lucky one."

Buddy the clown sat up.

"No!" Jason screamed.

"What's wrong?" Milo asked.

"Shoot him again!" said Amber.

"I don't have any more bullets," Jason cried. Buddy stood and Jason backed away. "This isn't fair! I stopped you! I'm the one who stopped you!"

Amber didn't have any other choice. She shifted and launched herself at Buddy, ignoring Jason's fresh cries of surprise and horror. She raked her talons across Buddy's face, leaving dusty furrows in his powdered cheek. He grabbed her arm as she kicked him in the balls, then pulled her closer and grabbed her horns. He swung her off her feet and let go and she went flying.

While she scrambled up again, Milo ran to Jason, pressed his gun into his hands, told him to fire. Jason shot Buddy over and over again and he kept coming. Amber picked up a decent-sized rock, ran up and jumped, slamming the rock down on to the clown's head. He turned and her black scales formed in plenty of time to cushion her against his fist. It still hurt, though, still knocked her back a little.

He moved faster than she'd anticipated, suddenly had both

hands around her throat. His thick fingers pressed into her scales. Milo ran through the clown, wrapped his arms around Amber's waist, tried pulling her free, but Buddy just raised her up off the ground. Milo redoubled his efforts, his grip tightening, so that when Buddy tossed Amber aside, Milo went with her.

They crashed to the ground. Amber went sprawling while Milo rolled and came up on to his feet.

"Run!" he shouted to Jason. "Get out of here!"

Jason took another step back as Buddy loomed over him. "I was supposed to beat you," he said bitterly.

Buddy hit him. The blow snapped his head back and Amber heard Jason's spine break. The boy collapsed and Buddy lashed a kick into him, sending him into a wild tumble across the grass. The clown was upon him again in two strides, picking him up by the ankle. He swung him high above his head and slammed him into the ground.

"Jesus," Milo whispered.

Buddy swung him again, and again, smashing every bone in Jason's body. He did it a third time, then looked down at him for a moment. He started to walk off, dragging the boy behind him. Another few steps and he discarded Jason and continued on, vanishing into the darkness.

Amber got up.

"Is he gone?" Milo asked.

"Yeah."

"Jesus."

"Yeah."

Amber reverted, and approached Jason. His body was a bloody mess, jagged bones bulging beneath his broken skin. His head was turned unnaturally and his face was unrecognisable.

"He looks so peaceful," Milo said.

Amber looked at him. "Are you being funny?"

He frowned. "Of course not. But the way he was thrown around, I expected massive bruising at the very least."

"You can't see it?"

"Can't see what?"

"He's ruined, Milo. Jesus Christ, there's blood everywhere."

Milo looked at Amber, then at Jason's body. "All I can see is a boy lying there like he's sleeping."

"Maybe that's how Buddy does it," said Amber. "Maybe that's how he's able to keep killing without the town going nuts looking for him. If everyone else sees what you see—"

"There's no trace of violence," Milo finished. "Jesus. They don't know these kids are being murdered."

31

BAD NEWS TRAVELLED FAST in Maple Lake. Amber sat with Milo, across the road and down a block from Jason Osmont's house. They'd watched friends and neighbours come by all day, a steady procession of sympathisers. A patrol car was parked in the drive. This was one unexplained death that the cops were immediately suspicious about.

"We should have picked up the bullets," Amber said. "Or, not the bullets. What are they called?"

"The shell casings," said Milo. "But that wouldn't have helped. Jason had gunpowder residue all over his hands. The cops would be here, anyway."

"I guess," said Amber.

It was hell, waiting here for something to happen. Amber had until Saturday night to trap Astaroth and it was already Tuesday. Time was slipping away from her and she was sitting in a car, watching a house. "Maybe we should go in," she said. "We need to talk to people, talk to his friends, see if they know what's going on."

"Not a good idea."

"No, it's not, but we have to do something."

"We are doing something," Milo said. "We're waiting."

"For what?"

He leaned forward. "For that."

Amber followed his gaze, back to the house. Three people were at the front door as it opened and someone welcomed them in. But at the side of the house a window was opening, and a jeans-clad leg emerged.

The girl who climbed out was blonde, about sixteen, and she held a notebook. She closed the window once she was out, sneaked to the sidewalk and checked she hadn't been seen. Then she started walking away, the notebook crammed into her back pocket.

"Stop her now," Amber asked, "or find out where she's going?"

"Option number two," said Milo.

Amber nodded, got out of the car and walked after her.

She followed her to the end of the street and then right, keeping a safe distance between them at all times. She needn't have bothered. The girl didn't look round once.

They reached the main street and the girl went into a cafe. Amber passed the window. Not many people inside, and the girl was sitting in the corner, reading the notebook, sipping a Coke.

The Charger pulled up beside a parking meter. Milo slid a few coins in, put the ticket on the dash, and together they entered the cafe. Music played. The guy behind the till was too busy wiping the countertop clean to notice them.

They went to the corner.

"Hi," said Amber.

The girl snapped the notebook closed.

"We're friends," Amber said quickly.

"With who?" said the girl.

"With you. We're on your side."

The girl frowned. "I don't know what you're talking about."

"We saw you sneak out of Jason Osmont's house," Milo said. "You had that notebook with you."

The girl slid it off the table, on to her lap. "This is mine."

"You picked a weird time to get it back."

She looked at them both suspiciously. "You knew Jason?"

"We met him last night," said Amber. "Right before he was killed."

"They're going to say he died of natural causes," the girl said. "Sudden Death Syndrome."

"There a lot of that going around?" Amber asked.

"More than you'd think," said the girl.

"I bet." Amber sat, and Milo pulled up a chair. "I'm Amber. This is Milo."

"I'm Sarah. What do you know?"

"We know about Cranston," said Milo. "Buddy the clown."

Sarah frowned. "How?"

"That doesn't matter. What matters is that we're here to help. What can you tell us about him?"

"How much do you know?"

"Not much," said Amber. "We know about his victims and how he was tracked down and how he was killed. The only thing we know about him now is that he's been killing kids in town, with Jason being the latest, and for some reason Milo here can't see him."

"Of course he can't," said Sarah. "He's too old. Anyone over eighteen can't see him, hear him, touch him... They can't even see what he does. Not really."

"Why is he here?"

"I don't know," Sarah said. "I don't think any of them knew."

"Them?"

"The other kids. The other... victims." She held up her notebook. "This belonged to the third victim. She'd seen what happened to her friends, so she started to document everything she found out, everything that happened. When Buddy got her, it passed to the next kid on the list, and the next, and the next."

"Wait," said Milo. "What list?"

Sarah almost smiled. "The birthday list. He's going after kids born sixteen years ago. I was born at the start of June. It's my turn now."

Amber sat. "And everyone has written in that notebook?"

Sarah nodded. "Every kid since the third. We're trying to help each other, give the next one a running start. I've already told the next guy on the list to prepare. He didn't take it well. I don't know if he'll survive long."

Amber frowned. "You're not dead yet."

"I will be soon," said Sarah. "We don't know how to stop him. One of the kids had his grave blessed. That didn't work. The next one dug up his bones, had them blessed. Didn't work, either. The one after that, she thought the bones were the things that were keeping him from passing on, so she destroyed them. Put them in a furnace, reduced them to ashes. Didn't make any difference. Jason, he did some reading – he thought if he could get the gun that killed Cranston, it might be able to kill Buddy. I don't know if he even got the gun."

"He did," said Amber. "It didn't work."

Sarah dropped the notebook and buried her face in her hands.

"I don't know what there's left for me to try. The others did everything and it made no difference."

Amber hesitated, then moved closer and wrapped an arm round Sarah's shoulders as she cried. Milo gently picked up the notebook and started flicking through the pages.

"We can help you," Amber said.

Sarah didn't look up. "How?"

"We don't know yet, but this is the sort of thing we do."

"You deal with the ghosts of killer clowns a lot, then?"

"First time," Amber admitted. "But we're quick studies."

Sarah raised her head. "You actually think you can help me?"

"We will try our best. I'm willing to bet you anything that Milo already has a plan to stop him. Milo?"

He looked up from the notebook. "Yes?"

"Do you have a plan to stop Buddy?"

He frowned. "No. Do you?"

Amber blinked. "No."

"I'm dead," said Sarah. "I am so dead."

"I don't think he can be stopped," said Milo. "But I don't think that's the question we should be asking."

Sarah looked at him. "What is?"

"One of the other kids found similar deaths all across the north-west," Milo said, flicking through the journal. "One murder, maybe two, in places like Seattle, Spokane, Boise... and then Buddy gets here and doesn't leave."

"So?" Amber asked.

"Why hasn't he left? What's keeping him here? Does he have a personal connection to Maple Lake, something from back when he was alive?"

"No," said Sarah. "Nothing that we've been able to find, anyway."

"But something is keeping him here," Milo said. "If we find that, we have a chance of stopping him. The first girl – who was she?"

"Tanya Ensor," said Sarah.

Amber watched Milo's face. "You're thinking why her," she said. "Why did Buddy pick her – or why did he stay once he'd killed her?"

"We need to find out more about her," said Milo. "Do you know her family?"

"Not really," said Sarah. "They moved away a few months after she died. The house has just been sold to a new family, but I don't think they've moved in yet."

"It's empty?"

"Yeah, I think. They might have some construction guys in doing some remodelling, but yeah."

"Maybe it's the house," said Milo. "The house or something in it. Can you show us where she lived?"

32

THEY TOOK THE CHARGER to Anchor Street, a cul-de-sac of large, handsome houses with decent-sized lawns, some of which had boats on trailers. Milo reversed up the drive to the Ensors' old house and parked in the shade. They went round to the rear and Milo used a crowbar to open the back door.

They passed through the open-plan kitchen and living room. One of the walls was half demolished, with support struts bracing what was left. The only piece of furniture was a sawhorse. Milo checked downstairs while Amber and Sarah went up to the second floor. The bedrooms still had beds, but everything else had vanished with the family.

On one wall of the main bedroom, someone had spray-painted a large question mark.

"Milo," Amber called. "Come look at this."

A few moments later, he was with them. He looked at the question mark, then went into the next room. He came back, stood outside the door for a moment, and re-entered. "The rooms should be bigger," he said.

"What do you mean?" Amber asked.

Milo walked up to the wall, and knocked. "I mean... either this wall is five-feet thick, or there's another room in here."

Amber raised an eyebrow. "A secret room?"

"I think so."

Sarah went to the window. "It's getting dark. Guys, it's already getting dark."

"Then let's hurry this along," Milo said. "I saw a sledgehammer downstairs."

He fetched it and started swinging. Amber did the best she could with the crowbar. In her horned-up form, she would have been a big help, but she wasn't about to shift, not with Sarah watching. Besides, the idea of shifting was making her more uneasy with every hour that passed. The thought of releasing that part of herself...

Milo's sledgehammer went through the wall and they all made the hole bigger. It was dark inside. They made the hole bigger still, until they could fit through.

Inside was a wooden crate lying on the floor, long and narrow.

"That's a coffin, isn't it?" Amber said.

"Maybe," said Milo. He went to the far side and crouched. "Ready?"

Amber hunkered down, dug her fingers in underneath, and they lifted. The crate was heavy, but she could manage it without shifting. They manoeuvred it out of the hidden room, and took it into the larger of the bedrooms. They laid it sideways on the bed, and Milo used the crowbar to pry the lid loose. Sarah stood close to Amber, and they watched until finally the lid tumbled off, revealing the body of the old woman inside.

"Huh," said Milo.

They peered closer. She wore a half-heart necklace.

"Any idea who she is?" Amber asked.

Sarah shook her head.

Amber looked up at Milo. "She seems unusually... fresh."

"I was just thinking that," Milo said. "For someone who's been buried in a secret room for God knows how many decades, she's surprisingly intact. Old as dirt, yeah, but intact." He reached out to touch her and immediately pulled his hand back. "Ow."

"What?"

He frowned. "Static electricity." He pressed his fingers to her throat. "I think she might still be alive."

Sarah stepped back. "How is that possible? That's not possible."

"I can't feel a pulse," Milo said, "but it might be too weak. She's warm, though."

Amber peered closer. "Can we wake her?"

"I doubt it," said Milo. "It might be a coma. It might be, I don't know, hibernation... Whatever it is, I doubt we stand a chance of snapping her out of it."

"Maybe she's Sleeping Beauty," said Sarah.

Amber laughed. "Ha, yeah, maybe Prince Charming took a wrong turn and never found his way back."

Sarah started to grin. "All it will take is true love's kiss to rouse her from her slumber."

"Both of you can cut that out right now," said Milo. "I'm not rousing anyone tonight, so you can forget it."

"Is she the one Buddy wants?" Sarah asked. "If we give her to him, will that do it? Will he leave me alone?"

"I don't know," said Milo. "Maybe."

"So let's do it," said Amber. "If it's the only way to save Sarah, we have to at least try. We carry the crate downstairs, leave it in plain sight."

"Yeah, maybe," Milo said. He grabbed the far end of the box. "Okay, let's go."

Amber took hold of the other end and they lifted and carried the crate out of the room, and started across the landing. "You think she's a good person or a bad person?"

"What?"

"Her," said Amber, looking at the old woman. "Think she's good or bad? What do you think Buddy's going to do with her?"

"I don't know," Milo said. They got to the stairs. Sarah helped Amber with her end, and they started down.

"You think Abigail knows about her?" Amber asked, straining a little.

"I think this old lady is the reason we're in town," Milo replied. "Abigail didn't send us to stop Buddy — she sent us to stop Buddy from getting his hands on Sleeping Beauty here. I just don't know why."

Sarah nearly slipped, and Amber grunted as she took the full weight while Sarah recovered. "It can't be that important if she didn't send her own people."

Milo didn't answer.

"What?" Amber said. They were halfway down.

"I don't agree," said Milo. "Abigail sending us was probably the best option she had."

"So... so Sleeping Beauty might be very important to her."

"Maybe."

They reached the first floor, carried the crate to the middle of the room and put it down. Amber rubbed the creases from her fingers.

"Abigail didn't know we'd find the old lady," Milo said. "She had a problem that she wanted fixed – a killer clown in a neighbourhood she wanted kept safe – and so she sent us. She sent us because she knew we could handle it... and we're not her people."

Amber frowned. "She wanted it kept secret."

"I don't know who Abigail is," Sarah said.

"She's a scary little girl who'd give you nightmares," Amber told her."

"She's a kid?"

"Sort of, yes."

"Like, an adult with the mind of a kid?"

"A kid with the mind of an adult, actually."

"You mean, she doesn't get older? How does she manage that?"

"This is how," Milo said suddenly.

They looked at him. "What?" said Amber.

"This is how she stays young," he said. "Think about it. This lady has presumably been in that wall for decades, doing nothing but getting older. And Abigail? She's back in Salt Lake City, staying the same age."

"I don't get it," said Sarah.

"They're linked," Milo said. "Look at the necklace. What do you bet Abigail has the other half? Sleeping Beauty does the ageing for both of them. Who knows how old she was when she fell asleep? Maybe she was Abigail's age. If there's a psychic link between them, it could be strong enough to draw in someone like Buddy. He's got no real thought processes of his own – he just kills in order to kill. He doesn't think. He probably doesn't even know why he's sticking around. Sleeping Beauty here is an anchor, keeping him in town, stopping him from leaving."

"What'll happen when he gets her?" Amber asked.

"I have no idea."

"If he harms her, if he kills her... what'll happen to Abigail?"

"Nothing good, I imagine."

"We need those chains," Amber said. "Maybe leaving this for Buddy is a bad move."

"What about me?" Sarah asked. "What's going to help me?"

Something moved on the other side of the front door.

"Aw hell," Amber whispered. "He's here."

33

THEY RAN BACK UP the stairs and ducked down at the banister, giving them a good view as Buddy walked through the door without opening it.

"He's inside," Amber whispered to Milo.

Buddy observed the box. He stepped forward slowly, gazing down at the old woman inside.

"What's he doing?" Milo whispered.

"Nothing," said Amber. "Just looking at her."

Buddy tilted his head like a curious dog and reached down, touched the old woman's face. He jerked his hand back, and Milo's hand twitched.

"*Jesus,*" Milo said.

Amber glared, her finger rising to her lips.

But Buddy had heard him, and he looked up, straight at Sarah. He started for the stairs, and Milo straightened.

"I can see him," he said. "The static electricity... maybe it's a psychic thing. But I can see him now. He's an ugly bastard."

Amber grabbed Sarah.

"We have powers," she said quickly. "Milo has powers and I have powers."

"What?" Sarah said, trying to twist out of her grip. "What are you talking about? Let me go! We have to run!"

In that moment, Milo shifted.

Sarah cried out and stumbled back. Amber made sure she didn't fall, and Milo launched himself at Buddy.

"See?" Amber said. "Powers."

Milo hit Buddy full force in the chest and they crashed through the banister and fell to the ground. Milo was first up, plunging his claws into Buddy's neck. Buddy took hold of Milo's arm and swung him off his feet.

"I'm really sorry about this," Amber said to Sarah, pulling off her sweatshirt and jeans to reveal the activewear beneath. "Please don't be scared."

She shifted and Sarah yelped again at the sight of her red skin and horns.

Amber turned away and popped the cork out of the vial in her hand. She downed the blood, felt the glorious rush as every nerve ending sang and her body grew and she became better, bigger and stronger with goddamn *antlers*.

She leaped over the banister.

She landed behind Buddy, grabbed the back of his costume and ran him forward, slamming him into the wall. Then she threw him across the room. He hit the ground and rolled once and got up in the same slow, unhurried way he walked. Amber stalked over, kicked him in the chest, driving him back a few steps.

Milo left her to it and ran upstairs. Amber didn't even ask where he was going. Her fist connected with Buddy's jaw and he went stumbling. She hit him again, and again. She was powerful and in control. She couldn't understand why she'd been so reluctant to shift lately. Power was good. Strength was good. She laughed as she reached for Buddy.

But Buddy reached for her first, and Amber couldn't understand what was going on as he forced her back. He hit her and the world shook. He grabbed her antlers, those stupid antlers, and threw her to the floor and kicked her.

Milo returned. He had the sledgehammer in his hands. He swung it into Buddy's back. The clown stumbled over Amber, turned, and Milo hit him again, this time in the face. Buddy dropped to one knee. Milo brought the sledgehammer down, aiming to smash it through the top of Buddy's head, but the clown caught it in both hands. Milo kicked him right under the chin, and Buddy lost his hold and toppled backwards. Milo slammed the hammer down on to him, cracking it into his head, his shoulder, his knee. It should have pulverised him, should have crippled him, but Buddy the clown just kept getting up, and when Milo stepped in too close Buddy lunged, wrapped him up in a bear hug, pinning his arms to his sides.

The sledgehammer fell and Buddy squeezed. Milo headbutted him three times in succession, like a pneumatic drill, but it did nothing.

Buddy fell forward, all his weight crashing down on to Milo. Before Milo could recover, the punches landed, and when Milo stopped struggling, Buddy grabbed the sledgehammer, holding it in one hand like it was a cheap plastic toy as he got to his feet.

Amber ran in and Buddy heard her. She ducked under the first swing, but didn't expect the return swing to come quite so quickly. It glanced off her shoulder and sent her spinning, despite the scales that had formed an instant before impact. As she rolled, she caught sight of a figure kicking open the front door.

Was that...?

When she came to a stop, the door was open but the figure was gone.

Buddy came after her. He raised the sledgehammer, went to bring it down, but a pale hand came to rest on the handle, preventing the swing.

Glen looked at Buddy with dead, dispassionate eyes.

The clown let go of the hammer and fell upon Glen, driving him back. He hurled him into the wall, and Glen crashed through the supports and the wall gave in to the abuse it had suffered and toppled onto him.

Buddy didn't even pause to celebrate his quick victory. He climbed the stairs. Going after Sarah.

Amber snarled and jumped up, followed Milo up the stairs. She got to the top in time to see Sarah backing into a bedroom. Milo grabbed the clown's shirt, dragged him away. Buddy turned, took Milo by the throat and lifted him, then tossed him through the glass like he was nothing.

Amber charged into the clown and he stumbled, almost going through the window himself. But he swung a punch and it was like being hit with a concrete block. Amber's knees buckled and he hit her again, and again.

"Hey!" Sarah yelled, and the fists stopped coming down. "Hey, Buddy, come get me! Let's go, asshole!"

Buddy left Amber where she was, slumped against the wall. Sarah ran down the stairs and Buddy lumbered after her. Amber toppled over, turned and lay on her back, looking up at the ceiling.

She could just stay here. The clown was too strong for her. Too strong for her and Milo combined, even. Glen too.

Sarah didn't stand a chance, but, when she was dead, Buddy would go away. He'd go for the next kid on the birthday list, but it'd be a kid Amber had never met. That would make it almost easy to walk away from this unfortunate little town. Groaning, she got up. There were other ways to get the chains they needed. Abigail couldn't be the only person who knew where to look. There were others. There'd have to be. Amber limped down the stairs, holding her ribs. Better to just chalk this up as a loss and get the hell out of here.

She got to the bottom of the stairs and crossed the floor, passed the old woman in the crate and went outside. Sarah was standing in the middle of the dark road, yelling at Buddy, staying just out of his reach. He really was a shambling, ambling mess of a monster.

Amber took a deep breath, and black scales rose to cover her entire body, and she broke into a run. By the time she slammed into Buddy, she was running full speed. She knocked him off his feet and kicked him in the head while he rolled. He got to one knee without missing a beat, but she kicked that knee from under him, and he dropped to all fours. She lashed a foot into his side, a kick that would have splintered the bones of a normal man, but drew not even a moan of pain from the clown. She kicked him again, but he caught her leg and he stood, so she hit him, and slashed him, and hit him again. He hit her and the blow rattled her scales. He let go of her leg and his right hand closed round her face. He lifted her off her feet and slammed her into the ground.

Lifted and slammed. Lifted and slammed. He didn't get tired.

He didn't grow weaker. He was relentless, and her scales couldn't take much more of this. Pretty soon she'd be nothing but a bloody smear on the road.

In the distance, a great beast roared, and red light lit them up.

Buddy let her go and straightened up, and Sarah had a hold of her arm and was pulling her off to one side as the Charger, Milo and the Charger, crept closer, their growls getting louder. Buddy looked at the car with that tilted-dog's head curiosity of his, and Milo put his foot down and the Charger charged.

It struck Buddy in the legs and bent him over the hood and slammed into the tree on the other side of the road with such force that the Charger's rear wheels left the ground for a moment, before settling back down with a crash. Steam billowed as the engine cut out. One headlight was smashed. The other kept on shining red.

Sarah helped Amber to her feet, and the scales faded and Amber reverted. She gasped at a whole new wave of fresh pain, but Sarah held her upright until she could stand on her own.

Milo kicked the Charger's door open, and got out. He, too, had reverted. Amber limped over, followed by Sarah. They stood there, looking at Buddy. Even though the lower half of his body must have been mangled beneath all that metal, Buddy looked back at them with a blank face. He wasn't even trying to free himself.

Lights were flicking on in the neighbouring houses, but as yet no one had ventured outside to investigate the noise.

"You okay?" Amber asked Milo.

"I ran over a clown," he said. "I'm great."

"So what now?" Sarah asked. "How do we kill him?"

"I don't know if we can," Amber told her.

"Then can we put him somewhere? Can we trap him?"

"Maybe. What about it, Milo? Think we can fit him in the trunk?"

Milo narrowed his eyes. "We are not putting a goddamn clown in my car."

"Where else are we going to put him? Milo, we really don't have a choice here, do we? And it doesn't have to be forever. We can take Sleeping Beauty with us when we go – we can even hand her back to Abigail, let her deal with Buddy. If we want to save Sarah, this is what we've got to do."

"I would appreciate being saved," said Sarah.

"Hear that?" said Amber.

"Goddammit," Milo muttered.

"Thank you," said Sarah, and hugged him. Amber watched, waiting for her turn. But, when they broke off the hug, Sarah turned her head and screamed.

Buddy was gone.

They'd taken their eyes off him and he'd disappeared.

Milo grabbed Sarah protectively and Amber spun, expecting the clown to lunge at her. But, apart from them, the street was empty.

"Where is he?" Sarah asked. "Where the hell did he go?"

Milo took a look under the car, came back up and scanned the area again.

Amber frowned. "Is he gone? You think he's had enough?"

"For tonight, maybe," Milo said.

"Okay," said Amber, "new plan. Sarah, we're taking Sleeping Beauty to Salt Lake City. You're coming with us, so we can keep you safe. Once that's done, Buddy won't have an anchor anymore to keep him here, so you can come back. Easy as pie, right, Milo?"

"Right," he said absently. Then he nodded. "That could work. We'll put the old lady in the trunk – drive there tonight."

"Your car is wrecked," Sarah said.

"It'll get better," Amber told her.

"Okay," Sarah said. "The journal's upstairs. I have to get it."

"Get me my clothes, too, would you?" Amber asked. Sarah nodded, ran back to the house.

"You're sure the car won't eat the little old lady?" Amber asked Milo.

"She'll be fine," he said. "You okay? That was quite a beating we took."

"And me with Astaroth's blood and everything," Amber said. "I'm bruised and hurt, but I'll be fine by morning. We're lucky we had help."

Milo grunted, and looked around. "Where is Glen?"

"In the house," Amber said.

Her eyes widened.

She ran for the house, Milo right behind her. The debris from the toppled wall had been moved. They got to the stairs. Amber's clothes lay on the landing where she'd dropped them. They ran to the bedroom, to where Glen was feeding from Sarah's neck.

"No!" Amber cried, lunging at him, but Milo caught her, yanked her back.

Buddy stood in the corner of the room, watching Glen feed from Sarah's limp body. Then, like he'd reluctantly accepted that the better man had won, the clown turned, stepped into the shadows and disappeared.

Amber broke free of Milo's grip and kicked Glen off the girl.

He retreated, hissing, then a strange look came over his face and he straightened, calm once again.

Milo dropped to one knee by Sarah's side, feeling for a pulse. "She's alive," he said.

34

APART FROM ABIGAIL SITTING at a table in the middle of the bar, The Dark Stair was empty.

"This feels like a really obvious trap," Amber muttered as she walked over. Milo didn't respond.

"There you are!" Abigail said brightly. "I was beginning to think I'd never see you again! Welcome back and congratulations! The good people of Maple Lake can rest easy once again! Take a seat!"

"We'll stand, thank you," Milo said. "It's good to stretch the legs."

Abigail giggled. "Be careful, Milo – I might start to think you don't trust me."

"Not about trust," said Milo, "it's about time. Something we don't have a lot of."

"If we could just pick up the chains," Amber said, "we'll be on our way."

Abigail looked at her, and nodded. "You did it, then? You beat the nasty clown? How did you manage it?"

"We had a talk," said Amber. "Convinced him to leave."

"So he's still out there?"

"We moved him on," Milo said. "We'll catch up to him again and put him down for good, but right now all we want are the chains."

Abigail rocked in her chair for a few seconds, like she was deciding on how best to break some bad news. "You see, I didn't expect you both to survive," she said. "I was kind of expecting only one of you to limp back here. That would have been ideal. It'd be much easier to only have to kill one of you."

Doors opened, and children emerged. A dozen of them. More. With big smiles and small knives.

"But we'll kill both of you if we have to," Abigail said, taking her own knife from her pretty purse.

Amber focused on her as the children closed in. "You were never going to get us the chains, were you?"

"I never even tried."

Milo's hand went to his hip, and Abigail laughed.

"Your bullets can't hurt me, Milo."

"Maybe not," Milo said, taking out his phone, "but if I press SEND then the little old lady we found in that crate is going to have her heart ripped out."

The children froze, and Abigail's smile faded.

"What?" she said quietly.

"You remember Glen, don't you?" Amber asked. "Irish guy? Annoying? He's with her now."

"I remember him," said Abigail. "He doesn't have the fortitude for murder."

Amber forced herself to remain calm. "You haven't heard? He's a vampire now. He doesn't speak much, but he listens, and he likes to protect me. In a few hours, the sun will go down and he'll wake, and once he picks up the phone I gave him, he'll know what to do. She's you, right? The little old lady? I reckon she's you. Milo thinks she might just be someone you're siphoning off, but I think I see a little resemblance around the mouth. Whichever it is, we're pretty sure that if she dies, you die. Would we be right, Abigail?"

Abigail glared at them. "Where is she?"

"Well, we couldn't leave her in Maple Lake," said Amber. "As soon as Buddy passed by, she drew him in like she was a magnet. So we took her somewhere else. Somewhere safe. For the moment, anyway. We'll tell you, if you keep your part of the deal and get us those chains."

"I can't get them," Abigail said. "They can't be got. You'd need someone to make them from scratch. It'd take me weeks to find someone who would even know where to start!"

"We don't have weeks," said Amber. "It's Wednesday now. We have until midnight on Saturday."

Abigail shook her head. "Impossible."

"Then I'm afraid we can't tell you."

"I'll find her," Abigail said. "I'll be able to find her."

"Eventually, maybe," said Milo. "You just better hope we hide her somewhere safe while you're looking." He looked around. "Places like this operate on a code, don't they? An *honour among thieves* kind of thing? What are your patrons going to think when they find out that you welched on a deal, Abigail? That you were going to have us killed? They may not like us, but do you think they're ever going to be able to trust you again?"

The little girl said nothing.

"We're leaving," Amber said. "If any of your little friends try to stop us—"

"They won't," Abigail snapped. "Go on. Get out of here. You're no longer welcome in this establishment."

The kids stepped back, and Amber walked towards the stairs, expecting an attack at any moment. Milo followed.

"Your friend," said Abigail, right when Amber's foot was on the first step, "the Irish one. He's burning in Hell, did you know that?"

Amber went cold.

"All vampires go to Hell," Abigail continued. "His body might be walking and talking, but his soul is being ripped apart as we speak. What do you think about that? He's in a kind of agony you can't even imagine, and he's got an eternity of it to look forward to. Maybe you'll pass him on one of your trips back to your Master, little doggy." .

Amber would have loved to have had a comeback, but she couldn't think of anything.

They walked up the stairs, through the darkness and out into the daylight, and crossed to the Charger. They got in and pulled on to the road.

"What do we do?" Amber asked. Her voice was hollow.

"We could go back to Desolation Hill," Milo said. "We have Shanks's key. It'd get us right into Naberius's cell. We could take the chains holding him. Of course, that'd mean freeing him, and, if that happens, everyone in that town is dead."

The seconds ticked by.

"Or we could forget about the chains," he continued, "forget about delivering Astaroth, and focus instead of getting Kelly back. I have no doubt your parents would be ready for that, but it looks like it might be the only avenue available to us. They're heading back to Orlando right now. We follow them, find them, wait for the right time, and make our move."

Amber hid her face in her hands. It was all going wrong. The lunatic trucker had Clarissa. Her lunatic parents had Kelly. Ronnie and the others were dead. Glen's soul was burning in Hell...

She looked up. "You think Abigail was telling the truth about Glen?"

Milo didn't say anything for a bit. "I don't know."

"Maybe she was lying, just to mess with us. A bit of torture, you know? We'd beaten her and that was the only way she could get back at us."

"Yeah," said Milo. "That's probably it."

Amber looked out of the window. "But what if it's true? What if Glen's soul really is in Hell? Would it be? He was a good person when he was alive. I think there might still be a bit of good in him, even now. But that means he'd go to... he'd go to Heaven, right?"

"I don't know much about Heaven, Amber."

"If there's Hell, there's Heaven. You can't have one without the other."

"Why not?"

"Because... because you can't. It doesn't make any sense."

"There are Demons, there's the Blood-dimmed King," Milo said, "and there's a plane of existence where souls go to be tortured and consumed. This place is called Hell. These things we know for sure, because we've seen them. We've experienced them. I've felt the touch of the Devil, Amber. I've never felt the touch of God. Have you?"

"No. But that doesn't mean there isn't one."

"True," said Milo. "It could just mean he's not interested in the likes of us."

"Could... could we find it?"

"Find what?"

"Glen's soul."

"What?"

"I've seen the Blood-dimmed King's palace, Milo. I'm pretty sure I can get there."

"And do what?"

She hesitated. "Bring Glen's soul back with me."

Milo pulled over. Turned off the engine. Looked at her. "How? How do you transport a soul? Do you even know what it'd look like?"

"Those offerings we've collected for Astaroth, some of them have been souls. Sure, the blood my parents offered up was pure power, but other offerings have been souls. I could feel them. Couldn't you feel them?"

"No, I couldn't."

"Well, I could. Probably another perk of the job, you know? The jar of hearts? They were souls. The head? That person's soul was still in there. Trapped."

"Then those souls were carried within those body parts. But what happens, then, when the soul is extracted? What does it look like? Does it stay in one piece? What form does it take?"

"Why are you so against this?"

"Because we don't know if it can be done, and, if it can be done, we don't know how to do it."

"Then we'll get help," she said. "Bigmouth will help me. I'll offer him a deal. I'll tell him I'll take him back with me."

"You're really going to trust Edgar, after what he tried to do?"

"I don't have much of a choice, do I? I'd just have to hope that his need to come home outweighs any desire to betray me."

"Amber, even if this worked, we don't know if he'd be able to survive outside Hell."

"Maybe he won't, but I'd say he'd prefer that to how he's living now."

"This is insane," Milo said. "You have enough to deal with right now without adding a jailbreak to the list." She didn't say anything, and his voice softened. "Look, if you're going to do this, then I'm coming with you."

"I don't think that's a good idea. I can come and go as I please," said Amber, "but the moment you set foot in Astaroth's castle, he's bound to know about it. I have to do this alone."

"Amber..."

"I have to try, Milo. Everything else is falling apart. I have to do something now, something good, something that'll remind me that I'm one of the good guys. Saving Glen's soul... I have to at least try."

Milo sighed, and scratched his stubble. "When?"

"Tonight. Let's get out of Salt Lake City and on the road home. How long's it going to take?"

Milo took a moment. "We'll drive to Cheyenne tonight, start early in the morning and push on to Kansas, get there by sundown. We'll get to Nashville late Friday, and Orlando early evening on Saturday."

"You're sure about that?" Amber asked. "We only have until midnight."

"If we don't make it, you've got Shanks's key."

"We can't take the Charger if we use the key," she said, "and if we can't take the Charger then you're at a disadvantage. Against Bill and Betty, you don't want to be at a disadvantage."

"We'll make it," he said. "We'll get there."

She nodded. "First stop Cheyenne," she said. "Let's go."

They left Salt Lake City and the mountains flattened to hills and then to nothing, and they passed mile after mile of this same nothing. Every so often, Amber would see a cow grazing. It stopped being a big deal after a while.

The Charger skipped round whatever car or truck they came to. No sign of the Peterbilt. Amber wondered if they'd seen the last of it, if the trucker had got what he'd wanted and driven off.

She tried not to think of what horrible fate had befallen Clarissa.

They passed through Laramie, and the grass started to get a little greener and the clumps of trees more frequent, but that didn't last long. They got to Cheyenne, drove through it and stopped at a motel on the far side. They took two rooms, but both of them went to Milo's. Amber got changed into her yoga pants and T-shirt in the bathroom, came back out to find Milo cleaning his gun.

He looked up. "You okay?"

She gave him a shaky smile. "Just kinda... worried."

"Understandable."

"No, not about what I'm going to do. I'm worried about... doing it as her. The other me. I'm worried that when I shift I won't care as much. Maybe I'll come back. Maybe I'll leave Glen's soul behind."

Milo put the gun down, and sat forward, elbows on his knees. "Hey," he said gently. "You might be more confident when you're red, you might be less thoughtful – but you're still you."

"You didn't see me go after that cop."

"You stopped yourself, didn't you? You're still in control. You just need to remind yourself of that. Shift. Go on. Shift and we'll continue this conversation."

Amber nodded, and shifted.

"How are you feeling?" Milo asked. "Still worried?"

"Yeah," Amber said.

He smiled, and sat back. "There you go. It's definitely you under those horns. You still want to go in there and bring Glen's soul back with you, right?"

"I guess."

"Then that's what you do. These forms we can take, they're our weapons. Our armour. They're tools we use to do what we have to do. That's all. It's like driving a car, Amber. As long as you stay in control, the car is an extension of the driver. It's when you lose control that bad things happen."

"So stay in control," said Amber. "Sounds so easy."

"You're sure you want to do this?"

She took a deep breath, and let it out. "I'm sure," she said.

"Then I'll be here when you get back."

She cut her palm and made a wide circle around herself. She didn't even get a chance to say goodbye before the circle burst into flames and Milo and the motel room vanished, and she was in Hell again.

35

SHE FOUND BIGMOUTH HIDING from Fool, cowering in a darkened corner while his master called his name in some distant part of Astaroth's castle. Amber coaxed him out, promising him that she wouldn't give away his location.

"I can help you," she said.

Bigmouth dipped his head.

"I have a friend who's trapped in the palace of the Blood-dimmed King," she said. "Back home, he's a vampire, but his soul is here. I need to get it out. If you help me do that, I'll take you with us when we go."

Bigmouth shook his head so vigorously that his jaw looked like it might detach itself with all the swinging.

"You're panicking," Amber said. "Don't panic. You don't have to panic. Nothing bad is going to happen to you."

He stepped backwards, still shaking his head.

"Bigmouth," she said, putting a little steel into her voice. "I am Lord Astaroth's representative. If I tell you that everything is going to be fine, then everything is going to be fine. Do you understand me?"

He stopped retreating, and nodded, eyes wide and fearful. She regretted her tone instantly.

Amber reverted, and the heat of the place rushed in on her, almost making her gasp. Bigmouth blinked, surprised at the change.

"I'm not here to hurt you," she said quietly, doing her best to ignore the sweat that was already trickling down the side of her face. "I'm not here to get you in trouble. I want to help my friend. I think I can do it. But I need your help."

Bigmouth hesitated, then tapped his own chest.

Amber nodded. "If you help me, I'll help you. You can come back with us. You can get away. I swear to you, Edgar, I won't leave you here."

Bigmouth looked around, like he was making sure Astaroth himself wasn't standing behind him, then hurried closer.

"Is it possible?" she asked him. "Can I take a soul out of Hell?"

Bigmouth nodded quickly.

"How do I do it?"

Chalk scribbled frantically on his slate.

Cross river. Enter palace. Find soul.

"How do I cross the river?"

Need coin. I give you.

"Why do I need a coin? To pay for something? One of the boats?"

Pay boatman. He take you across.

"And how do I get into the palace?"

Bigmouth made a sound that could have been a tittering laugh.

Representative go where she likes.

"So I can walk in? I can just walk in and no one will try to stop me? Okay, that's good. That's good news. But how do I find my friend? What does a soul look like?"

Here, a soul is physical being. Physical beings are easier to torture. They have parts to cut off.

"So it looks like him? My friend's soul will look like my friend?"

Bigmouth nodded.

"And then I just sneak him out?"

Sneak him back here. No coin for return journey. Sorry.

"Don't worry," said Amber. "I'll improvise."

Then take him home. Take me home, too? Promise?

"I promise," she said.

Go back. Meet you there.

She barely had time to read it before he spun and hurried away, wiping the words off the slate as he moved.

Amber shifted again. She had to. The heat was unbearable otherwise. She headed back the way she'd come and waited in the chamber for Bigmouth to join her. The circle still burned, and would do so until she stepped into it once again.

Minutes later, she heard Bigmouth's footsteps. He emerged from a corridor to her right, and waved her over to the central tapestry. He pulled it back, revealing a narrow gap in the stonework. He squeezed through, and beckoned her to follow. Amber ducked her head in first. It was a tight squeeze, but she managed it.

They were in a narrower corridor now, and Bigmouth shuffled ahead. They found a stone stairwell leading down. Bigmouth nearly went tumbling a few times, but Amber was there to keep him upright. His unsteadiness didn't slow him, though. Down and down they went, around and around. They must have been in a tower of some sort, perhaps a tower nobody used anymore, one with a door at the bottom. Either that or Bigmouth had double-crossed her, and was leading her into the dungeons.

Amber glared at him, but could glean nothing from the back of his head.

Then they reached the bottom, and there was a door. It was big and old, and required all of Amber's strength to open it. She stepped out into warm air. It was night here but it was always night. The sky above was tinged with red, the grass beneath was yellow, and the forest ahead was dark. The palace on the horizon was huge.

Bigmouth rapped his knuckles on the door, and she turned. "You can't leave the castle?" she asked.

He shook his head, and showed her a large silver coin. A flick of his thumb and it spun through the air, into her hand. She slipped it into her pocket.

"Is there a trail through the forest?" she asked.

He shook his head.

"Anything in the forest I should avoid?"

He nodded.

She sighed. "Wonderful. Any advice you can give me?"

Bigmouth scribbled on his slate, and showed her.

Beware the water.

"Well, that's creepy," she said. "That's very frikkin' creepy. Thanks."

He gave her the thumbs up.

Amber sighed.

"Be ready for when I get back," she said. "I don't want to wait around for you."

Bigmouth nodded, and Amber took off.

The trees were dark, their branches sharp and probing. They snagged on her clothes and in her hair, but the forest was a lifeless thing. No creatures awaited her. No monsters sprang out at her. It was dark and quiet and that was all.

There was long grass on the other side that came up to her knees. This, too, was sharp, but her scales protected her from its scratches. She reached the pebbled shore, went to the nearest boat.

"Uh... hi."

The boatman moved slightly. His hooded robes hid his head. Only his hands were visible. They were long and thin and covered in broken scabs.

"I, um, I was wondering if you could take me across?" she asked.

No response.

"I have business in the palace," she said. "I am Lord Astaroth's representative. It's a very urgent matter. I must deliver a message to the Blood-dimmed King personally."

No movement.

Amber frowned. "I can pay."

The boatman raised his head, and she could see what was under his cowl. The middle of his face was steadily being eaten away by maggots, and the flesh beneath was rotten and brown.

"Uh, I have this," she said, and held out the silver coin.

He took it from her, held it up, and then brought it close. His tongue, a rotten slug of a thing, dragged itself across the surface of the coin until he was satisfied. Depositing the money in his robes, he took hold of the pole and moved aside. Amber climbed on board and he pushed off from the shore even as she was sitting. She almost fell out. The water was dark, and, as they left the shore behind them, it got darker. There were things in the water. They moved like fish but were not fish. Some of them were quite close to the surface. They had faces.

Amber stopped looking at the water and kept her eyes on the palace. It was getting bigger, and not merely because she was drawing closer. It was growing, accommodating her perception of what qualified as "big" and then expanding beyond it.

The boat rocked suddenly, and she thought they were about to capsize before she saw that they had reached the other shore.

"Thank you," she said, clambering out. "Will you be here for the return journey? I don't have another coin but—"

He pushed the boat away, and left her there.

She found steps leading up. Many of them. Even in her demon form, her muscles were singing by the time she got to the top. She joined a trickle of people heading into the palace. One of them was a demon, like Gregory Buxton except smaller. He ignored her. She ignored him.

A man and a woman stood guard at either side of the gate, their heads down. Their bodies were masterworks of pain, bloodless gashes intersecting at vicious angles. Only their faces, so peaceful in sleep, were untouched.

Amber walked between them, certain that they were going to look up and grab her.

She got through, and allowed herself to breathe again as she entered the palace of the Blood-dimmed King.

36

THE SCREAMING WAS LOUDER here, but so was the laughter, and none of it seemed to come from any one particular place. Rather, it drifted around, like it was caught on the warm, stifling breeze.

Amber moved away from the others, who walked with blank expressions, seemingly oblivious to everything around them.

She came to a vast opening into a cavernous room and she looked at what stood in the centre for a full ten seconds before she realised what it was. A throne, as big as a cathedral. Amber backed out, struggling to make sense of the scale.

"You're lost."

She turned. A priest walked up, his white collar smudged and his vestments torn. He was balding, with a long, lined face. "Maybe I can help you," he said. "Where do you need to go?"

"I'm not lost," said Amber.

The priest smiled. "Of course not. My mistake. I have a tendency to believe that everyone is lost except me. You are one of Lord Astaroth's demons, are you not?"

"I'm his representative, actually."

"Oh, I see," said the priest. "I do apologise."

"Not at all. Feel free to, uh, go about your business."

Amber walked on, down a corridor of black stone, but he followed.

"And what are you doing here?" he asked.

"Sorry?" she said, not slowing down.

He caught up with her. "Here, in the palace of the Blood-dimmed King."

"Oh. Yeah. Business," she said. "Lord Astaroth's business. I can't discuss it, sorry."

"Nor would I expect you to," said the priest. "But, if you need a guide, I do know this palace quite well."

Amber considered this. "Well, since you're here," she said, "I have to deliver a message to the soul of a young man. A vampire."

"This way," said the priest. She followed him into an adjoining corridor. "They're very well organised down here," he continued. "Infernal bureaucracy is what they do best, if I'm to be honest. Wicked souls to your left, innocent souls to your right, damned souls straight ahead, that sort of thing."

"How long have you been here?" she asked.

The priest smiled. "A long time. Sometimes it feels like I've been here forever."

"I'm Amber, by the way."

"Very pleased to meet you," the priest said, but did not offer his own name in return.

"What did you do?" she asked. "To come here?"

He frowned for a moment, then smiled. "Oh, I see. You think I sinned? No, no. In this palace, there are priests who have volunteered to be here, to live in this Hell in order to offer salvation to the tortured and the suffering."

"The Blood-dimmed King allows this?"

"Of course," said the priest. "Without hope of salvation, there can never be true despair. There is only acceptance."

"You volunteered to be here?"

"I came of my own volition, yes."

"How do you do it? How do you live here with all this pain?"

"I could ask you the same question," he responded. "How do you live out there, among the living, with all that pain? Here, you know what to expect. Out there? Every cut is deeper, because the people wielding the knives have the choice not to cut. And yet they still draw blood."

"We're messed up, I'm not denying that, but it's not all bad."

"And I would submit to you that it is not all bad here, either."

"Isn't this a place of eternal torture?"

"Well," he said, "yes, but friendships can still flourish, honour still exists, and it is not unheard of for two souls to find love. Even here."

"Have you seen him? The Blood-dimmed King? Is he really that big? Was that actually his throne?"

"The Blood-dimmed King can be as tall as a mountain or as small as a mouse. He can take any form." The priest took a leather-bound flask from his robes, held it out. "Water?"

Amber hesitated, then took it. The water was surprisingly cold. It soothed her parched throat and, without realising it, she'd soon drained the whole thing. "Sorry," she said, handing it back.

The priest smiled. He didn't seem to mind.

He took her into the bowels of the palace. The stench of bile and excrement and rotting meat oozed from the walls, and Amber put her hands over her mouth as she walked.

The priest noticed, and laughed. "Oh dear," he said, "is it really that bad? I'm afraid I must be quite used to it by now. It's funny how smell is the first thing you can ignore, isn't it?"

"It'd take a lot to ignore this," she muttered, and the priest laughed again.

They turned a corner and he held up his hand. Ahead of them was a chamber full of men and women, their bodies slashed, their eyes closed.

"Move slowly," the priest whispered. "The Scarred Ones won't wake if you don't make a sound. The damned souls are just beyond them."

She nodded, and they crept forward.

Up close, the Scarred Ones were even more distressing. The gashes that covered their bodies appeared to have been made without pattern or design. They were just gashes, moments of pain inscribed into flesh. Amber moved slowly, her sneakers silent on the rough stone floor. She watched their eyes as she passed, searching for a telltale flicker to warn her that they were waking.

She made it through the chamber and turned as the Scarred Ones raised their heads and their hands shot out, clamping hard on to the priest's arms. She dived for cover behind the doorway.

"Ah," the priest said, "I'm afraid the jig is up. Run now, Amber, I'll do my best to buy you some—" He frowned suddenly as they crowded him. "Now wait a moment, I'm not the one you want."

He tried to pull free, but they started to drag him away.

"No," he said, panic rising in his voice. "You're making a mistake. *You know me.* Amber, tell them."

Amber stayed hidden, but the priest's eyes found her. "Tell them!" he shouted. "They'll condemn me to this place! *Tell them!*"

Amber's hand rose to her mouth to stop herself from crying out.

"I helped you!" the priest screamed. "I helped you!"

Through a door he went, and then they were gone.

Her heart beating wildly in her chest, Amber sagged against the wall. She'd left him. He'd helped her and she'd left him.

He'd get out of it. Amber started walking. The Scarred Ones would realise their mistake and they'd release him. He wasn't in any danger. He wasn't.

"Balls," she whispered to nothing but the stench, and she turned back, sprinted through the chamber, following the priest. She got to the door and threw it open, and stopped.

The door led outside, to a long pathway that stretched from one tower to the next. On this side of the palace, she was on the top of an impossible mountain, looking down on a valley where winged creatures preyed on each other in mid-air. It was freezing here. The path was covered in ice.

The Scarred Ones were halfway across, walking away from her. The priest walked with them. Their hands were no longer clasped to his arms. He was no longer struggling, or shouting.

He looked over his shoulder, like he knew she'd be there, and he smiled, and walked on.

Frowning, Amber stepped back, closed the door to the freezing cold. She turned, hurried back through the chamber until she got to the cells.

Metal walls, with bars of black iron, and people behind them, reaching out to her as she passed, begging her for help, for release or for an end to their pain. She couldn't help them. She couldn't slow down, couldn't listen to their words. She could only listen for voices.

"Glen!" she called, and got a cacophony of responses.

She saw a key hanging from a nail, snatched it as she passed.

"Glen Morrison!" she called, running now. She turned a corner and ran on. "Can you hear me? Glen!"

And then a voice. His voice.

She backtracked, peering through the bars. "Glen? Glen, where are you?"

One hand among all the others waved out, yet somehow she knew it was his.

She took his hand, crouched down, stared into the darkness of the cell.

"Glen?" she said softly. "Glen, it's me. It's Amber."

She saw him. He was Glen, and he wasn't. He looked like Glen, had the same face, the same hair, but there was something different about him. She blinked to clear her vision, but when she looked back it hadn't changed. It was like he was the *essence* of Glen, instead of the real thing. He was naked and covered in grime, slathered in filth.

"I've come to rescue you," Amber said. "I'm going to take you to a better place. Do you want to go to a better place?"

A small voice. "Yes."

"Come on, then. We have to be quick. Do you understand? We have to hurry."

She used the key to open the cell. There were many figures in here and they surged out. She let them. All she cared about was Glen.

He reached for her, his cold fingers wrapped around her hand, and Amber led him back the way she'd come.

Or she thought she did. There were suddenly a lot more turns than she'd remembered, and the freed souls were making too much noise to hang around. She chose a corridor at random and sprinted, Glen barely keeping up.

Behind her, she heard screams of terror.

And then a familiar voice called out to her. "Amber? Is that you?"

She stopped, her insides suddenly cold.

Grant Van der Valk, her parents' friend, stared at her from behind the cell bars. "You're free," he said. "You're not... you're not trapped here."

Kirsty pressed to the front. "Amber? Is that Amber? Help us. Please help us."

Amber backed away.

"Where are you going?" Grant asked. "Amber, you can't leave us here. You can't just abandon us. Please help us."

"You have to," Kirsty wept.

Someone moved behind them, and Amber's eyes widened when she saw the grime-smeared face of the woman who had helped her, who had saved her, who had shown her the only love she'd ever experienced as a child. "Imelda?"

Amber ran to the next set of bars, Glen stumbling after her, and Imelda reached her hand through and stroked Amber's face.

"You're not dead," Imelda whispered.

"No," said Amber. "Not dead. Me and Milo, we're still alive."

Imelda smiled so brilliantly, so brightly that Amber just knew it was the first time she'd smiled since she'd been here.

"That's my girl," Imelda whispered.

"I can get you out," said Amber. "I got my friend out – I can get you out, too."

But Imelda shook her head. "I'm not leaving. Can never leave. Go on, go before they find you."

"You're coming with me."

"No, Amber. This is my place now."

"This is Hell. You don't belong here."

"Oh, but I do. And so do your parents. When can I expect to see them?"

"I... I don't know."

"I'm looking forward to seeing them," Imelda said. "I'm looking forward to sharing all this with them."

Down the corridor, there were shouts. Screams.

"Go now," said Imelda. "The Twisted are coming. Run, Amber. Run!"

Tightening her grip on Glen's hand, Amber ran, but the corridors ahead were filled with tormented bodies in ragged robes, the Twisted, and they moved quickly and with purpose. She backed off, took another route, but the way ahead was blocked and the path behind was suddenly alive with their pursuers.

Glen whimpered and she pushed him to the wall and stood there, guarding him, snarling as the Twisted closed in.

37

THE TWISTED THINGS ROWED Amber and Glen across the water to the castle of the Shining Demon. They marched them through the massive doors and up the worn steps, and they climbed and walked and climbed and finally she was brought before Astaroth, forced to kneel with Glen beside her.

Astaroth stood up from his throne. "I do not know what to make of you, girl. I bestow upon you an honour that few have ever possessed, and this is how you act? You sneak. You steal. You betray."

Her mouth was dry. "It's my—"

"Pardon?" the Shining Demon said, moving down the steps. "You wish to speak? By all means. Let me hear what you have to say."

Amber licked her lips. "It's my fault he was there."

"This boy?"

"Yes, Lord. It's my fault. He died because of me."

Astaroth peered at Glen, who kept his head down and trembled. "A vampire took his life, is that not true?"

"Yes, that's how he died, but—"

"Then is the vampire not responsible for the death?"

"He wouldn't have been there if it wasn't for me," Amber explained. "I let him down. I wasn't there to save him."

"Then you merely failed to keep him alive," said Astaroth. "You are not responsible for his death. This... confuses me. For this, you attempted to steal a soul from the Blood-dimmed King?"

She dropped her eyes. "Yes, Lord."

"I fear I may have chosen unwisely in selecting you to be my representative. If you have acted in this fashion against our King, what have you done against me?"

She looked up quickly. "Nothing, Lord, I swear."

Astaroth sneered. "I can taste your lies, girl."

"I promise, I haven't done anything," said Amber. "I didn't think anyone would notice if I took my friend's soul back with me. I didn't mean anything by it. I didn't mean to betray anyone."

"And yet you have," said Astaroth. "I fear our arrangement has come to an end. Your friend will be taken back to the palace, where he will no doubt endure a fresh eternity of unknowable pain. You, meanwhile, will assume another post, as plaything to the vicious."

"Lord Astaroth, please."

"Away with you."

"Please, don't do this! I'm close to finding my parents!"

"You need not concern yourself with them any longer," Astaroth said, turning away. "My next representative will deliver them to me."

"I know where they are!"

"Farewell, girl."

"They want me to trap you!"

Astaroth stopped, and looked back at her.

"They have someone I care about. They'll give her back to me in exchange for..."

"Me," said the Shining Demon.

"Yes, Lord. They know about your brother, how he was trapped."

"And they want to trap me as I trapped Naberius. To what end?"

Amber hesitated. "They wanted me to bring you to them, in chains. And they'd... they'd consume you."

"The audacity," Astaroth breathed. But he was smiling. "The sheer, brazen, magnificent *audacity*. Your parents were indeed worthy of the power I gifted them. Their schemes and machinations are truly wonderful..."

"I can bring them to you," said Amber. "I'll find a way to make them come here..."

Astaroth thought for a moment. "No," he said. "Such a daring plan deserves to be seen through to the absolute end. They wish you to deliver me, powerless and in chains, and this you will do."

She frowned. "Lord?"

"Naberius tried to trick me, a hundred years ago," said Astaroth. "What happened when I found out, little girl?"

"You... you played along," said Amber.

"Yes," said Astaroth. "I played along. I let him enjoy his moment. I let him savour the anticipation of a well-executed plan. Then what did I do? What is that phrase? With the rearranging of the furniture?"

"You turned the tables."

"I did indeed. I turned the tables. He fell into his own trap. That is what should happen here."

"I don't understand..."

"Rise."

Amber got to her feet.

"You will deliver me in chains," the Shining Demon said. "Only these chains will do nothing to diminish my strength. I wish to see their faces. I wish to see the delight in their eyes. I wish to hear the words they speak as they gloat, and boast... And then I wish to taste their terror when they realise their lives are at an end.

"You will do this, girl. I will let you keep the little soul you have salvaged, and you will remain as my representative. A hundred years of doing my bidding will scrub your sentimentality away, have no fear of that. I will ensure you become my most vicious of representatives."

"Yes, Lord."

"Go now. Return when it is time to deliver me to your parents."

"Yes, Lord. Thank you."

The Twisted stepped back, and Amber pulled Glen to his feet and hurried him out of the Hall of a Thousand Mirrors. Once back in the corridors, she speeded up, expecting at any moment to hear Astaroth's voice, to realise that he'd changed his mind.

They got back to the chamber with the tapestries. The circle of fire was still lit, and Fool stood beside it.

It turned, thick liquid leaking from its ruined eyes, and sniffed the air. "Is that a soul I smell?"

"It is," said Amber, keeping a tight grip on Glen's hand. "I'm taking it with me."

"You're taking it to the realm of the living?"

"I am. The Shining Demon is allowing me to."

Fool tittered. "What fun! How exciting! What'll happen to it, then? What happens to a soul in the realm of the living?"

"I... I don't know. But anything is better than this."

"Than what?"

"Hell, Fool. Anything is better than Hell."

Fool frowned. "But this is home."

"Not for me," said Amber. "Not for all those souls that are being tortured. It's not your home, either. What was your life like before this?"

"There was no life before this."

"Then how did you get here? Were you born here?"

"I..."

"Did you grow up here? When you were a child?"

Fool laughed. "I was never a child! I was Fool! Always! Forever!"

"We all come from somewhere, Fool. We don't just appear. We all have lives before this."

It shook its head. "Not I. My life has always been this castle, always Lord Astaroth."

"And what about Naberius?"

Fool's face darkened. "We do not speak of Lord Naberius."

"You remember him?"

"We do not speak of the betrayer."

"Do you know what happened to him?"

"We do not speak."

"Okay, Fool. Okay. If Lord Astaroth doesn't want us to talk about his brother, we won't talk about his brother. That's fine. No need to get upset."

"It is the Master's will."

"And that's fine. I didn't know that and now I do. Thank you for explaining that."

"The Master will be very angry if he finds out."

"Well, I'm not going to tell him."

"The Master has no time for betrayers."

"No one's betrayed him, Fool. I asked a question and you answered. There has been no betrayal."

"I have no time for betrayers, either."

Amber looked around. "Where is Bigmouth?"

Fool smiled. "Bigmouth has been naughty."

"Where is he?"

"Bigmouth opened a door Bigmouth was not supposed to open."

"Can I see him? Where is he? Is he through here?"

She started walking, taking Glen's soul with her. Fool followed.

"Bigmouth tried to run," Fool continued. "Bigmouth is not allowed to run."

"What did you do to him, Fool?" she asked, just as she passed through the doorway. The room beyond was lit with candles, casting a warm glow on to cold stone. Bigmouth hung on the far wall, suspended by chains wrapped around his torso. He blinked at her, and tears ran down his face.

"Oh God," Amber whispered.

"Bigmouth opened a door," said Fool, "so I took Bigmouth's arms away."

Amber lowered her head.

"Bigmouth tried to run," said Fool, "so I took Bigmouth's legs away."

She could hear the dripping of the blood from the raw stumps, and she knew those stumps could drip forever and Bigmouth would never be offered the release of a true death.

"I'm sorry," she said, looking Bigmouth in the eyes.

He turned his head away.

She took Glen back to the chamber, made him stand in the circle. She stood beside him, keeping a firm grip on his hand. Then she stamped on the flame and it went out, and she was back in Milo's room, just outside of Cheyenne.

Her hand was empty as Milo jumped to his feet.

"It worked," she said, looking around. "I found him. Took him with me. I... I think. I was holding his hand just two seconds ago."

"It's a soul," said Milo. "You can't see a soul, Amber, not here."

She reverted. She was suddenly cold, so she pulled on a sweatshirt. "You think he's gone?" she asked. "Where? Where do you think he is?"

Milo didn't answer right away. "If there is a Heaven, maybe his soul's gone there. He was a good person, right? I think... I think if Heaven exists, that's where it's gone."

The corners of her lips twitched upwards. "I like that. He deserves it, y'know?"

"Yeah."

"And the other part of him?"

"I don't know. That's a vampire. That's... unknowable. The only thing you've got to remember is that your friend is free, and the thing that remains, the vampire, is just something that happens to look like him. I'm assuming you got the soul out without anyone noticing? Amber?"

Amber hesitated.

"Oh, Amber," said Milo, closing his eyes.

38

THEY DROVE FOR MOST of the next day. Amber managed to keep her mouth pretty much shut until they were an hour from Kansas City.

"Obviously—" she blurted.

"*Jesus!*" Milo said, jumping.

"Sorry."

"A little warning next time." He settled. "Anyway, what?"

"I was just going to say that, obviously, he's still a problem," Amber said. "Astaroth, I mean. I don't want him pulling my strings and he's pulling my strings. But one thing at a time."

Milo glanced at her. "I have a feeling you've gone over this conversation a few times in your head."

"I have, yes," she said. "Trying to anticipate your responses. I want him and my parents off my back. Doing what Astaroth wants gets my parents off my back. Which is good."

"Yes, it is."

"But with my parents taken care of," she continued, "then I have nothing to distract myself from being the Shining Demon's representative. So that's not good."

"No, it isn't."

"But what choice do I have? There are three things on my list. Rescue Kelly. Deliver my parents. Cheat Astaroth. This takes care of two of them. I'll bring them Astaroth, he'll be in chains, they'll think he's helpless, and then... *bam*."

Milo nodded. "*Bam*."

"And, while he's killing them, I'll swoop in and rescue Kelly and get her the hell out of there."

"And then?"

Amber faltered. "And then... I don't really know."

"You'll have crossed off the first two things on your list, but you'll still have a Duke of Hell to either run from, cheat, or kill."

"Or," she said, "they'll kill *each other*. What do you think of that?"

"It's unlikely to happen."

"But it's a possibility."

"Your parents aren't that strong," Milo said. "If you do what Astaroth wants, and it works and your parents are taken out of the game, then the Shining Demon has to be next on your list."

"Do you have any idea how to kill a Duke of Hell?"

"Not a one."

Milo's phone buzzed, and he handed it to Amber.

"Caller ID is blocked," she said, "but they're requesting a video call."

"May as well answer it," he said. "Only a handful of people know my number."

She frowned, and answered, and stared at her mother.

"Hello, sweetie!" Betty cooed, smiling at her from a thousand miles away. "Just checking in! Oh, are you in the car right now? Is Milo with you? Hi, Milo!"

Milo scowled.

Bill took the phone and his face filled the screen. Amber couldn't tell where they were. "We're going to assume you're on your way to get us what we want," he said. "Are you close?"

"Let me speak to Kelly," Amber said.

"First you answer my question."

"No," Amber said, her anger rising. "First I talk to Kelly. Then I answer your question."

Bill sighed, and then he was walking. It was a house Amber had never seen before. A door opened and now Amber got a good view of Kelly, chained to a chair in the middle of an empty room. She watched Bill's fingers pull the gag from Kelly's mouth. "Say hello."

Kelly opened and closed her mouth a few times before speaking. Her face was covered in cuts and bruises. "Hey, Amber. Don't know where I am, sorry."

"You okay?" Amber asked.

Kelly smiled. "I burned down the first house they kept me in," she said. "Then I took their phone and used it to transfer all their money to different charities across the—"

Bill's hand came into shot again, and he fixed the gag back into place before turning the phone back to him.

"Your little friend here is lucky we're so patient," he said, clipping his words the way he always did when he was trying not to appear angry. "So tell me now, or I'll break her fingers. Are you close to getting us what we want?"

"We're doing our best," Amber said.

"What does that mean?"

"It means I'll get it done, Bill. That's what it means."

"You'd better. Because if you don't—"

Amber ended the call.

She looked at the phone in her hand, but they didn't call back.

"Did I make it worse?" she asked.

"Don't see how it could be worse," Milo said. "But, for the record, no, I don't think you did. They were calling for an update. Nothing's changed. Good idea that, demanding to speak to Kelly. At least you know she's okay."

"She burned down a house."

"I heard."

"And gave all their money away."

"Don't know why you're happy about that one. That's your inheritance."

They looked at each other, and burst out laughing.

"I knew she'd be the worst kind of hostage anyone could ever take," Amber said. "I just knew it."

"She's doing you proud."

"Yes, she is."

They reached Kansas City and found a Motel 6 on the outskirts, opposite a Cracker Barrel and a Subway. It was pretty early, but they still went straight to their rooms. Amber fell asleep watching TV, and in her dream she was in a warehouse, and there was gunfire.

She passed a man on the stairs. He was wearing a suit and was quite dead. Someone had pulled his guts out of his belly. She kept climbing.

There were two more men in suits lying dead on the stairs.

Another man burst out onto a landing, bleeding badly and carrying Molly. She was unconscious and pale, her arm twisted.

Amber kept going. She got to the top of the stairs and went through.

Her parents and their friends, Imelda included, had poor Carolyn surrounded. They leered at her with demon faces and Carolyn spun to face anyone who got too close. She held a gun in her trembling hand.

"One bullet left," said Grant.

"Better make it count," said Alastair, reaching for her.

Carolyn turned, made him back off. "Get away from me."

"Why are you fighting?" Bill asked. "Grant and Kirsty's kid didn't fight. Alastair and Imelda's kid didn't cause us this much trouble. You're just like your brother, you know that?"

"My brother was a hero," Carolyn snapped back.

Bill laughed. "You don't know the first thing about your brother."

"I know more than you."

Betty frowned. "Do you, now? And how do you know this? The old woman you were with. Who is she?"

Despite her circumstances, Carolyn found the strength to smile. "You'll never find her, even with all your resources. She has more."

Imelda leaped at her, grabbed her arm and pointed the gun into the floorboards as Carolyn fired her last bullet. The gun dropped from her hand and the others closed in.

"Tell us who she is," said Betty.

Carolyn spat at her, and in return they devoured her.

"Jesus," Amber said as she woke.

She pulled on her sneakers and left the room. She was too wired to get back to sleep. And too hungry.

She crossed to the Subway and sat at a small table near the back. She thought about Kelly and smiled, but pretty soon the worry started to kick in again, and the doubts, and the doubts

271

brought with them images of Ronnie and Warrick and Linda, and her brother and sister. She abandoned the sandwich halfway through, but she felt a little better after it. A little stronger. But also like she was about to throw up.

A girl wandered in, looked at the worktop dumbly, ignoring the offers of help that were coming from the staff. Amber glanced up.

"Clarissa?"

Clarissa looked at her blankly.

Amber rushed over. "Jesus, Clarissa, are you okay?"

It took a few seconds for Clarissa to answer. "Amber...?"

"Come on," Amber said, "come with me." She took Clarissa's hand and led her outside. No sign of the Peterbilt. They crossed the road, got back to Amber's room, where she sat Clarissa on the bed. "What happened?" she asked. "We saw you get in the truck."

"Truck," Clarissa echoed, and started to shiver. "Truck. No. *Please*."

"You're safe," Amber said quickly. "You hear me? It's over. You're free. You're safe."

"Please don't let him take me," Clarissa said, tears rolling down her cheeks.

"You're safe," Amber said again. She used her strong voice this time. "He's gone. No one will hurt you now. Clarissa, I need you to tell me what happened. When you got in the truck."

"Oh God," Clarissa said, "it was... He wasn't human, Amber. His skin was black. I mean... *black*. Like night."

"I know," said Amber.

"And his eyes. His eyes were red. Steam came out of them. They were just, they were red eyes. I thought, I thought he'd drugged me or... but they were red. Later on, when he smiled, the red light, it was coming from his mouth as well."

"What happened, Clarissa?"

"I was hitching," she said, "and he stopped. I opened the door and he was, he looked normal. Then I got in and the moment, the moment the door shut he changed, and I tried to jump out, but I couldn't get the door open, and we were driving so fast."

Amber grabbed a box of tissues from the nightstand and passed it over. Clarissa took a handful. "I was shouting. I told him to let me out and he... and nothing. He didn't even look at me. And Jesus, Amber, the screaming."

"What screaming?"

"From the radio. All the screaming, the begging. He turned it up louder. He enjoyed it. It got stuck in my head. I couldn't get it out. It got underneath my thoughts. All the people he killed. Their souls. It was their souls, screaming."

Amber sat next to her, patted her back. "You're okay now," she said softly. "Where did he take you?"

"Nowhere," said Clarissa. "We drove around. We didn't stop. I had to pee and I — I told him. I told him I had to pee and he didn't say anything, didn't stop, didn't look at me. I tried to hold it in, I held it in for hours, but I... I wet myself. Like a toddler, I wet myself. I had to."

Amber rubbed her back. "You didn't stop? Not at all?"

A small laugh escaped Clarissa's lips. "Not even after I pissed on his seat."

"Did he say anything?" Amber asked. "Did he talk to you?"

"Didn't say a word. The whole time. Not one word."

"How did you get out?"

"What?"

"How did you get out of the truck, Clarissa?"

Clarissa frowned at her. "Out?"

"How did you escape?"

"I didn't escape," Clarissa said. "I'm still there now."

"What?"

Clarissa moved, plunging something long and cold and sharp into Amber's belly. "This is how I get out."

39

Amber fell back, off the bed, hands at her belly, the blood running through her fingers.

Clarissa stood. "This is how I escape. When he has what he wants, he won't need me anymore. He'll pull over and open the door and let me out." She still held the knife. It was a long one.

The pain was a tight thing that twisted with every beat of her heart. Amber started crawling for the door, but Clarissa shook her head.

"You can't leave," she said. "If you leave, he won't let me leave." She stood over Amber and leaned down, stabbing her quickly in the side.

Amber cried out and turned over on to her back. Clarissa's eyes were wide and glassy, but she was calm. Amber's own blood dripped from the blade on to her face.

"Shh," said Clarissa. "You won't even notice it."

Amber gritted her teeth and shifted. The pain flared, making her cry out, but once she was horned up it fell away to a dull throb. Clarissa didn't register any surprise at the transformation. She may not have even noticed.

She leaned down again. The knife scraped off scales and Amber took hold of her wrist and squeezed, and Clarissa yelled in pain and dropped the weapon. She tried to pull away, but Amber held on until the time was right – then she let go and Clarissa flew backwards, hit the corner of the bed and flipped over it.

Amber got to her feet slowly, one arm pressing against the scales covering her wounds. She watched Clarissa stand.

"Where is he?" Amber asked.

"I have to kill you," said Clarissa.

"Tell me where he is and I'll kill him, instead."

A smile rose. "He's a monster. You can't kill monsters. Monsters kill you. That's what they do."

"But you're not a monster, are you?"

"No. No, I am not."

"You just got in the wrong truck."

"The very wrong truck."

"You're in the truck right now, are you?"

Clarissa nodded. More tears came. "He won't let me go."

"He's beside you, is he?"

"Yes."

"He wants you to kill me, but only a monster would kill me, and you're not a monster, Clarissa, are you?"

Her face crumpled. "But... but if I don't kill you he'll never let me go."

"Look at him, Clarissa. Look at his face. He's never going to let you go no matter what you do, is he?"

She sobbed. "No, he's not."

"He wants to turn you into a monster."

Clarissa shook her head. "He won't."

"What does he want, Clarissa?"

"He wants me to kill you. He wants to take your friend."

"He's going after Milo himself?"

"Yes. I don't know how I know these things. His thoughts... I think they got in my head a little bit."

"I have to leave now, Clarissa. I have to help my friend."

Clarissa shook her head. "You have to die."

"Okay then, kill me. Come on, I'll let you do it."

"You will?"

"Yes, I promise."

Tears of gratitude came to Clarissa's eyes as she stepped forward. "Thank you, Amber! Thank you so much!"

Amber slapped her hard and Clarissa fell straight back, unconscious before she hit the ground. Even that movement tore up Amber's insides. She hurried to her bag, took the second to last vial from the box and stuffed it in her pocket, then she walked quickly to Milo's room, leaving a trail of blood behind her. The door was open. Inside, the bed was shoved to one side and the table was smashed. Gritting her teeth, she ran for the parking lot, reaching it just in time to see the Peterbilt pull out on to the road and drive north.

Hissing, she retraced her steps, got back to Milo's room, tore the place apart looking for his keys. She grabbed them and ran to the Charger, but her legs failed her and she fell. She heard someone groaning and realised it was her.

She crawled onwards, on her hands and knees. She reached for the handle, but the door seemed to open by itself. She dragged herself in, took a moment to get her breathing under control. She was cold and getting colder and bleeding all over the seat.

The key scraped at the ignition a few times before slipping in. She twisted it. The engine sprang to life and the radio crackled.

Adrenaline shot through Amber's system, but before she could turn the radio off a voice rose from the speakers, thin and tremulous.

"Hello?"

Amber breathed out. The last time the radio had been on the car had been filled with a screaming that still haunted her nightmares. She reached out to click it off.

"Can anybody hear me?"

Her fingers paused.

"Help me." The voice was female. "Please, someone help me. Is anybody there?"

Another voice now. Male. "Is someone there? I'm scared. I think I'm dead."

More voices rose, as if to the surface of a lake.

"Are we dead? Can you help us? Please help me. We can hear you breathing. Why aren't you saying anything?"

Amber frowned. "Me?" she asked quietly.

"Help!" the voices cried, so fiercely it shocked her. "Help us! We're stuck here! Let us out! Let me out! Am I dead? Where are we?"

More voices joined the chorus, all of them shouting to be heard, adding to the cacophony that filled the car, that filled her head, those voices like drum beats on the inside of her skull, pounding an ever-growing rhythm behind her eyes until her fingers – trembling now, and weak – found the dial and twisted them all to silence.

Breath coming in shallow rattles, Amber sat there with her head down, tears on her face.

She put the Charger into gear, and eased out on to the road.

40

She found the Peterbilt and followed at a safe distance. The Charger, usually so responsive, strained against her. It surged forward with the slightest tap on the gas, its engine complaining against the restraint she was forcing upon it. But Amber battled and she won, and the distance between her and the truck stayed the same for over fifteen minutes. Then the truck slowed, and took a dirt track, and Amber killed the headlights and followed.

The Charger trundled over the uneven ground, and every bounce made Amber wince. She worked to keep the Peterbilt's tail lights in view at all times. It wasn't easy, but she managed. Trees loomed on either side as she made her way down the tunnel of wood and leaves.

The Peterbilt swung off the track, into a clearing, and Amber stopped the Charger and turned off the engine. It growled with displeasure before it quietened, and she got out.

She popped the stopper of the vial, drank the blood within. The power exploded inside her, surging through her system, pulsing through her body, healing it, making it stronger, her injuries knitting themselves closed even as she grew bigger and taller and her horns turned to antlers.

Feeling better – feeling much, much better – Amber crept through the trees. She heard the Peterbilt's door slam closed and she ducked her head under low branches and got closer. The truck's engine was off, though still ticking, and its headlights were on, catching the trucker in full beam.

He was a big man in jeans, with a brown leather jacket, the kind with a fur collar, zipped up over his gut. Beneath the battered cowboy hat his skin was pitch black, and red light shone from his eyes and mouth. He dragged Milo by the scruff of the neck, then dropped him and took a pouch from his jacket. He poured the black powder inside on to the ground, making a circle. When he was done, he went back for Milo.

Amber stepped out. "Don't touch him."

The trucker looked at her, his red mouth smiling.

"I'm not going to tell you to walk away," Amber said, walking closer. "I know you won't. Anyone who loves killing as much as you do, they're not going to listen to reason. And you do love killing, don't you?"

The smile widened.

"Yeah, that's what I figured. You a representative, like me? Maybe you are. Something tells me that you don't have any moral quandaries about it, though. You like that word? Quandaries? Yeah, Milo taught it to me. It's a good word. It means that there is a little bit of a good person left inside me. I haven't completely snuffed her out. I'm not entirely reprehensible. You like that word, too? You can have it. It suits you.

"But I'm going to be honest with you, Mr Trucker. The only way you're going to stop is if I stop you, and that's what I'll try to do. And, I admit, I might not succeed. You look like you've been doing this a long time. But I'm going to try. I'm going to do my best to beat the crap out of you and stomp on your head until it's nothing but a puddle. I just thought you ought to know that, before we begin."

The trucker took a box of matches from his pocket and walked back to the circle. He struck a match and let it fall, and the powder caught fire.

A figure appeared in the circle. Thin and robed, its face hidden by the hood it wore. It carried a spear, the blade of which was the deepest, darkest black. Amber didn't need an introduction. She knew who it was. The Whispering Demon.

"Demoriel," she said.

The Demon observed her for a moment before his thin hands rose to his hood and pulled it back. Demoriel's face – his real face – would appear to have been sliced off long ago. The one he wore now, pinned in place by rusted nails, was stretched too tightly over the glistening muscles beneath.

"You're one of Astaroth's," he said. Although he spoke in the gentlest of whispers, she heard him as clearly as if his flayed lips were at her ear.

"I'm more than that," she responded. "I'm his representative. And I'm here to take Milo back. You can't have him. I won't let you."

Beneath the skin-mask he wore, his eyes flickered to Milo, then back to Amber. "I admire your loyalty to your friend," Demoriel said, "but, when a deal is broken, there must be consequences. It is that single principle upon which our entire system is based. There can be no exceptions."

"Then let this be the first," said Amber.

"An exception such as the one you suggest could only be the result of exceptional circumstances – and your friend, though obviously important to you, fails to meet the requirements for exceptional."

Amber stepped closer. "I'm not going to let you take him."

"There is precious little you can do to prevent it."

"I can kill your trucker-demon here."

Demoriel shook his head sadly. "Little demon, why must violence be your only recourse?"

"Because talking's not getting me what I want. Listen to me – if I fight him, I'll win, that's guaranteed, and I'll take Milo back with me. So why not just skip the fight, and your guy gets to walk away and I get Milo?"

Demoriel smiled. "Because you are Astaroth's representative."

"So?"

"So I have a strong dislike of your Master."

"Join the club."

Demoriel laughed. "Well, this is interesting," he said, and the trucker attacked.

He took Amber by surprise, grabbing her and punching. Those hands were big and heavy and they moved fast. She lost her footing in the scramble. He had hold of her antlers. Those things were always getting in the way. She fell and his knee came down on her belly and he kept punching. She tried to cover up. His fists got through to her scales anyway, rattling them on her face. This was not how she had wanted this fight to start.

Amber squirmed free and he straightened and kicked her. The scales absorbed most of it, but even so she went rolling. She got back to her feet as he closed in, and threw a punch of her own. He ducked under it, grabbed her and flung her against the side of the Peterbilt, sent two punches crunching into her ribs for good measure. Then he grabbed her antlers again.

"Stop doing that!" she shouted, clipping him under the chin. He took a step back and she hit him again and his hat flew off. She tried to kick him in the balls, but he caught her foot, held it and drove her backwards against the truck once more. He let go and threw a punch, but now it was Amber who slipped by. She plunged her talons into his gut, raked them out and as the trucker stumbled she took him off his feet and kicked him in the head. He sprawled in the dirt, and for a moment Amber thought the fight was over. But he started to get up again.

And then Glen dropped from the night sky, stomping the trucker's face into the ground.

Glen straightened. The Peterbilt's headlights caught on his pale skin, throwing one side of his face into darkness.

Demoriel dipped his head. "And who are you?"

"I am darkness," said Glen. "I am death. Leave this place, Demon. I have seen your kind. I have heard your twisting words. I have no fear left in my heart, and so I do not fear you. I say to you again, leave this place of light, of love, of life, and return to your squalid shadows of pain and tormented— *Balls*."

The trucker's outstretched hand closed around Glen's ankle as the trucker sat up. Glen hopped in place.

"Let go, you dick."

The trucker got to his feet and swung Glen round, slamming him into a tree.

Amber charged and the trucker turned to her, fists ready, but just before she reached him she reverted. The trucker swung a punch.

"Stop!" Demoriel commanded.

The trucker's fist stopped inches from Amber's face.

His red eyes narrowed.

"You hit me when I'm like this," she said, "you'll probably kill me. And your boss doesn't want to upset my boss, do you, Demoriel?"

She turned her back to the trucker, feeling his breath on her neck, but ignoring it, focusing on the Demon. She saw Glen, back on his feet and baring his fangs, but he stayed in the darkness.

"You are clever," the Whispering Demon said. "And reckless. You would start a war in Hell over this?"

"Hell, yeah," said Amber.

"And yet," Demoriel said, "deals are deals."

"Milo can't even remember making his deal," Amber said. "He doesn't know how or why it happened. Did you do that? Did you take his memories?"

"He did it," said Demoriel. "He wanted to forget. It was a clumsy procedure he embarked on, could easily have left him without even the ability to form thoughts. But he had help, and he blocked those memories off like a dam stops up a river. The memories are still there, of course. I can see them, swirling and churning on the other side of his dam."

"I want you to release him from his contract," said Amber.

Demoriel laughed. "Whyever would I do that?"

"Because I'm asking you to. We both know Milo's never going to work for you again."

"Yes, we do," said Demoriel, "which is why I take him back with me today."

"If you do that, I'll kill your trucker here."

"Very well."

"And I'll hunt down your next demon," she continued, "and

284

your next, and your next. I'll kill them one by one, and, every time you make a new deal with some desperate idiot, I'll kill them, too. It'll be my life's work, and it'll be my hobby. I'll kill your demons because I'm not allowed to kill Astaroth's."

"You would kill your Master's demons?"

"Oh yes," she said. "I've met them. I know who they are and where they are and what they've done. I'd like nothing more than to go after them. Going after yours wouldn't be as satisfying, but, nonetheless, it might even balance a few scales."

Demoriel watched her and said nothing.

"Or you can let Milo off the hook," she said. "He's already been gone twelve years, right? So let him go. Is he really worth the hassle? Really?"

Demoriel didn't speak for another few moments. Then he said, "I will require something of you."

"No," said Amber. "Forget it. No more deals."

"This is not a deal," Demoriel said, "it is an agreement. You say you hate Astaroth, yes? How much do you hate him?"

"I'd say I hate him just enough."

"Do you hate him enough to act against him?"

"You asking me to betray him?"

"I am merely enquiring as to—"

"Yes," she said. "I hate him enough to betray him."

"I see."

"Release Milo from his contract, and trust me to hate Astaroth when the time comes."

"Very well," said Demoriel. "Come closer."

Amber frowned. "You're going to break the contract?"

"I am, but deals are sealed with a handshake, little demon.

This is how they must be dissolved. I can hardly shake your unconscious friend's hand, can I? So it must be yours."

Amber hesitated. "If this is a trick..."

"I don't lie, little demon."

She walked over, and extended her hand.

"Closer," he said.

"You can reach my hand from there."

"To do so, I would have to leave the circle. And I never leave the circle."

Amber took a deep breath. Keeping an eye on the black spear he carried, she took his other hand. It was cold, like shaking the hand of a dead person.

"There," said Demoriel. "It is done."

He released her hand without trying anything tricky.

She took a step back. "What is? What did you do?"

"Your friend is no longer one of mine," said Demoriel. "He is no longer a demon."

"You... you took his power?"

The Whispering Demon smiled. "It was never his to begin with. He has his life back, his soul is scrubbed clean, and he is free to squander it as he sees fit."

"Right. Well, uh... thanks." She resisted the urge to wipe her hand on her pants.

"Be careful how you go, little demon. And don't forget what we discussed. If you get the chance to betray Astaroth—"

"I'll take it," said Amber. "Don't you worry about that."

41

AMBER TOOK MILO BACK to the motel, laid him on his bed and turned out the light. She went back to her own room. Clarissa was gone.

She walked out, went to the parking lot, stood beside the Charger and waited.

From overhead, the sound of fluttering clothes, and then a voice from behind her. Amber turned. Glen stood there.

He cleared his throat, and gave a little wave. "Hello."

She frowned. "Glen?"

"Yes," he said, excitement bubbling. "It's me! I'm me again!"

"How?"

He came forward. Still deathly pale, but his eyes sparkled. "It was you, right? I don't know exactly how, or what you did, but you did something, didn't you? I have this, this feeling that you did something and now I... I'm me again. What did you do?"

"I brought you back," she said. "Your soul."

"Where was it?"

"In Hell."

His face screwed up. "Why was it in Hell?"

"Anyone who gets turned into a vampire goes to Hell. You don't remember it? You don't remember anything about a palace, or the Blood-dimmed King, or meeting the Shining Demon?"

"I met the Shining Demon?" Glen asked. "Wow. I don't remember, like, any of that. I *do* remember being in that motel room, back when I was alive, and a dude coming in and, basically, biting me. It was confusingly intimate. I remember being on the bed and thinking, y'know... why am I liking this so much? Am I gay? But it wasn't a gay thing, as it turned out. He was just killing me. Then it all went dark. And, when I woke up, I wasn't me. I couldn't think the same way, I couldn't... I was sad. I suppose that's the only way I can describe it. I was sad and I couldn't get happy. My brain wouldn't let me."

Amber hesitated, then squeezed his arm.

"It didn't help that I was killing people," he said.

"Yeah."

"I feel kinda bad about that."

"You probably should."

"I can't let it affect me too much, though."

"Why not?"

"I was a creature of the night, Amber. I can't be held responsible for what I did or didn't do when I was a creature of the night."

"So what *didn't* you do?"

"I... well, I didn't *not* kill people."

"Yeah," she said slowly. "I don't know, Glen, I think you should probably still feel bad about that."

"It wasn't me, though. That was Vampire Me. He doesn't count."

"But aren't you still a vampire?"

"I am, yeah."

"And are you going to kill more people?"

He frowned. "Yeah..."

"Don't you see a problem with that?"

"Oh, I do!" he said. "Yes, absolutely! I can't be going around killing people, willy-nilly. And no more innocent people, either. They are right off the menu and that is that."

"No one's saying otherwise."

"But I reckon all I need to do is be more selective in my... snacking, as it were. How about this – how about I only go after bad guys?"

"Okay."

"Yeah?"

"Sure. Where will you find them?"

"Ah, they're everywhere," said Glen. "I'll be able to find them, no problem. They hang out in dive bars and places like that. And, like, with all the enemies you make, I'm sure I'll be kept well fed."

"So you're planning on sticking around?"

"Well, yeah," said Glen. "If you'll have me. I could be such a resource, Amber. I have all the strengths of a vampire and none of their weaknesses."

"None of them?"

"None," he said, nodding. Then he shook his head. "Well, okay, all, but I can use my vampire powers for the benefit of mankind. I can punish the guilty. Avenge the innocent. Do other stuff."

"Yeah," said Amber. "Maybe."

"Of course," he continued, "I'd really only be effective on night-time adventures, for obvious reasons."

"Sure."

"During the day I'll be in a hole in the ground."

"Not a hotel, then?"

"Too risky. What if a maid comes in while I'm sleeping and opens the blinds? Instant barbeque."

"I guess so."

"But I can fly, really fast if I have to, so if you guys drive during the day, I'll catch up with you at night and, y'know, help out."

"Mm-hmm. Although we do tend to sleep at night."

"Oh yeah."

"But I'm sure we can work something out."

"Cool," said Glen, grinning happily. Then his eyes widened. "Hey, you're gay!"

"Uh yeah."

"That's so cool! Why didn't you tell me back when I was alive?"

"I don't know, Glen. I didn't feel like sharing."

"That's cool, that's cool. Like I said, I thought I was gay for a minute, but, well..."

"It was just the vampire killing you."

"Pretty much, yeah. But I think that minute has really changed me. As a person, like. It's given me a newfound respect for you and your people."

"Oh dear Jesus, Glen."

"I'm serious, Amber. And, as a vampire, I feel I now understand what it's like to be persecuted for who I am."

"Is that right?"

"I'm, like, a metaphor for gays."

"You're not, though."

"I could be."

"You haven't been a vampire that long, and not enough people know vampires exist for you to actually be persecuted for it."

"But isn't that what they said about gay people?"

"No."

"Then Martin Luther King died for nothing."

"I'm going away now."

"What'll I do?"

She thought for a moment. "We're on our way to Orlando. We'll meet you there."

He brightened. "At Disney World?"

"No, Glen, at my home."

"You're from Orlando?"

"I told you I was."

"Did you? I'm terrible at remembering places."

Amber sighed. "You still have that phone we gave you? Get to Orlando and keep it charged. We'll call you when we arrive."

"That's a plan," said Glen. "Hey... you think he'll be all right? Milo, I mean?"

"I don't know," she said. "I hope so."

Glen nodded.

She gave him a smile, walked back to the motel with that fluttering noise passing overhead.

She let herself into Milo's room. He was awake, sitting up. The bedside lamp was the only light.

"How are you feeling?" she asked.

He didn't answer.

"Demoriel, he... he released you from your contract," she said. "Your soul is clean, apparently. He won't be coming after you again." No response. "He took your power, too," Amber continued. "You're not a demon anymore. I don't know how you feel about that."

His face was impossible to read.

Amber talked on, filling the void. "Clarissa's gone," she said. "The trucker... I don't know what he did to her mind, but... In her head, she's still trapped in that truck. Do you think she'll get better?" She sighed. "I hope she does. I hope I see her again, maybe get a chance to really help her, you know?"

No response.

She brightened. "Glen's back. His soul is in his body again, I mean. Isn't that cool? He's a little freaked out, but he's his old self. I think. He wants to stay with us. You're probably going to hate me for this, but I said he could. Is that okay? I have no idea how this is going to work, though. What do you do with a happy vampire? What's he going to do with his life? I think we're stuck with him, though. Do you mind?"

Milo murmured something.

"Sorry? What was that?"

"I've lost track of time," he said. "How long before we have to meet your parents?"

She hesitated.

"Amber? How long?"

"It's still Thursday," she said. "The exchange isn't until midnight on Saturday. But..."

"What is it? What's wrong?"

She met his eyes. "I'm going to do it alone."

"No, you're not," he said immediately.

"This is my fight, Milo."

"It's our fight. Me and you. What's brought this on?"

"You're not a demon anymore. If you get hurt, the car can't heal you."

"Then I won't get hurt."

"Milo..."

"You've given me my life back, Amber. Do you understand what you've done? I can start living again. I can stop running, stop hiding, I can... I can grow old. For twelve years, I was in stasis. Limbo. But every day *means* something now. Every moment is something I can... I can reach out and touch. And you did that for me. You made me human again. So I'm not abandoning you, and you're not abandoning me. Are we clear?"

"Yeah," she said. "Yeah, okay."

"Besides," he said, "I have a plan."

Amber blinked. "What?"

"A plan," he repeated. "A way to take down your parents and Astaroth with one move. If it works."

"Seriously?"

"I'm not as strong as I was, so it's time to be smarter. It stands a chance of working. Not a big chance, not a good chance, but a chance."

"Well, that's great," Amber said. "That's excellent. Will it take long?"

He frowned at her. "You have a pressing engagement elsewhere?"

"Kind of," she said. "We have two days left, and, if we're making a move against Astaroth as well, I want to take down as many of his demons as possible before we do."

"We're going to be lucky to get to Orlando in time," said Milo, "and you want to make detours?"

"We have Shanks's key," she reminded him.

"But, to use it, you need to keep a particular door in mind. How are you going to remember all the doors?"

Amber took out her phone, and opened up the pictures of her standing in front of door after door after door.

"Your selfies," he said.

She grinned. "My generation kicks ass."

42

They passed through St Louis, driving with shades on and the windows down.

When they stopped off at Mount Vernon, Amber's hair was a petrified mess.

She wrangled it under control, and picked up Shanks's key. They went to the first locked door they could find, and Amber focused on the picture on her phone, letting the memory swim into her mind, solidify, and then she slid the key into the lock.

Tumble. Click.

THE HOUSE WAS OLD and dusty and unfurnished. The plainly-dressed man and woman stood against the wall, their backs to the room and their heads down, like they were waiting to be activated.

Amber crossed to the stone fireplace and they raised their heads, turned, and Milo started firing. The bullets jerked them back, but didn't stop them, and Amber tore away the grate, grabbing for the sack that she knew was buried underneath.

The man and woman realised what she was doing, and their impassive features stretched in dismay. Amber pulled the blackened baby's skull from the sack and threw it, and Milo shot it in mid-air.

The skull exploded in fragments. A moment later, so did the man and woman.

THEY GOT TO CLARKSVILLE.

When she hooked the iPad up to the motel Wi-Fi, Amber found a message waiting for her on the *Dark Places* forum. It was from Balthazar's-Arm-Candy, and it simply read, *Tick-tock. Tick-tock.*

She shut off the iPad, and Milo came to her room and she took the key from her pocket.

Tumble. Click.

THE UNSTOPPABLE KILLING MACHINE that had once been known as Jack Devries stepped through the trees, and saw them.

"We should probably hurry," said Milo.

They ran for the twisted tree in the centre of the forest and Jack came after them, machete swinging. Milo emptied his gun right into his chest, but Jack didn't seem to mind in the slightest. He swung at Milo and Milo dodged, barely.

Amber took a knife and ran it over her forearm, crying out in pain. Her blood spilled and dropped to the ground, and the ground churned and rumbled and split apart as Jack's body, his original body, rose to the surface. While Milo kept Jack busy, she pulled away the roots that had intertwined with his skeletal remains, grabbed the dog tags from around the neck and yanked them free.

Jack froze, his machete poised to come down on Milo's head. Milo rolled out of the way, and got to his feet as Jack started to rot. It spread quickly, and the machete fell, embedding itself in the ground as Jack turned to putrid mush that sank into the undergrowth.

THEY PAID FOR TWO hotel rooms an hour outside of Nashville, then Amber took out the key.

Tumble. Click.

AMBER APPROACHED MR AND Mrs Paget with a smile on her face.

"Hello there," she said. "Did you enjoy your meal?"

"We did," said Mr Paget, glancing at his watch.

"We're just waiting for your colleague to bring our car around," Mrs Paget said.

Amber's smile didn't dim. "Oh, I don't work for the restaurant," she said, "or the valet service. You probably don't recognise me, do you?"

"Should we?" Mr Paget asked.

"Ah, maybe not. I look a lot different tonight. I met you about three weeks ago? You were, and I don't mean this in a bad way, but you were acting kind of drunk?"

Mrs Paget raised an eyebrow. "We don't drink, so I don't think it was—"

"You had red skin and horns," Amber continued, "and you'd just eaten your son? It was around then?"

They stared at her, giving Milo plenty of time to walk up behind them and put a bullet in each of their brains before they had a chance to shift.

Tumble. Click.

THE CATCHING Z'S MOTEL was open for business, but at this time of night there was no one in the manager's office.

Amber led Milo through the secret door, and they found their target in the corridor beyond. He had his snarling surgical mask pushed up to his forehead as he worked on repositioning the camera behind one of the windows.

They watched him until he noticed them, and his eyes widened and he tried to run.

Milo didn't let him get very far.

The next day they passed through Georgia, but their schedule was too tight to make a detour. So they used the key.

Tumble. Click.

SHE STEPPED THROUGH THE blackened debris, and with each moment came a quiet insight that burst from the back of her mind. This was the cabin Mauk had lived in, back when he was alive. After his arrest, someone had burned it down in an attempt to scrub his existence from the world. But it remained, a dark smudge on the edge of town, and not even the bravest of souls would venture here. The townspeople believed this place to be haunted. They were right.

She found Mauk lying on a table. His eyes were closed, but he wasn't sleeping – not really. He was simply shut down. Even monsters raised from the dead needed to rest, to recharge their dark batteries. Amber picked up a burnt plank of wood, careful not to make any noise.

"Wakey-wakey, sleepyhead," she said softly, and slammed the plank down on to his head.

Mauk howled, rolled off the far side of the table, and Amber dropped the plank and wiped the soot from her hands.

He stared at her. "What the hell did you do that for?"

"Hi, Elias," she said.

"What did you—"

"I heard you the first time," she said. "I just didn't want you sleeping through our final conversation together, that's all."

He straightened up, squaring his shoulders. "You're moving on, are you?"

"You are, actually," Amber said.

Mauk didn't reply for a few seconds. "Why don't you have your horns on? If this... if the Shining Demon sent you, you'd have your horns on."

"I probably would," she said. "Very well spotted. I'm not here in my official capacity as Lord Astaroth's representative. I'm off duty."

Mauk took off his cap, revealing the band of burnt skin circling his skull. He bent the cap, adjusted the brim, and put it back on. "Why are you here?"

"You know why, Elias."

"Is this because of the name-calling?" he asked.

"No," she said. "This has nothing to do with that."

"Then I don't know why you're here."

"I'm here to kill you."

He didn't laugh at her, or curse at her, or try to run. He just said, "You can't do that."

"Yes, I can," said Amber. "I'm about to."

"When the Shining Demon finds out—"

"I'm going to take care of him, too," she said.

Now he did laugh, but it was short, and nervous. "You're nuts."

"Maybe."

"You're gonna take on Astaroth? You? You stand zero chance of making it outta that alive."

"Maybe."

"Hell," he said, taking his hammer from his belt, "you stand zero chance of making it outta here alive. You tried killing me already, remember?"

"But now I know how to do it right," said Amber, and the burgeoning cockiness in Mauk's eyes dimmed instantly. "There's always something physical to keep you creeps here," she continued, "but, while the others tried to bury it, tried to hide it, you thought you were the smart one, didn't you? You figured you could keep it on you at all times. Well, I say on. I mean in."

Milo stepped over a fallen rafter, and Mauk turned to him.

"A heart-shaped locket," Milo said. "Funny, I wouldn't have pegged you as the sentimental type."

"This ain't right," said Mauk. "The Shining Demon will tear you apart for this."

"We know where it is, too," Milo told him. "You cut yourself, pushed the locket into the meat of your left shoulder, didn't you?"

"It ain't fair!" Mauk said, backing away.

"So that means we just have to separate your arm from your body, and you'll never kill anyone again." Milo showed Mauk the hatchet he was carrying.

Mauk roared and attacked, and Milo stepped inside the swing of the hammer and flipped Mauk over his hip. Milo tried to pull the hammer away, but Mauk grabbed it with both hands, and immediately Milo seized Mauk's left wrist. He extended the arm and Mauk cried out and Milo chopped.

Amber turned away from that bit. She'd seen enough blood. Mauk kept screaming, and she started to feel sorry for him. But then she reminded herself of how many people Mauk had killed, and her sympathy dried up.

And then it was over. She looked back as Milo straightened up. The arm he was holding started to decompose, and he dropped it onto Mauk's shrinking, rotting body. Milo put the hatchet on the table and nodded to her.

"That's as many as we can do for now," he said. "Maybe when this is over we can go after the rest."

"If we're still alive," said Amber.

He shrugged.

43

THEY GOT INTO ORLANDO a little before five on Saturday afternoon. The sky was blue and the sun was beating down and the air was thick with heat, so much so that Milo was forced to turn on the air conditioning.

Amber didn't like being back here. She didn't like the heat, didn't like how it made her feel. Didn't like the memories it conjured. Her childhood. The friends she'd never had. The discomfort she'd always felt. The love she'd never known she was missing.

"That's the first time I've had to use the a/c in a long time," Milo muttered.

Amber shook herself free from her thoughts. "You want to try the radio?"

"Not yet," he answered. "And I won't. Not for a while."

"It turned on when I was driving," she said. "I could hear... I could hear voices."

He nodded. "Yeah," was all he said.

It was weird treating the car like an ordinary car. Treating Milo like an ordinary man. Now the car needed refuelling and Milo got hungry on the road, just like Amber did. He needed water, and rest stops, and when he got out of the car after a few hours his back was stiff and he groaned.

It was a lot to take in.

And so was being back in Florida. They passed her school. She didn't mention it to Milo. It wasn't relevant anymore. They passed landmarks she knew well, landmarks that should have bathed Amber in the reassuring glow of familiarity. But they were different now. Or, rather, *she* was different. She viewed them through new eyes, eyes that had seen things she'd never before imagined. The sights offered by her hometown were insignificant in comparison.

They stopped a few miles from her house, pulled in at a gas station as the Charger's fuel gauge hovered over red. The restroom was out of order, so Amber went to the bar across the road. She peed and washed her hands, examined herself in the mirror. She looked tired. She looked exhausted. But she didn't look bad. She had to admit that.

"Are you kidding?" her demon-self said, standing beside her. "You look awful."

"I'm not listening to you," Amber said, fixing her hair.

"Fine. Be like that." Her demon-self fixed her own hair in the mirror. "So how many vials you got left? One, is it?"

"You know it is."

"You used up the other one healing yourself from stab wounds you could have avoided. I mean, that's just *sloppy*. Why didn't you just kill that brat the moment she knifed you the first time?"

"Clarissa is not my enemy."

Her demon-self laughed. "Whatever, dipshit. The point is, you got one more vial left. Do you think that'll be the one that sends you insane?"

"I feel fine."

"You're talking to a hallucination in a restroom."

Amber straightened. "Good point." She walked to the door.

"One more vial, babycakes," her demon-self called after her. "One more vial and then I'm moving in permanently."

Amber left the restroom, headed for the exit as two people entered. She froze.

The FBI agents stood in front of her.

For a moment, nobody moved. Nobody spoke.

Then the woman said, "Amber, we've been all over the country looking for you. I'm—"

"I know who you are," said Amber. "FBI. Agent Sutton, right?"

"Byrd," said the woman. "He's Sutton."

"How do you do?" Agent Sutton asked.

"I don't want any trouble," Amber told them.

"No trouble," Byrd assured her. "We sincerely just want to chat. Do you mind if we take a booth? We've got a lot to talk about."

"Sure," Amber said.

They waited for her to move first, and flanked her as she crossed to the booth at the back. She took a seat. They slid in opposite.

"We're not actually FBI agents," said Sutton. "You're not in any trouble."

"We're here to help," Byrd said.

"You have FBI badges."

Sutton put his elbows on the table and leaned forward. "We're part of an organisation with a lot of resources and pretty deep pockets. It's called the Foundation of Light – maybe you've heard of it?"

"Sorry."

He shrugged. "Not to worry. It just means we're doing our job."

"And what is your job?"

"We handle things," said Byrd. "The kind of things you've been encountering on your travels. Sometimes it's people like the Gundersons – evil and twisted but pretty much human. Quite stoppable. And then sometimes it's not. Sometimes it's more complicated."

"Like vampires," said Sutton. "We've encountered a few towns suffering from the same problem as Cascade Falls, but never quite so widespread. You certainly did a number on them. We were very impressed."

Byrd nodded. "Very."

Amber watched them. "So your organisation—"

"The Foundation."

"—the Foundation, you're like cops tracking down all the monsters out there?"

"That's exactly what we are," Byrd said. "We each have our reasons for joining. I'm ex-FBI, but Sutton here was born into it."

"That's why we're here," Sutton said. "The Foundation was set up in the 1970s by a woman named Molly Harper. I don't expect that name to mean anything to you, but—"

"She knew my brother," Amber said, eyes widening. "And my sister."

Sutton frowned. "Uh... yes. How did you know?"

"I've been dreaming about it. My brother helped her. Saved her. She tried to do the same in return for my sister."

"That's... that's right," said Sutton. "If it wasn't for your

315

brother, Molly wouldn't have lived to see her seventeenth birthday."

Despite her wariness, Amber smiled.

"They only had a brief time together," Sutton continued, "but what they had was enough. I don't know how much you've dreamed, but it might give you some solace to know that your brother finally experienced love in his last few days, before your parents and their friends caught up with him."

"It does," Amber said quietly.

"After James's death, Molly devoted her life to finding out more about the monsters that killed him. This led to her uncovering all kinds of killers and demons roaming this great country of ours, and she realised something had to be done. There had to be someone out there willing to walk into the shadows to fight them.

"And, as you said, she tried to help your sister. It wasn't easy tracking your parents down, not back then. She managed it, but she was too late. By the time she found her, Carolyn had already turned sixteen. Molly just didn't have enough time to get her to safety."

"I saw her," Amber said. "She did her best."

"So she set up the Foundation of Light," Byrd said, "a privately funded organisation made up of mostly ex-military and law-enforcement personnel, people who have either been scarred in some way by these monsters, or have some other connection. Like Sutton, here."

"Molly Harper was my great-grandmother," Sutton said.

"So now you're here," said Amber. "Why? To help me or kill me?"

"To help you, of course," said Byrd.

"It could have helped me long before now," Amber said. "It's been around since the 1970s, right? The Foundation could have sent you or someone like you to kill my parents at any part of my childhood. Why wait until now to pop up?"

"There have been some issues," Sutton said hesitantly.

"I am eager to hear them."

Byrd chose her words carefully. "Molly died twenty years ago. Since then, there has been something of a power struggle within the Foundation."

Sutton took over. "There were some who felt that you, as a demon-in-waiting, should be on our hit list. They were of the opinion that not killing you along with your parents amounted to nothing more than sentimentality."

"Wow," said Amber. "All of these conversations going on to decide my fate that I knew nothing about. Well, I guess that pretty much sums up my life."

"But the power struggle has since been resolved," said Byrd. "Sutton's parents are now in control. And our number-one policy, from which your parents are naturally exempt, is we don't kill family."

Amber frowned. "Family? What?"

"Sutton failed to mention something about Molly's time with your brother," said Byrd. "They grew very close, very quickly. And contraception was not an option."

The frown deepened. "She got pregnant?"

"And nine months later, she gave birth to your niece," said Sutton. "Who grew up to give birth to my father. And then my father met my mother, and they had me."

"What?"

"It's very good to meet you, Great-Grand-Aunt Amber."

Amber didn't realise she had jumped out of her seat until she was standing and staring at Sutton. "You're kidding."

"I am not."

"Oh my God... I have family?"

"That doesn't want to kill you. Must be weird."

"It is," she said. "Very."

"If it makes you feel any better," Byrd said, "you and I are not related in any way."

"Thank you," said Amber.

"Maybe when this is over," Sutton said, "we could catch up. Get to know each other better. We're family, after all."

"When what's over?" Amber asked, frowning.

Sutton shrugged. "Whatever it is you're planning. We assume it's got something to do with your parents, yes? We would like to offer our assistance." He frowned. "You do have a plan, don't you?"

Amber smiled.

44

MILO WATCHED SUTTON AND Byrd drive away. "The Foundation of Light, huh?"

"I've got a good feeling about this," Amber said. "It's like my brother and sister are lending me a hand. What did you think of them — Sutton and Byrd, I mean?"

"He's okay," Milo said. "Couldn't get a read on her."

"I think she may be resistant to your charms," Amber said.

He grunted, checked his watch. "If we're going to do this, we better get to it."

Amber sighed. "Yeah, I know."

They went to the out-of-order restroom around the side of the gas station.

"Ready?" said Milo. "No going back now."

"Ready," Amber said.

She slid Shanks's key in, and twisted.

She took a breath to calm her nerves, opened the door, and they stepped through.

TWO HOURS LATER...

45

THEY PUT THE SHINING Demon in the Charger. His eyes never left Amber's the entire time. Even when Milo closed the trunk, she could feel them boring through the metal, seeking her out.

She shivered, and got in the car.

Night had fallen, and brought with it the thunderclouds. The sky lit up with lightning as the rain lashed against the Charger's windshield.

"How can you see in this?" Amber asked as they drove.

Milo shrugged. "It's not about seeing," he said. "It's about knowing your car and knowing the—"

A car braked ahead and Milo slammed his foot down, barely stopping short of a collision.

Milo looked at Amber. She didn't say anything.

They took the next left and pulled over. A blurry figure hurried towards them. Amber moved her seat forward as the door opened, and Glen climbed into the back seat. She let her seat fall back, and Milo pulled out on to the road.

"That's some rain," said Glen.

Amber turned to him. "How was the journey?"

"Fine," he said, nodding. "Got lost a few times. The phone's

GPS helped me out, though, so that's okay." He turned to Milo. "So, uh... How's it going, Milo?"

Milo nodded as he drove. "Glen."

"Good to see you again."

"I suppose it is."

"This is some rain, isn't it?"

Milo grunted in agreement.

"Yep," said Glen. "It is. We don't have rain like this in Ireland. I mean, we have rain, we have all kinds, but this... this is something different. Even when it lashes in Ireland, it's still pretty gentle compared to this. And the thunder and lightning! Isn't it mad? I wouldn't be able to fly in this weather. Did you know that? That I can fly now?"

"I knew," said Milo.

"I can do other things, too," Glen said. "Well, I'm trying to. The whole turning into mist and bats thing, that still eludes me, but I'm gonna keep practising. I'll get there eventually. I really want to turn into a wolf. I think that'd be cool. So you're human now."

Milo shot him a look in the rear-view that Glen totally missed.

"Must be a shock to the system," Glen continued. "To go from being strong and cool to... well, to being normal, I suppose. It's funny when you think about it, isn't it? You started off cool and I started off normal, and now you're normal and I'm cool."

"You're a vampire," said Milo.

"Yeah," Glen said.

"Who was the last person you fed from?"

"Uh..."

Amber narrowed her eyes. "Glen?"

"Okay, I couldn't find a criminal," Glen said. "I didn't have time to go looking for one. I thought it'd be much, much easier to find them. So, y'know... I took a little, just a little, blood from this nice old lady on her porch. She didn't even mind, though, so you don't have to worry about that. And I didn't kill her, so she won't turn into a vampire. She'll just... she'll just have some pretty saucy dreams about me for a week or two and then she'll go back to normal."

"You shouldn't be hurting innocent people, Glen."

"I didn't hurt her! I swear! Just a tiny little bite! You wouldn't even notice it with all the wrinkles!"

Amber sighed but said nothing.

Glen looked around. "Wasn't the Shining Demon supposed to be back here?"

"He's in the trunk," Milo said.

"Is he chained up?"

"Of course."

"Can I see him?"

"He's not a puppy."

"I'm not gonna *pet* him."

"You'll see him soon enough," said Amber. "Here's the plan, okay? We get to my house. We take him out of the trunk. We march him up to the front door. We knock. It's all very civilised. My parents open the door. They invite us in. We make the exchange. Then we get the hell out of there. You got that?"

"Seems pretty straightforward. Will I need to use my vampire powers?"

"Don't call them that," Milo said.

"Will I, Amber?"

"My parents cannot be trusted," Amber said. "If they can

pull off a double-cross before we get to pull off our double-cross, there's going to be trouble."

"And I'll use my vampire powers," Glen said, nodding.

Milo gripped the wheel tighter.

They got to the house, and Milo pulled up at the kerb.

"You live *here?*" Glen asked, peering out.

"Lived," Amber corrected.

"Look at the gaps between the houses," he said. "You could fit three more houses and a tennis court in each one. Your folks like their privacy, huh?"

"Yes, they do," said Amber.

The rain eased off as they got out of the car. It was hot and humid. The air smelled of rain and heaviness and freshly disturbed dust. It was a smell Amber was familiar with. It was the smell of home.

"Lights are on," Milo said. "Looks like they're here." He glanced at her. "You okay?"

She nodded.

"I'll knock," said Glen, walking forward.

"Glen, no!" Amber called.

He turned. "I'll knock. They'll open the door. If they have any kind of trap planned, it won't work on me, will it? I'm already dead."

Amber bit her lip, then nodded, and Glen walked up to the front door, raised his fist, and right before his knuckles struck, he was blasted backwards off his feet.

He landed on the lawn, but was up immediately.

"The *mur du sang*," said Milo. "Had a feeling they'd have one in place."

Glen frowned. "What was that?"

"A blood barrier," said Amber. "Only I can go in. You two will have to stay out here."

Glen frowned. "But... but I won't be any use out here."

"You won't be any use in there," said Milo.

"I'd be more use than you," Glen shot back. "You've got no powers, you've got no cool stuff you can do, but me? I'm a creature of the night."

Milo took a tiny crucifix from his pocket and held it up, and Glen hissed and shielded his face with his arms.

"Guys," said Amber, "please, have a little self-respect. Milo, will I be able to take our prisoner through?"

Milo put the crucifix away. "A *mur du sang* wouldn't be able to stop a Demon."

Glen frowned. "But Kelly's in there, right? How did they get her in?"

"They brought her in first," Milo told him. "Then they put up the barrier. Do you need everything explained to you?"

Glen ignored him. "Amber, I don't want you to worry about Milo. If something dangerous happens, I promise I'll protect him."

"Kid, the day I need your protection—"

"Milo," said Amber sharply, "it's almost midnight."

"Sure," Milo said, and walked over to the car.

"He doesn't like me," Glen said.

Amber tuned him out. She wanted to pee, and puke, and sit down and run away. She could feel the final vial of blood in her pocket, snug against her hip. Drinking that would soothe her nerves, she knew. Even shifting would help.

But she didn't shift. For her plan to work, she needed to be in complete control.

She turned at the sound of clinking chains. Shackles bound the Shining Demon at the ankle and wrist, and he had a sack over his head. The small amount of rain that still fell hissed and turned to steam when it landed on the glowing embers of his body. Milo held out the chain and Amber took it.

She walked up the path, passing the spot where she'd fallen as a kid. She'd cut her knee open and had run to her mom. Betty had almost been a normal mother back then, or at least a better actress. Amber remembered the Band-Aid and the kiss. Then Bill had come home, and Betty had shed her motherly instincts as easily as taking off a coat.

Amber knocked on the door. No answer. She turned the handle. It was unlocked, and it swung open. She looked back at Glen, and then at Milo, and they stood there, eager to help, but powerless to do so.

Amber walked into the cool of the house, and she took the Shining Demon with her.

46

THE HOUSE SMELLED OF a recently-cooked roast, the kind her father made so well. The place was so familiar to her, and yet so alien, like someone had built a set of her real house and was trying to fool her. It was an odd, disjointing sensation.

Bill and Betty were in the living room in their demon forms, holding Kelly between them. Bill laughed when he saw the Shining Demon.

"I told you she'd do it," he said. "I told you she wouldn't let us down!"

Amber ignored him and looked straight at Kelly. She was okay. That was the important thing.

"How did you manage it?" Betty asked.

Amber hesitated, looked at the Shining Demon and reached for the shackles around his wrists.

"She's releasing him!" Betty cried, lunging for Kelly with her claws out.

But Amber yanked on the chain and the Shining Demon fell to his knees with a grunt. "I told him," she said. Betty stood behind Kelly, talons at her throat. "I had to. He caught me releasing my friend's soul from Hell. I had to tell him about your plan. It amused him. He wanted to play along. He wanted me to bind him with ordinary chains, and then he'd snap them and turn the tables."

Bill regarded her with wary eyes. "But?"

"But that couldn't guarantee Kelly's safety," said Amber. "And, once he'd killed you, I'd still be his representative. So these chains... they're not ordinary."

"And he allowed himself to be shackled?"

"Yes."

Bill laughed. Hard.

Betty looked at Amber with a smile on her face. "You chose us over him?"

"Better the devil you know," Amber said.

Bill glanced at Betty, then started towards them. Amber liked the look on his face. It was trepidation. It was fear.

"Nervous?" she said, and a smile of her own broke out.

His eyes flickered to her, then back to her prisoner, like he expected that skin to start radiating light at any moment.

"I could be lying," Amber said. "This all might be part of Lord Astaroth's plan. He likes his games, as you know."

Bill stopped walking.

"You're aware that the mayor of Desolation Hill trapped his brother, right? But you don't know how he did it. See, Naberius plotted with the mayor to trap Lord Astaroth, but Lord Astaroth is no fool, and he played along. And at the last moment, just when Naberius thought he'd succeeded... the tables were turned."

"Is that what you're doing now, Amber?" Bill asked, his voice quiet. "Are you playing along?"

"There's only one way you're going to find out," Amber told him, and pulled the hood off the Shining Demon.

Beneath, he wore an iron mask that wrapped around his head and clamped over his jaws. His eyes, though calm, betrayed an endless reservoir of rage at his indignities. A Demon, a Duke of Hell, one of the Blood-dimmed King's most loyal subjects, on his knees before three of Hell's mongrels and a mortal girl.

Bill smiled down at him. "You can't even curse us, can you?"

The Shining Demon glared.

"I've done my part," said Amber. "Let Kelly go."

"Do it," said Bill, not taking his eyes off his prey. "We have what we want."

Betty released her hold and moved, like she was sleepwalking, to her husband while Kelly rushed to Amber's side. They started backing out.

"Oh, Bill," Betty said. "I've never been so happy."

Amber's parents turned to each other, and kissed with a love so deep it made Amber uncomfortable just to look at it.

Then Bill and Betty fell upon the Shining Demon, fangs tearing through his flesh, his screams caught by the mask he wore and whittled to mere murmurs of pain as they began to devour him.

Kelly took Amber's hand and they ran outside.

"Move it!" Amber shouted to Milo and Glen. "Let's go!"

"That might be a problem," Milo said.

Stromquist stood between them and the Charger.

47

"Mr Stromquist," Amber said. "I would really appreciate it if you'd step aside."

Stromquist sneered. It was an expression his face was obviously accustomed to. "You're not leaving, I'm afraid."

"I've given my parents what they want," Amber said.

"Nevertheless, they asked me to make sure you stay."

"I'll take care of this guy," said Glen, striding up to him. "Move aside, old man, or I'll move you aside."

Stromquist arched an eyebrow. "You, boy?"

"I'm no boy, old man. I've been touched by darkness. I'm the undead. I'm a vampire."

"As am I," Stromquist said, smiling.

Glen faltered. "Seriously?"

Stromquist swung his arm lazily outwards, caught Glen in the face and launched him back off his feet.

Milo watched Glen land and roll and groan, then he took out his gun and aimed. "Vampire, huh?"

"Indeed," said Stromquist.

Milo fired, the bullet entering Stromquist's chest. Stromquist didn't fall, and no blood stained his white shirt.

Milo nodded. "He's a vampire, all right." He held up the crucifix. "This do anything?"

"Hardly," Stromquist said.

Milo sighed and put it away. "Watch out for him. He's a tricky one."

"Don't worry," said Amber. "I've seen him in action." She shifted, and turned to Kelly. "Sorry."

Kelly shook her head. "You do what you gotta do."

Amber gave her a smile, turned back to Stromquist.

"You've seen me kill?" Stromquist asked as she closed in.

"In my dreams," she said. "I know you snatched Molly Harper."

"I snatched a lot of people," Stromquist said.

"Molly was a friend of my brother's."

"Ah," said Stromquist. "Her. Yes, your brother interfered and she escaped my grasp. If only he had not. If only he had walked away, then I would never have discovered him, and I would never have had to contact your parents."

Amber nodded. "So it's his own fault he's dead?"

"Oh no," said Stromquist, smiling. "It is entirely mine."

"Yeah, it is," she said.

She hit him and he grabbed for her and she hit him again and put him on his ass. Stromquist got up, already annoyed. He lunged at her, the teeth in his palms snapping, but she ducked and swayed back out of his reach.

"You think you know me," he said.

"I know enough to kill you."

He smiled, and raised his right hand. The mouth in his palm grinned at her — and then shot out from his hand on a tendril of flesh, and Amber jerked back just in time to avoid those teeth.

The mouth, the tentacle, the whatever it was, coiled and sprang at her again, and she stumbled, rolled, slashing at it as it got too close. The second mouth shot out from his left hand now, and he advanced, twin tentacles swaying like snakes.

Amber backed off, just enough to allow Stromquist to smile in triumph. Then she let the black scales cover her, from head to foot.

His smile faltered.

The tentacles came at her. She ducked one of them. Grabbed the other. Squeezed. Stromquist gasped, fell to one knee.

Amber slashed at the tentacle, severing that nasty little mouth from the rest of him.

Stromquist cried out, the tentacles retracting into his palms. Amber was on him before he had a chance to recover. She stomped on his knee, bending it sideways, and Stromquist grunted and fell.

He glared up at her. "Your brother put up a fight, too."

"I heard."

"But, when he died, he died begging for mercy."

"I doubt that."

"I can still hear his screams, even now."

"That might be tinnitus," said Amber. "And y'know what? Even if he did die begging, so what? The point is he fought back. He did his best. Makes me proud to be his baby sister."

"You would not be so proud if you had heard his pathetic squealing."

"We've just established that I don't give a damn about that stuff. Pay attention. We've moved on. We are now at the point where I destroy you."

His gaze flickered behind her. "I doubt that very much."

She turned. Bill and Betty walked into the open, holding hands. They were taller, stronger, even more beautiful, and their antlers scraped the lintel as they passed underneath.

Stromquist laughed. It was both booming and hollow at the same time. "Our time here is over," he said to Amber. "Your parents have come to punish you for your wicked ways."

Bill and Betty looked over, and said nothing.

"I don't think they care," Amber told him. Her fingers grew to claws.

Stromquist frowned. "We had a deal!" he bellowed to Amber's parents. "I delivered your son to you! I have been your ally for a century!"

Amber grabbed him. "They've just eaten a Duke of Hell," she whispered into his ear. "They don't need you anymore."

"Unhand me!" Stromquist shouted. "Unhand me at once!"

"Ha," she said. "I bet when my brother died, he didn't sound half as pathetic as you."

Stromquist roared and she swiped her claws across his throat, dug her fingertips into the wound, and tore his head from his shoulders.

His chest turned to dust beneath his clothes and it spread outwards quickly, until his hands and feet and head were crumbling and the warm breeze swept him away.

Amber turned to face her parents. "Nice meal?" she asked.

Betty smiled. "Intoxicating. This level of power is... something to behold."

Amber nodded, waited for them to say something else. When they didn't, she filled the silence. "You're going to kill me, aren't you?"

Betty laughed. Bill smiled.

"Why would we do that?" he asked. "What a waste that would be. No, no, sweetheart, you have it all wrong. We've all come this far, we've grown so close as a family – why would we want any of that to end? Besides, we're going to need our very own representative, aren't we?"

Amber stared. "What?"

"We have consumed the Shining Demon. The logical next step is to take his place as the brand-new Duke and Duchess of Hell."

"And you can come with us," said Betty. "We can be Hell's first Royal Family. Would you like that?"

Amber shook her head in disbelief. "You think you'll just be able to take over? You think that'll be allowed?"

"We think the Blood-dimmed King will recognise our potential," said Bill. "We're going to walk in there, take over Astaroth's castle, and begin our negotiations from a position of power. He'd be a fool to say no."

"You're taking a huge risk."

"Life without risk is life without worth," said Betty. "We taught you that." She held out her hand. "Come with us."

"No."

"Come with us or we'll kill everyone here."

Amber glanced at Kelly, then at Milo and Glen, and she sagged. "Why can't you leave me alone? Why can't all this just be over? I did what you said – I brought you Astaroth. You don't need me anymore. Why can't you just stop, and let me have a normal life?"

"Because you're our daughter," said Betty, walking over. "You're the first child we've had that has survived this long. You're the first to have surpassed our expectations. You changed

334

everything. Because of you, our friends are dead. Because of you, we've had to evolve. At first, we wanted to kill you for the trouble you've caused, but we've realised that what you've done is a wonderful thing. Without you, we'd have stagnated. You gave us the shove we needed."

Betty extended her arms and Amber tensed, but all she was doing was hugging her.

"My child," Betty said softly. "My sweet, beautiful child."

48

Amber made a half-circle of her blood, and her parents joined her inside it, and when the circle was complete it caught fire and they were inside Astaroth's castle.

Bill and Betty looked around the chamber, examining the atrocities depicted in the tapestries and the stained-glass windows. They'd been here before, but had been robbed of the chance to fully appreciate their surroundings. Amber waited for them to finish their inspection.

"What is this?" said a soft voice from the shadows.

Fool emerged into the light. It had removed the glass shards from its eyes and scooped out the mess within. It had two new eyes now, eyes that dangled from their sockets on frayed strings and tapped its cheeks when it moved. It took hold of those eyes, lifting and pointing them at Amber and her parents. "What is this?" it asked again.

Amber frowned at it. "Where'd you get those eyes, Fool?"

"Do you like them?" Fool giggled. "They're Bigmouth's. He didn't need them anymore."

Amber felt herself deflate slightly.

Fool angled the eyes towards Bill and Betty. "I don't understand."

Bill walked over to it, looked down and smiled. "We've killed your Master. We ate him. Ate every last bit."

Fool's mouth fell open. "No. No. Why would you do that? Why would you say that?"

"We're in charge now," Bill said. "And I don't see why we would need something like you."

His hand closed around Fool's throat and Amber hurried over.

"Bill, wait, Fool can be useful."

Bill looked at her. "You think I should spare its life?"

"You're going to need help getting to know how things work around here, right? Fool can help you with that. You'd help, wouldn't you, Fool?"

"I'd help," Fool gurgled.

Bill thought for a moment. "Betty, what do you think?"

"Our daughter may have a point," Betty said, walking over to join them. "She is a smart girl, after all."

"That's true," Bill murmured. "Very well. I'll let you live, Fool, providing that Amber refers to us by our titles from now."

Amber frowned. "Duke and Duchess?"

Betty laughed. "Heavens, no, sweetie. Mom and Dad."

Something recoiled deep within Amber's chest, but she forced herself to nod.

"Sure," she said. "I can do that. Mom. Dad."

Bill released Fool, and smiled broadly. "We're becoming a family for the first time," he said. "I have truly never been happier."

Amber took Fool by the shoulders and pointed it in another direction. "I'll take them to the throne, Fool. You go somewhere and stay out of our way."

Fool nodded and walked off, confusion on its painted face, and Amber looked at her parents.

"This way," she said.

She led them through the corridor with the windows. They gazed outside, enraptured by the palace of the Blood-dimmed King.

"Magnificent," said Betty.

"One day," Bill said, squeezing his wife's hand.

"Is that it?" Amber asked. "That's your goal?"

Betty smiled at her. "Why not? We've just taken over a castle. Taking over a palace shouldn't be much harder."

"We'll get in the good graces of the King," said Bill, "we'll get him to trust us... and then we'll kill him. We'll feast on his flesh and absorb his strength, just like we did with Astaroth."

Betty wrapped an arm round Amber's shoulders. "And then you can take over this place," she said. "Would you like that? To be a fully-fledged Demon? Think of the strength, Amber. Think of the power."

Amber frowned. "I'd be in charge?"

"Of your own little corner of Hell," Betty said, and laughed. "This is more than a dream come true. This is everything we never *dared* dream. You've turned our lives around, Amber."

"You have," said Bill. "Before you, we were limited. We shared our power with others. We lived our lives sixteen years at a time. We were content with the morsels we were fed, with the terms of our contract... And then you shook us free of our mooring, and allowed us to think bigger."

They turned the corner to the giant doors of the throne room. Amber didn't need to tell them what lay beyond. They knew.

"We owe you so much, sweetie," Betty said.

Amber managed a smile. "Thanks, Mom."

Betty laughed. "No, no, thank *you*, sweetheart! Thank *you*! We finally have a family. Isn't that amazing? For so long it's just been Bill and I... and now we have you." Betty hugged her. "I love you so much, my beautiful girl."

Betty stepped away and Bill came in for a hug next. Amber remained frozen in place. A tear trickled down her cheek.

Bill laughed at her reaction. "It's going to take a little while to get used to this, isn't it? That's okay, kiddo, we've got an eternity to make up for lost time. Come on, let's get in there."

Her parents walked over to the door. Amber reverted, and hurried to catch up.

Right before they pushed the door open, Bill smiled at her, and the smile faded a little. "Sweetheart?"

"Yes, Dad?"

"Why are you, uh, why are you like that?"

Amber smiled back, a little confused. "Like what, Dad?"

"Like your old self, sweetie," said Betty. "That girl's gone. You don't have to wear her face anymore."

"But... but I like her face. It's not perfect, and I haven't always liked it, but it's... comfortable."

Her parents glanced at each other.

"But wouldn't you prefer to be beautiful?" her mom asked. "Don't you feel better when you're tall and strong and beautiful? You never have to wear this face again. That's why we're doing this. We are royalty here. And, as royalty, we must be our true selves at all times."

"But I feel more like me when I'm like this," Amber said. "Does it matter? We're a family now, right? You love me. You said so."

"We do love you," said Betty. "But we love you when you're like us. So, for one last time, shift into your true self, and never look back."

"But... but Mom... this is my true self."

"Amber," Bill said, his voice tight, "you will not ruin this for us. Shift this instant."

"I... I don't want to, Dad."

"Bill, it's okay," Betty said. "We need to give her a little more time, that's all. It's a lot to adjust to. It's a big decision."

"It isn't any kind of decision," Bill replied, his narrowed eyes still on Amber. "There's only one choice to make when offered something like this, and that's to say yes, immediately and without equivocation."

She gazed up at her father. "But you said you loved me, Dad."

"Give her some time," said Betty, laying her hand on his arm.

Her touch calmed him, and his eyes moved from Amber to Betty. He even managed a smile. "She gets it from your side of the family."

"I know, dear," Betty said, and they laughed and pushed open the giant doors.

The Hall of a Thousand Mirrors reflected her parents' beauty back at them, and it was a wondrous sight. They held hands as they climbed the steps to the throne. Amber stayed down below.

Betty sat first. She closed her eyes and tilted her head back like she was lying out in the sun. "Glorious," she said. "But it could be better." Then she stood up, and it was Bill's turn.

He took a seat, and smiled. "I think you're right," he said. "We should get new thrones. I want mine made from the bones of my enemies."

Betty kissed him. "And I want mine made from the blades that slew them."

And then came the moment Amber had been waiting for.

A click from the corridor, a shushing of bare feet against stone.

And then Astaroth strode into the room, the orange light blazing beneath his skin, power in his every move, his face twisting in something far beyond anger.

"What is the meaning of this?"

49

BILL LEAPED FROM THE throne, and Betty shot a glare at Amber.

"What did you do?" she demanded. "What did you do, you treacherous little witch?"

Amber smiled up at her. "I fed you his brother, Mom. I went back to Desolation Hill and fetched Naberius for you, instead. Do you think you've got room for dessert?"

"You dare enter my castle?" Astaroth roared, coming forward. "You dare sit atop my throne?"

"They're here to take your place!" Amber shouted, retreating to the doors. "They're here to kill you!"

Bill launched himself at Astaroth, but the Shining Demon merely batted him aside. Betty charged, her talons slashing the Demon's chest. He snarled and grabbed her, slammed her into the floor.

Bill plunged his claws into Astaroth's back, and Astaroth roared again, but whether it was with anger or pain Amber couldn't be sure. Bill hit him, though, and Astaroth stumbled.

He *stumbled*.

The Shining Demon was as shocked as Amber, and almost as shocked as Bill himself.

Astaroth's hands closed around Bill's head, and Bill screamed as his skin started to blister and boil. Betty tore some meat from the back of Astaroth's leg, and Astaroth released Bill and swiped at her. She ducked under his arm and hit him and Astaroth stumbled again, his injured leg buckling beneath him.

Astaroth snarled, reappraising his foes, and then he shifted, transforming into something huge and monstrous and blinding. Amber had to turn her head from the brilliant light, but she glimpsed her parents leaping into it, talons slashing. Giant shadows danced on the walls and then, as quickly as they'd appeared, they were gone. Amber looked back, saw Betty rolling across the floor, saw Bill on his knees and Astaroth standing over him.

A quarter of Astaroth's head was missing. Sliced off, by the looks of it. Liquid light ran from his wound, splashing to the ground.

He wobbled, and stumbled against Bill. He reached his hands down, took hold of Bill's head.

Betty got to her feet. Fell to one knee. "No," she said. "Please."

Astaroth wrenched Bill's head to one side, then tore it from his shoulders.

Betty screamed and fell and screamed again, and Amber watched her father's body crumple.

The Shining Demon dropped the head, and walked unsteadily towards Betty.

But then something shifted in the room, something Amber couldn't quite see, and there was a robed man behind Astaroth.

"This is disappointing," said the priest, the one Amber had met in the palace of the Blood-dimmed King.

Astaroth turned. "My Lord," he mumbled. Missing a piece

of his head was obviously slowing him down, and not just physically.

The priest, in his tattered robes. "Your insistence on playing games meant you were always vulnerable to those who played them better," he said. "I gave you power and this is how you chose to wield it. Your brother was treacherous, but you... you are foolish."

"My apologies, my King," said Astaroth, and dropped to one knee before him, his head down. "I shall strive to... to prove worthy."

"Your time for striving is over," said the priest, who was the Blood-dimmed King, who was many names and many faces.

Demoriel, the Whispering Demon, stepped from the darkness with his spear in his hand, and Astaroth looked up, watched him come.

"My King," said Astaroth, "what is the meaning of this?"

"Your time is at an end," said the priest.

"No, my Lord," Astaroth said, struggling to stand. "I can still be of use."

"Only as target practice," said the Whispering Demon, and plunged his spear through what remained of Astaroth's head. Astaroth staggered back three steps and collapsed, and the wondrous light that burned beneath his skin stopped burning and turned grey, and the Shining Demon stopped shining.

The priest stepped over Astaroth's body and walked slowly to Amber. "You don't belong here," he said.

"No," she responded, her voice tiny.

The priest touched her cheek with one cold, slender finger. "Go now," he said. "Before you are locked in here forever."

She nodded, stepped back, turned and ran.

Amber passed a room, a room she'd seen before, and she turned left and then right. The sweat was streaming down her face as she entered the room where Bigmouth hung from chains.

She shifted, she had to in order to reach up and take his weight, and she freed him from the chains and carried him.

"It's okay," she said. "You're coming back with me. Like I promised."

Bigmouth whimpered.

She got back to the chamber with the tapestries, with the circle of fire, and she stepped into it, and right before she stamped out the flames she saw her mother sprinting towards her, hatred burning in her eyes. But the flames went out and Amber was in Florida again, on her front lawn, in a different kind of heat and a different kind of night, and the thing that had once been Bigmouth, that had once been Edgar Spurrier, fell to pieces in her arms and dropped to the ground.

She reverted, and Kelly ran into her arms and Amber hugged her, hugged her tight, and closed her eyes and cried.

"You okay?" Kelly whispered in her ear. "You okay?"

Amber could only nod into Kelly's shoulder.

Milo and Glen joined them.

"Is that it?" Glen asked. "Is it over?"

Amber would have told him yes, it was all over, were it not for the circle of flames that appeared behind him, and her mother lunging from it.

50

BETTY LAMONT POWERED THROUGH Glen and Milo and tossed Kelly to one side like she wasn't even there. She grabbed Amber and took her off her feet, screaming all the while, then threw her. Amber shifted at the last moment, black scales covering her body an instant before she smashed through the front window of their house, and she landed in the living room, wrapped in torn curtains and struggling to get her bearings.

Betty jumped through the window after her.

"You ungrateful wretch," Betty said. "You ungrateful little wretch."

She hurled Amber into the far wall, grabbed her as she staggered and shoved her through the doorway into the kitchen.

Amber rolled over, watching Betty follow her in even as she got to her feet.

"What did you expect, Betty?" she asked. "Did you expect loyalty? Love?"

"We are your parents!"

"You tried to kill me."

Still brimming with Naberius's power, Betty struck Amber and Amber went sliding across the floor.

"I'm through having this conversation with you," Betty said. "Now I understand, now I finally understand all those other parents and their complaints about the sullen teenager who never listens, who thinks it's their lot in life to rebel against the people who've nurtured them."

"That's what I am?" Amber asked as she got back up. "A sullen teenager? This is my fault?"

"This is all your fault!" Betty screamed. "We gave you life! We owned you! Why couldn't you have just died when you were supposed to?"

Amber grabbed a kitchen knife, held it before her. "Your mind is so warped, Betty, that it's pointless explaining just how warped it is."

"You led us into a trap," Betty said. "You got your father..." She couldn't bring herself to say it.

So Amber did, instead. "Killed?"

Betty snarled. "You betrayed us."

"I betrayed Astaroth, too," said Amber. "Everyone who thought they could tell me what to do. Who thought they could order me around. Who thought they could control me or diminish me. Hey, wow, I guess you're right, Betty. I guess I am the typical rebellious teenager." She smiled. "How clichéd."

Betty charged, sent Amber crashing through the door behind her in an explosion of splinters, the knife spinning from her grip.

"You think this is funny?" Betty roared. "You think this is something to laugh about? Bill is dead! He was the love of my life and you got him killed!"

Amber groaned as she stood up. "That's what you get for putting all your eggs in one basket."

Betty kicked and pain exploded and Amber went tumbling.

"You're a little fool," Betty said. "You let your hurt feelings get in the way of true power. We were offering you a place by our side in Hell."

"I've been to Hell," Amber managed to say, "and I've been at your side. Got no interest in either."

Betty watched her as she got to her hands and knees. "You're so sure, aren't you? So self-righteous. But of course you are. You're young. You're a child. To a child, everything is simple. It's when you grow up that you realise that life is complicated. You can be sure of nothing except, if you're lucky, the person you fall in love with. And you've taken that from me."

Amber stood, dusted herself down, and said, "Boo-frikkin'-hoo."

Betty lunged and Amber ducked under her. Her mother turned, but stood on a bit of wood that slid out from beneath her. She fell, and Amber laughed.

"Don't laugh at me!" Betty screeched.

This made Amber laugh harder.

Betty scrambled up and dived at her so fast that Amber didn't have a chance to dodge out of the way. Betty's hand closed round her throat and she smashed Amber into one wall, then hurled her against the other, then tossed her into her own bedroom.

Amber straightened up, coughing but still laughing. "You're a joke," she said.

"I'll kill you," Betty said. "And then I'll kill all your friends."

The laughter stopped. Amber's hand went to the vial in her pocket. Still intact. Still full of Astaroth's blood.

"Mr Sebastian..." said Betty, walking in to the bedroom, "I'm going to tear his arms and legs off. The vampire boy... I'll take his head. But the cute little redhead? I'll carve my name into her face and then I'll rip out her heart."

Amber pulled the stopper and brought the vial to her lips, but Betty smacked it out of her hand, and it smashed against the Dark Places poster on the wall, and with it went any chance Amber had of living through this.

Betty's first punch knocked out teeth. The second broke her jaw. Amber tried to push Betty away, but her mom snapped her arm like it was kindling. More punches came down, punches that scattered the scales that tried, in vain, to protect her. They fell like confetti.

Betty took hold of one of Amber's horns, the left one, with both hands, and dragged her across the floor. Every time Amber tried to push herself up with her good arm, Betty kicked that arm out. Then she twisted, and Amber cried out, feeling the tendons in her neck about to tear. But Betty wasn't trying to break her neck.

There was a pain unlike any Amber had felt before, and Betty was stumbling away and blood was running down Amber's face and she went to clasp her horn protectively, but there was nothing there to clasp. Her mother held up Amber's horn for her to see, and tossed it aside.

Breathing fast through clenched teeth, Amber started to get up, and Betty brought her foot down on Amber's leg. The bone snapped and Amber's skin bulged, and Amber toppled against her bed and lay in a broken heap.

Betty wiped tears from her eyes. "I wish he was here to see this," she said. "I wish your father was here to watch you die. He would have loved it. He would have..."

Betty broke down in sobs, and a distant part of Amber's mind, the part not clouded with pain, thought, *What a dick.*

But then, incredibly, she heard footsteps behind them, in a house with a blood barrier keeping everyone else out.

Betty whirled. "Bill?"

Sutton stepped into Amber's bedroom, gun in hand, and Betty froze.

"Molly Harper says hello," he said, and fired.

The bullets drove Betty backwards, despite the scales rising on her body. Sutton emptied his gun, but before Betty could recover he'd rammed in another magazine and he was firing again. Some of the bullets hit the scales on Betty's head and she spun, her knees buckling under her. She stumbled against Amber's desk, fell to the floor.

The smell of gunpowder filled the air and the shooting stopped. Amber's ears rang.

Sutton stood there, looking at Betty, and Betty sat there, looking at Sutton.

"Who?" Betty said at last.

"Never you mind," Sutton said. "You can die anytime now."

But Betty got to her feet. Her scales retracted, revealing her red-skinned beauty once again. "You thought you were going to come in here and save the day? You thought you'd be the one to put me down?" Her hands turned into claws. "Not you, I'm afraid."

Betty strode forward and Sutton backed off and Amber threw herself on to Betty and plunged her severed horn into her mother's throat.

"Well, how about me, Mom?" she asked as blood gushed.

51

SOME OF THE BLOOD splashed against Amber's face. She swallowed it, her body becoming warm, shockingly so. Wounds started to heal as Betty fell slowly sideways to the wall, Amber still clinging on. She pulled the horn out and Betty tried stopping the flow of blood with her hands.

Amber fell, jarring her broken bones.

Betty slid down the wall, gasping, gurgling, hands at her throat.

She had fear in her eyes – real, genuine fear – and her red skin was losing its lustre. She tried to get up, and collapsed again.

She stopped trying to stem the blood flow.

One hand fell into her lap.

The other fell to the floor, fingers curling.

Amber crawled forward. She took her mother's blood-slicked hand and held it so that she wouldn't be alone in her final moments.

Betty squeezed her hand in return.

It took her another four minutes to die.

52

SUTTON LEFT THEM, AND Amber did what she had to do in order to heal her injuries. When she was done, she reverted, moaning at the pain. In the bathroom, she washed the blood from her face and hands, then limped through the wreckage of her home, out into the night. Her leg was back in one piece. Her arm was tender, and she held it close, flexing her fingers. Her jaw was no longer broken, but it was still sore. Her whole body ached, and yet beneath the aches she buzzed, even as she cried for her mother.

After everything that had happened, she was crying for her mother.

Kelly hurried over. "You okay?"

Amber nodded, and closed her eyes as Kelly hugged her. When she opened them, Milo and Glen were there.

"You did it," Milo said.

She managed a smile. "You don't look surprised."

He shrugged. "You never gave me a reason to doubt you."

"Is that it?" Glen asked. "Is it over?"

"Not quite," said Byrd, walking over with Sutton. She glanced at her partner, almost nervously, before looking away. "The

Foundation of Light was set up by Molly Harper as a direct result of Betty and Bill Lamont and who they were. Amber, the fact that we were able to help you, in some way, to stop your parents... I think that's everything Molly could have hoped for."

Amber nodded, and did her best to stand on her own.

"Of course," Byrd continued, "the Foundation has expanded over the years. It's not just about demons, anymore. Now we tackle whatever monsters we find. And we draw in recruits from all over the globe. People who've seen the darkness. People who know that there is true evil in the world. I'm one of those people. My parents and my brother were murdered when I was a kid. I've been hunting for their killer ever since. It's why I joined. It's why all of us join."

Glen frowned. "Are you offering us a job?"

She looked at him, quite blankly. "No," she said. "I just wanted you all to understand why." Then she raised her arm and she was holding her gun and she shot Milo three times in the chest.

Amber screamed and Sutton lunged, knocking Byrd to the ground while Glen caught Milo as he fell. Glen laid him on the ground and Amber dropped to her knees beside him.

"I'm sorry, Amber," Byrd said as Sutton cuffed her hands behind her back.

"Milo," said Amber, tears already spilling down her cheeks. "Milo, please. Please don't die. Please, we'll, we'll get you into the Charger, it'll be fine, it'll be fine."

"The Charger can't heal him anymore," Glen said softly.

"It will!" Amber shouted. "It's not going to let him just die! You hear that, Milo? The Charger won't let you die. I won't let you die."

"I'm sorry," said Byrd.

Amber hated her with every ounce of her soul.

"He killed them," Byrd continued. "He ran us off the road. I was the only one who survived. I remember his red eyes. I remember his car. He murdered my family."

Sutton, pale and shaking, picked his partner up off the ground and led her away.

Amber leaned closer, speaking into Milo's ear. "You're not him anymore. I know you're not. The Ghost of the Highway was a different person. You're a good man, Milo Sebastian. A good man."

"Amber..." Kelly said gently.

Amber shook her hand off. "Milo, get up," she ordered. "I'm paying you a goddamn salary, and you get up right this minute and earn your pay. Please get up, Milo. Please."

"Amber," said Glen, "he's dead."

"No. No, he's not. Help me get him to the Charger."

"He's not a demon anymore, Amber, it won't—"

"*Help me.*"

They helped her. They carried Milo's body to the Charger, laid him across the front seats and closed the doors. Amber sank to her knees and cried. Kelly stayed with her arms around her. Glen stood nearby.

Sutton came back. He tried to talk, but couldn't. His partner sat in their car with her head down.

Ten minutes later, Sutton left, taking Byrd with him.

A half-hour before sunrise, Glen left. He kissed the top of Amber's head, and then he was gone.

Only Kelly stayed with her until morning. Only she was there to help her stand, and only she was there to watch Amber open the door of the Charger and start to cry all over again.

53

AMBER DRANK HER SPRITE and looked out of the window and thought about stuff.

New York City in the middle of summer. It was hot, but not Florida hot. Not Hell hot. It was a bearable kind of hot, and all kinds of people passed the deli window as she sat there. She'd heard all her life about how rude New Yorkers were. She didn't find them rude. She found them upfront. They talked fast and they talked loud and it was refreshing to just be here. She liked New York. This was her kind of town.

Kelly came back from the restroom, sat opposite. She had a Sprite of her own that she drank from, slurping noisily with her straw. Kelly didn't mind if she annoyed people with the slurping. Amber didn't, either.

Beneath her light jacket, Kelly was wearing her *Dark Places* T-shirt. The show had been all over the news ever since the attempt on Annalith Symmes's life and the discovery of three dead people and a dog. There was closed-circuit camera footage of Kelly's face, and a blurry picture of Amber, but so far no one had recognised them on their travels. The more time passed, the less likely it was to happen. Amber had recently decided that the whole thing was just going to fade away.

"Terrible, isn't it?" said a man waiting at the counter.

They looked at him. "Sorry?" Amber said.

The man, a quiet-looking guy with neat hair and spectacles, nodded at the TV in the corner. For a moment, Amber thought they'd been recognised and was about to start cursing her own stupidity, but the news report was about the other big story dominating the summer. The police chief's son.

"The kid who was taken," the guy said. "That psycho has had him for, what, months? More? Definitely dead by now. Terrible."

"Yeah," said Kelly.

The quiet guy shook his head sadly, seemingly content to let the conversation settle right there.

"Takes all kinds," said Amber.

"I guess it does," the quiet guy replied. He took off his glasses and cleaned them.

"Ever been up that way?" Kelly asked.

He squinted at her slightly. "Where?"

"Keene. Where the kid was snatched."

"Me?" said the quiet guy, and put his spectacles back on. "No. Never. Well, I guess I've passed through once or twice. Never stopped, though. Looks like a nice town. Terrible that something like this should happen there."

"Terrible it should happen anywhere," said Amber.

"True," he said, nodding. "You never can tell, can you? Like you said, it takes all kinds."

"It does," Amber said. "It certainly does. When you think about it, just about anyone could be a serial killer and you'd never know it, would you? They could be your best friend, your neighbour, that lonely guy in the office... Could even be a random stranger you get to talking to while you're out for a bite to eat."

The quiet guy smiled sadly and nodded, turned his head to check on his order.

"The thing is," said Kelly, "they can look just as normal as anyone. They don't all have to wear blood-stained overalls or freaky masks or carry chainsaws – though there are those, too."

"That there are," said Amber. "Those are the easy ones to spot. *Oh look, a guy the size of a mountain, dressed in festering rags and holding a machete – I bet he's the one who's been killing all those pretty co-eds.* Easy, right? But it's the other ones, the not-so-obvious ones... It's the quiet ones you have to look out for, isn't it?"

The quiet guy smiled politely. "I guess so."

"But here's the thing," said Kelly. "Once you've met one of them, you're bound to meet more. It's the way of things. From the moment you're touched by darkness, it never lets you go."

"I guess so," he said again. He was handed his sandwich and he took it and paid, counting out the exact change. Then he looked at Amber and Kelly and gave them a farewell nod. "Have a nice day," he said.

"See you around," said Amber.

He left.

Amber looked at Kelly and Kelly drained the last of her Sprite, and they got up. They went outside, watched the quiet guy walking away.

It was too warm for a jacket, and Kelly took hers off. She would normally have put it in the trunk of the Charger, but that's where Glen was sleeping, covered in a blanket. So she slung the jacket on the back seat and took the gun from the glove box, clipping it on to her belt, and pulled her T-shirt down to hide it.

Amber locked the car and they went walking. Part of Kelly's forearm was wrapped in plastic to protect the new additions to her tattoo sleeve. Ronnie, Linda, Warrick and Two, all done cartoon-style, bordering her wrist, keeping the monsters and the killers from sliding off and escaping. It looked good. It looked cool.

They walked hand in hand and didn't say much. There were a few people who gave them a second look, but they were all gazing at Kelly, and Amber could understand that. Kelly was a beautiful girl, after all – tall and slim and stunning. But what Amber knew, what those people did not, was that Kelly was as beautiful on the inside as she was on the outside. She was strength and love and happiness, despite everything that had happened to her. She was positive. She was a light in the darkness. She was hope.

And Amber needed hope. She needed that light in her life, a light that had been denied her for so long. She had someone to love. Someone to fight for, to fight beside. Maybe she'd never lose all that weight. Maybe she'd never be all that pretty. So what? She'd stopped caring. So long as her smile made Kelly smile and her laugh made Kelly laugh, that was all that mattered.

"What?" Kelly asked. "What are you grinning about?"

"You."

Kelly looked amused, and pleased, and she raised Amber's hand to kiss it.

Two young men coming the other way saw the kiss. They didn't whistle or catcall or leer. They just passed on by.

Amber and Kelly got to the end of the street, and watched the quiet guy climb the steps to his front door and let himself in. It was a nice house, identical to all the other nice houses in that row, the kind with narrow windows near the ground, allowing a little light into the basement.

They crossed the road. There were no cars. They went straight to those narrow windows and lay down, had to wipe the grime from the glass in order to peer through. There was a washing machine along one wall, some odds and ends on an old bookcase, but, apart from that, the basement was empty.

The quiet guy walked into view. He went to the bookcase and pulled. It swung wide, like it was on hinges. Behind it was a door. The quiet guy slid back the bolts and opened it. There was someone there, in the small room. Someone sitting on the floor, drawing their legs in.

The quiet guy didn't move inside. He was talking. He held out the sandwich and a bottle of water, then stepped in, put them on the ground, and stepped back again. He rubbed his palms on his legs like they were sweaty, then came out, closed the door and bolted it. He swung the bookcase over and stayed there with his head down for a moment. Amber and Kelly ducked back before he turned. They took a peek a few seconds later and he was gone.

They went round the side of the house, looked through the kitchen window. The quiet guy stood at the sink, eyes closed. He was muttering to himself. He looked angry.

Finally, he calmed down, and washed his hands. He took forever. When he was done, he started making dinner. He was fastidious. Every chop was precise, every measurement exact. Every bit of leftover ingredient was added to a plastic bag at the end of the worktop. When the bag was full, he tied it off, took it to the back door.

Amber nudged Kelly and they hurried round the corner, watching the quiet guy take the bag to the trash. They went quickly over to the door while his back was to them, making it inside before it completed its slow swing closed. Keeping low, they passed through the kitchen, went down the corridor, got to the basement door. Amber turned the handle. It was unlocked. They hurried through, hearing the back door close.

Amber led the way down the steps. She tried pulling the bookcase back. It rattled slightly, but didn't move. She skimmed her fingers over the spot she'd seen the quiet guy grip, and found a latch. She pressed it and pulled, and now the bookcase swung open easily. She slid back the bolts on the door, and knocked.

"We're here to help," she said quietly. "There are two of us – we're going to get you out of here. When I open the door, I don't want you to make a sound, okay?"

There was a moment of silence, and then a soft, tentative, "Yes."

Amber opened the door, the diffused light spilling into the darkness. The boy was on his feet, the half-eaten sandwich in his hand. He stood on a thin mattress and he had blankets wrapped around his shoulders. The police chief's son.

"Come on," Amber said, holding out her hand.

He shook his head, pointed to his ankle, where a thin chain was binding him to the wall. Amber nodded, stepped into the room. The boy didn't shrink back.

"Hey there," Kelly whispered. "My name's Kelly. Are you injured? Are you hurt?"

The boy looked at Kelly while Amber hunkered down behind him and gripped the chain with both hands. She shifted, snapped the chain and immediately reverted before the boy looked down.

"All done," she said, straightening up. "Let's go."

He frowned at the chain, but nodded, and she took his hand and led him out, and they followed Kelly up the steps and out of the basement. They turned for the front door. The quiet guy stood in the doorway to the kitchen, looking at them, his eyes wide in surprise. He had a large knife in his hand.

Not a word was spoken. He looked at Kelly, then at the boy, then at Amber and back to the boy again. His gaze settled on Kelly. She was the closest. He didn't know that she had the gun on her hip, but, if he ran at her, Amber didn't know if she'd be able to draw and fire in time. Kelly wasn't a quick draw, not like Milo.

The quiet guy shook his head. He started crying. He raised the knife, pointed it at them like he was going to say something, but all he did was cry. Then his face contorted, flushing in anger, and he took two steps towards them and broke into a run. Amber pushed the boy behind her, was about to shift when Kelly drew the gun at her hip and fired twice. The quiet guy's legs went out from under him as he ran, and he sank to his knees and toppled.

Keeping the gun trained on him, Kelly kicked away the knife. She didn't bother shooting him in the head. This wasn't a killer who'd made a deal with a Demon, the kind that popped back up just when you thought they were finished. This was just your garden variety, made-in-America serial killer.

Takes all kinds, as the man said.

They left the house, and Amber and Kelly walked back to the

deli, the police chief's son between them. He went inside and they hung around for a few moments until they saw everyone make a big fuss over him, and then they got in the car.

Kelly put the gun back in the glove box as Amber buckled her seat belt. As Kelly buckled hers, Amber started the engine. The radio sprang to life, zeroed in on an eighties music station. 'Here I Go Again' by Whitesnake.

They had a lot to do. Somewhere out there was seven-foot homicidal clown who needed to be stopped. Somewhere out there was a homeless girl with a broken mind who needed to be helped. Somewhere out there was a fresh horror waiting to unfold.

Amber checked the mirrors, then swung out on to the road and drove. They took the Lincoln Tunnel out of town.